Ray Bradbury, one of the greatest writers of fantasy and horror fiction in the world today, has published some 500 short stories, novels, plays and poems since his first story appeared in *Weird Tales* when he was twenty years old. Among his many famous works are *Fahrenheit 451*, *The Illustrated Man* and *The Martian Chronicles*. He has also written the screenplays for *It Came from Outer Space*, *Something Wicked This Way Comes* and *Moby Dick*. Mr Bradbury was Idea Consultant for the United States Pavilion at the 1964 World's Fair, has written the basic scenario for the interior of Spaceship Earth at EPCOT, Disney World, and is doing consultant work on city engineering and rapid transit. When one of the Apollo Astronaut teams landed on the moon, they named Dandelion Crater there to honour Mr Bradbury's novel, *Dandelion Wine*.

By the same author

# RAY BRADBURY

# The Martian Chronicles

## (The Silver Locusts)

*An Imprint of* HarperCollins*Publishers*

Grafton
An Imprint of HarperCollins*Publishers*
77—85 Fulham Palace Road,
Hammersmith, London W6 8JB

Published by Grafton 1977
9 8 7

First published in Great Britain by
Rupert Hart-Davis in 1951
under the title *The Silver Locusts*
Panther Books 1977 publication
also entitled *The Silver Locusts*

The Author asserts the moral right to
be identified as the author of this work

ISBN 0 586 04362 4

Set in Times

Printed in Great Britain by
HarperCollinsManufacturing Glasgow

For My Wife Marguerite
with all my love

'It is good to renew one's wonder,' said the philosopher. 'Space travel has again made children of us all.'

# Chronology

## Chronology

## *Rocket Summer*

One minute it was Ohio winter, with doors closed, windows locked, the panes blind with frost, icicles fringing every roof, children skiing on slopes, housewives lumbering like great black bears in their furs along the icy streets.

And then a long wave of warmth crossed the small town. A flooding sea of hot air; it seemed as if someone had left a bakery door open. The heat pulsed among the cottages and bushes and children. The icicles dropped, shattering, to melt. The doors flew open. The windows flew up. The children worked off their wool clothes. The housewives shed their bear disguises. The snow dissolved and showed last summer's ancient green lawns.

*Rocket summer*. The words passed among the people in the open air, airing houses. *Rocket summer*. The warm desert air changing the frost patterns on the windows, erasing the art work. The skis and sleds suddenly useless. The snow, falling from the cold sky upon the town, turned to a hot rain before it touched the ground.

*Rocket summer*. People leaned from their dripping porches and watched the reddening sky.

The rocket lay on the launching field, blowing out pink clouds of fire and oven heat. The rocket stood in the cold winter morning, making summer with every breath of its mighty exhausts. The rocket made climates, and summer lay for a brief moment upon the land . . .

# *Ylla*

They had a house of crystal pillars on the planet Mars by the edge of an empty sea, and every morning you could see Mrs K eating the golden fruits that grew from the crystal walls, or cleaning the house with handfuls of magnetic dust which, taking all dirt with it, blew away on the hot wind. Afternoons, when the fossil sea was warm and motionless, and the wine trees stood stiff in the yard, and the little distant Martian bone town was all enclosed, and no one drifted out their doors, you could see Mr K himself in his room, reading from a metal book with raised hieroglyphs over which he brushed his hand, as one might play a harp. And from the book, as his fingers stroked, a voice sang, a soft ancient voice, which told tales of when the sea was red steam on the shore and ancient men had carried clouds of metal insects and electric spiders into battle.

Mr and Mrs K had lived by the dead sea for twenty years, and their ancestors had lived in the same house, which turned and followed the sun, flower-like, for ten centuries.

Mr and Mrs K were not old. They had the fair, brownish skin of the true Martian, the yellow coin eyes, the soft musical voices. Once they had liked painting pictures with chemical fire, swimming in the canals in the seasons when the wine trees filled them with green liquors, and talking into the dawn together by the blue phosphorous portraits in the speaking-room.

They were not happy now.

This morning Mrs K stood between the pillars, listening to the desert sands heat, melt into yellow wax, and seemingly run on the horizon.

Something was going to happen.

She waited.

She watched the blue sky of Mars as if it might at any moment grip in on itself, contract, and expel a shining miracle down upon the sand.

Nothing happened.

Tired of waiting, she walked through the misting pillars. A gentle rain sprang from the fluted pillar-tops, cooling the scorched air, falling gently on her. On hot days it was like walking in a creek. The floors of the house glittered with cool streams. In the distance she heard her husband playing his book steadily, his fingers never tired of the old songs. Quietly she wished he might one day again spend as much time holding and touching her like a little harp as he did his incredible books.

But no. She shook her head, an imperceptible, forgiving shrug. Her eyelids closed softly down upon her golden eyes. Marriage made people old and familiar, while still young.

She lay back in a chair that moved to take her shape even as she moved. She closed her eyes tightly and nervously.

The dream occurred.

Her brown fingers trembled, came up, grasped at the air. A moment later she sat up, startled, gasping.

She glanced about swiftly, as if expecting someone there before her. She seemed disappointed; the space between the pillars was empty.

Her husband appeared in a triangular door. 'Did you call?' he asked irritably.

'No!' she cried.

'I thought I heard you cry out.'

'Did I? I was almost asleep and had a dream!'

'In the daytime? You don't often do that.'

She sat as if struck in the face by the dream. 'How strange, how very strange,' she murmured. 'The dream.'

'Oh?' He evidently wished to return to his book.

'I dreamed about a man.'

'A man?'

'A tall man, six foot one inch tall.'

'How absurd; a giant, a misshapen giant.'

'Somehow' – she tried the words – 'he looked all right. In spite of being tall. And he had – oh, I know you'll think it silly – he had *blue* eyes!'

'Blue eyes! Gods!' cried Mr K. 'What'll you dream next? I suppose he had *black* hair?'

'How did you *guess*?' She was excited.

'I picked the most unlikely colour,' he replied coldly.

'Well black it was!' she cried. 'And he had a very white skin; oh, he was *most* unusual! He was dressed in a strange uniform and he came down out of the sky and spoke pleasantly to me.' She smiled.

'Out of the sky; what nonsense!'

'He came in a metal thing that glittered in the sun,' she remembered. She closed her eyes to shape it again. 'I dreamed there was the sky and something sparkled like a coin thrown into the air, and suddenly it grew large and fell down softly to land, a long silver craft, round and alien. And a door opened in the side of the silver object and this tall man stepped out.'

'If you worked harder you wouldn't have these silly dreams.'

'I rather enjoyed it,' she replied, lying back. 'I never suspected myself of such an imagination. Black hair, blue eyes, and white skin! What a strange man, and yet – quite handsome.'

'Wishful thinking.'

'You're unkind. I didn't think him up on purpose; he just came in my mind while I drowsed. It wasn't like a dream. It was so unexpected and different. He looked at me and he said, "I've come from the third planet in my ship. My name is Nathaniel York—" '

'A stupid name; it's no name at all,' objected the husband.

'Of course it's stupid, because it's a dream,' she explained

quietly here, soundless, not moving until this thing occurred,
this thing expected all day, this thing that could not occur
but might. A drift of song brushed through her mind.

'I—'

'Do you good,' he urged. 'Come along now.'

'I'm tired,' she said. 'Some other night.'

'Here's your scarf.' He handed her a phial. We haven't
gone anywhere in months.'

'Except you, twice a week to Xi City.' She wouldn't look
at him.

'Business,' he said.

'Oh?' She whispered to herself.

From the phial a liquid poured, turned to blue mist, settled
about her neck, quivering.

The flame birds waited, like a bed of coals, glowing on the
cool smooth sands. The white canopy ballooned on the night
wind, flapping softly, tied by a thousand green ribbons to
the birds.

Ylla laid herself back in the canopy and, at a word from
her husband, the birds leaped, burning, towards the dark
sky. The ribbons tautened, the canopy lifted. The sand slid
whining under; the blue hills drifted by, drifted by, leaving
their home behind, the raining pillars, the caged flowers,
the singing books, the whispering floor creeks. She did not
look at her husband. She heard him crying out to the birds
as they rose higher, like ten thousand hot sparkles, so many
red-yellow fireworks in the heavens, tugging the canopy like
a flower petal, burning through the wind.

She didn't watch the dead, ancient bone-chess cities slide
under, or the old canals filled with emptiness and dreams.
Past dry rivers and dry lakes they flew, like a shadow of
the moon, like a torch burning.

She watched only the sky.

The husband spoke.

She watched the sky.

'Did you hear what I said?'

'What?'

He exhaled. 'You might pay attention.'

'I was thinking.'

'I never thought you were a nature-lover, but you're certainly interested in the sky tonight,' he said.

'It's very beautiful.'

'I was figuring,' said the husband slowly. 'I thought I'd call Hulle tonight. I'd like to talk to him about us spending some time, oh, only a week or so, in the Blue Mountains. It's just an idea—'

'The Blue Mountains!' She held to the canopy rim with one hand, turning swiftly towards him.

'Oh, it's just a suggestion.'

'When do you want to go?' she asked, trembling.

'I thought we might leave tomorrow morning. You know, an early start and all that,' he said very casually.

'But we *never* go this early in the year!'

'Just this once, I thought—' He smiled. 'Do us good to get away. Some peace and quiet. You know. You haven't anything *else* planned? We'll go, won't we?'

She took a breath, waited, and then replied, 'No.'

'What?' His cry startled the birds. The canopy jerked.

'No,' she said firmly. 'It's settled. I won't go.'

He looked at her. They did not speak after that. She turned away.

The birds flew on, ten thousand firebrands down the wind.

In the dawn the sun, through the crystal pillars, melted the fog that supported Ylla as she slept. All night she had hung above the floor, buoyed by the soft carpeting of mist that poured from the walls when she lay down to rest. All night she had slept on this silent river, like a boat upon a soundless tide. Now the fog burned away, the mist level lowered until she was deposited upon the shore of wakening.

She opened her eyes.

Her husband stood over her. He looked as if he had stood there for hours, watching. She did not know why, but she could not look him in the face.

'You've been dreaming again!' he said. 'You spoke out and kept me awake. I *really* think you should see a doctor.'

'I'll be all right.'

'You talked a lot in your sleep!'

'Did I?' She started up.

Dawn was cold in the room. A grey light filled her as she lay there.

'What was your dream?'

She had to think a moment to remember. 'The ship. It came from the sky again, and the tall man stepped out and talked with me, telling me little jokes, laughing, and it was pleasant.'

Mr K touched a pillar. Founts of warm water leapt up, steaming; the chill vanished from the room. Mr K's face was impassive.

'And then,' she said, 'this man, who said his strange name was Nathaniel York, told me I was beautiful and – and kissed me.'

'Ha!' cried the husband, turning violently away, his jaw working.

'It's only a dream.' She was amused.

'Keep your silly, feminine dreams to yourself!'

'You're acting like a child.' She lapsed back upon the few remaining remnants of chemical mist. After a moment she laughed softly. 'I thought of some *more* of the dream,' she confessed.

'Well, what is it, what *is* it?' he shouted.

'Yll, you're so bad tempered.'

'Tell me!' he demanded. 'You can't keep secrets from me!' His face was dark and rigid as he stood over her.

'I've never seen you this way,' she replied, half shocked, half entertained. 'All that happened was this Nathaniel York person told me — well, he told me that he'd take me away into his ship, into the sky with him, and take me back to his planet with him. It's really quite ridiculous.'

'Ridiculous, is it!' he almost screamed. 'You should have heard yourself, fawning on him, talking to him, singing with him, oh gods, all night; you should have *heard* yourself!'

'Yll!'

'When's he landing? Where's he coming down with his damned ship?'

'Yll, lower your voice.'

'Voice be damned!' He bent stiffly over her. 'And *in* this dream' — he seized her wrist — 'didn't the ship land over in Green Valley, *didn't* it? Answer me!'

'Why, yes—'

'And it landed this afternoon, didn't it?' he kept at her.

'Yes, yes, I think so, yes, but only in a dream!'

'Well' — he flung her hand away stiffly — 'it's good you're truthful! I heard every word you said in your sleep. You mentioned the valley and the time.' Breathing hard, he walked between the pillars like a man blinded by a lightning bolt. Slowly his breath returned. She watched him as if he were quite insane. She arose finally and went to him. 'Yll,' she whispered.

'I'm all right.'

'You're sick.'

'No.' He forced a tired smile. 'Just childish. Forgive me, darling.' He gave her a rough pat. 'Too much work lately. I'm sorry. I think I'll lie down awhile—'

'You were so excited.'

'I'm all right now. Fine.' He exhaled. 'Let's forget it. Say, I heard a joke about Uel yesterday, I meant to tell you. What do you say you fix breakfast, I'll tell the joke, and let's not talk about all this.'

'It was only a dream.'

'Of course.' He kissed her cheek mechanically. 'Only a dream.'

At noon the sun was high and hot and the hills shimmered in the light.

'Aren't you going to town?' asked Ylla.

'Town?' he raised his brows faintly.

'This is the day you *always* go.' She adjusted a flower-cage on its pedestal. The flowers stirred, opening their hungry yellow mouths.

He closed his book. 'No. It's too hot, and it's late.'

'Oh.' She finished her task and moved towards the door.

'Well, I'll be back soon.'

'Wait a minute! Where are you going?'

She was in the door swiftly. 'Over to Pao's. She invited me!'

'Today?'

'I haven't seen her in a long time. It's only a little way.'

'Over in Green Valley, isn't it?'

'Yes, just a walk, not far, I thought I'd—' She hurried.

'I'm sorry, really sorry,' he said, running to fetch her back, looking very concerned about his forgetfulness. 'It slipped my mind. I invited Dr Nlle out this afternoon.'

'Dr Nlle!' She edged towards the door.

He caught her elbow and drew her steadily in. 'Yes.'

'But Pao—'

'Pao can await, Ylla. We must entertain Nlle.'

'Just for a few minutes—'

'No, Ylla.'

'No?'

He shook his head. 'No. Besides, it's a terribly long walk to Pao's. All the way over through Green Valley and then past the big canal and down, isn't it? And it'll be very, very hot, and Dr Nlle would be delighted to see you. Well?'

She did not answer. She wanted to break and run. She wanted to cry out. But she only sat in the chair, turning her fingers over slowly, staring at them expressionlessly, trapped.

'Ylla?' he murmured. 'You *will* be here, won't you?'

'Yes,' she said after a long time. 'I'll be here.'

'All afternoon?'

Her voice was dull. 'All afternoon.'

Late in the day Dr Nlle had not put in an appearance. Ylla's husband did not seem overly surprised. When it was quite late he murmured something, went to a closet, and drew forth an evil weapon, a long yellowish tube ending in a bellows and trigger. He turned, and upon his face was a mask, hammered from silver metal, expressionless, the mask that he always wore when he wished to hide his feelings, the mask which curved and hollowed so exquisitely to his thin cheeks and chin and brow. The mask glinted, and he held the evil weapon in his hands, considering it. It hummed constantly, an insect hum. From it hordes of golden bees could be flung out with a high shriek. Golden, horrid bees that stung, poisoned, and fell lifeless, like seeds on the sand.

'Where are you going?' she asked.

'What?' He listened to the bellows, to the evil hum. 'If Dr Nlle is late, I'll be damned if I'll wait. I am going out to hunt a bit. I'll be back. You be sure to stay right here now, won't you?' The silver mask glimmered.

'Yes.'

'And tell Dr Nlle I'll return. Just hunting.'

The triangular door closed. His footsteps faded down the hill.

She watched him walking through the sunlight until he was gone. Then she resumed her tasks with the magnetic dusts and the new fruits to be plucked from the crystal walls. She worked with energy and dispatch, but on occasion a numbness took hold of her and she caught herself singing that odd and memorable song and looking out beyond the crystal pillars at the sky.

She held her breath and stood very still, waiting.

It was coming nearer.

At any moment it might happen.

It was like those days when you heard a thunderstorm coming and there was the waiting silence and then the faintest pressure of the atmosphere as the climate blew over the land in shifts and shadows and vapours. And the change pressed at your ears and you were suspended in the waiting time of the coming storm. You began to tremble. The sky was stained and coloured; the clouds were thickened; the mountains took on an iron taint. The caged flowers blew with faint sighs of warning. You felt your hair stir softly. Somewhere in the house the voice-clock sang. 'Time, time, time, time . . .' ever so gently, no more than water tapping on velvet.

And then the storm. The electric illumination, the engulfments of dark wash and sounding black fell down, shutting in, forever.

That's how it was now. A storm gathered, yet the sky was clear. Lightning was expected, yet there was no cloud.

Ylla moved through the breathless summer-house. Lightning would strike from the sky any instant; there would be a thunder-clap, a boll of smoke, a silence, footsteps on the path, a rap on the crystalline door, and her *running* to answer . . .

Crazy Ylla! she scoffed. Why think these wild things with your idle mind?

And then it happened.

There was a warmth as of a great fire passing in the air. A whirling, rushing sound. A gleam in the sky, of metal.

Ylla cried out.

Running through the pillars, she flung wide a door. She faced the hills. But by this time there was nothing.

She was about to race down the hill when she stopped herself. She was supposed to stay here, go nowhere. The doctor was coming to visit, and her husband would be angry if she ran off.

She waited in the door, breathing rapidly, her hand out.

She strained to see over towards Green Valley, but saw nothing.

Silly woman. She went inside. You and your imagination, she thought. That was nothing but a bird, a leaf, the wind, or a fish in the canal. Sit down. Rest.

She sat down.

A shot sounded.

Very clearly, sharply, the sound of the evil insect weapon.

Her body jerked with it.

It came from a long way off. One shot. The swift humming distant bees. One shot. And then a second shot, precise and cold, and far away.

Her body winced again and for some reason she started up, screaming and screaming, and never wanting to stop screaming. She ran violently through the house and once more threw wide the door.

The echoes were dying away, away.

Gone.

She waited in the yard, her face pale, for five minutes.

Finally, with slow steps, her head down, she wandered about the pillared rooms, laying her hand to things, her lips quivering, until finally she sat alone in the darkening wine-room, waiting. She began to wipe an amber glass with the hem of her scarf.

And then, from far off, the sound of footsteps crunching on the thin, small rocks.

She rose up to stand in the centre of the quiet room. The glass fell from her fingers, smashing to bits.

The footsteps hesitated outside the door.

Should she speak? Should she cry out. 'Come in, oh, come in'?

She went forward a few paces.

The footsteps walked up the ramp. A hand twisted the door latch.

She smiled at the door.

The door opened. She stopped smiling.

It was her husband. His silver mask glowed dully.

He entered the room and looked at her for only a moment. Then he snapped the weapon bellows open, cracked out two dead bees, heard them spat on the floor as they fell, stepped on them, and placed the empty bellows-gun in the corner of the room as Ylla bent down and tried, over and over, with no success, to pick up the pieces of the shattered glass. 'What were you doing?' she asked.

'Nothing,' he said with his back turned. He removed the mask.

'But the gun — I heard you fire it. Twice.'

'Just hunting. Once in a while you like to hunt. Did Dr Nlle arrive?'

'No.'

'Wait a minute.' He snapped his fingers disgustedly. 'Why, I remember now. He was supposed to visit us *tomorrow* afternoon. How stupid of me.'

They sat down to eat. She looked at her food and did not move her hands. 'What's wrong?' he asked her, not looking up from dipping his meat in the bubbling lava.

'I don't know. I'm not hungry,' she said.

'Why not?'

'I don't know; I'm just not.'

The wind was rising across the sky; the sun was going down. The room was small and suddenly cold.

'I've been trying to remember,' she said in the silent room, across from her cold, erect, golden-eyed husband.

'Remember what?' He sipped his wine.

'That song. That fine and beautiful song.' She closed her eyes and hummed, but it was not the song. 'I've forgotten it. And, somehow, I don't want to forget it. It's something I want always to remember.' She moved her hands as if the rhythm might help her to remember all of it. Then she lay back in her chair. 'I can't remember.' She began to cry.

'Why are you crying?' he asked.

'I don't know, I don't know, but I can't help it. I'm sad and I don't know why, I cry and I don't know why, but I'm crying.'

Her head was in her hands; her shoulders moved again and again.

'You'll be all right tomorrow,' he said.

She did not look up at him; she looked only at the empty desert and the very bright stars coming out now on the black sky, and far away there was a sound of wind rising and canal waters stirring cold in the long canals. She shut her eyes, trembling.

'Yes,' she said. 'I'll be all right tomorrow.'

# The Summer Night

In the stone galleries the people were gathered in clusters and groups filtering up into shadows among the blue hills. A soft evening light shone over them from the stars and the luminous double moons of Mars. Beyond the marble amphitheatre, in darknesses and distances, lay little towns and villas; pools of silver water stood motionless and canals glittered from horizon to horizon. It was an evening in summer upon the placid and temperate planet Mars. Up and down green wine-canals, boats as delicate as bronze flowers drifted. In the long and endless dwellings that curved like tranquil snakes across the hills, lovers lay idly whispering in cool night beds. The last children ran in torchlit alleys, gold spiders in their hands throwing out films of web. Here or there a late supper was prepared in tables where lava bubbled silvery and hushed. In the amphitheatres of a hundred towns on the night side of Mars the brown Martian people with gold coin eyes were leisurely met to fix their attention upon stages where musicians made a serene music flow up like blossom scent on the still air.

Upon one stage a woman sang.

The audience stirred.

She stopped singing. She put her hand to her throat. She nodded to the musicians, and they began again.

The musicians played and she sang, and this time the audience sighed and sat forward, a few of the men stood up in surprise, and a winter chill moved through the amphitheatre. For it was an odd and a frightening and a strange song this woman sang. She tried to stop the words from coming out of her lips, but the words were these:

'She walks in beauty, like the night
  Of cloudless climes and starry skies;
And all that's best of dark and bright
  Meet in her aspect and her eyes . . .'

The singer clasped her hands to her mouth. She stood,
bewildered.

'What words are those?' asked the musicians.

'What song is that?'

'What *language* is that!'

And when they blew again upon their golden horns the
strange music came forth and passed slowly over the
audience, which now talked aloud and stood up.

'What's wrong with you?' the musicians asked each
other.

'What tune is that you played?'

'What tune did *you* play?'

The woman wept and ran from the stage. And the
audience moved out of the amphitheatre. And all around
the nervous towns of Mars a similar thing had happened.
A coldness had come, like white snow falling on the air.

In the black alleys, under the torches, the children sang:

'—But when she got there, the cupboard was bare,
  And so her poor dog had none!'

'Children!' voices cried. 'What was that rhyme? Where
did you learn it?'

'We just *thought* of it, all of a sudden. It's just words
we don't understand.'

Doors slammed. The streets were deserted. Above the blue
hills a green star rose.

All over the night side of Mars lovers awoke to listen to
their loved ones who lay humming in the darkness.

'What is that tune?'

And in a thousand villas, in the middle of the night,
women awoke, screaming. They had to be soothed while

the tears ran down their faces. 'There, there. Sleep. What's wrong? A dream?'

'Something terrible will happen in the morning.'

'Nothing can happen, all is well with us.'

A hysterical sobbing. 'It is coming nearer and nearer and *nearer*!'

'Nothing can happen to us. What could? Sleep now. Sleep.'

It was quiet in the deep morning of Mars, as quiet as a cool and black well, with stars shining in the canal waters, and, breathing in every room, the children curled with their spiders in closed hands, the lovers arm in arm, the moons gone, the torches cold, the stone amphitheatres deserted.

The only sound, just before dawn, was a night watchman, far away down a lonely street, walking along in the darkness, humming a very strange song . . .

## *The Earth Men*

Whoever was knocking at the door didn't want to stop.

Mrs Ttt threw the door open. 'Well?'

'You speak *English*!' The man standing there was astounded.

'I speak what I speak,' she said.

'It's wonderful *English*!' The man was in uniform. There were three men with him, in a great hurry, all smiling, all dirty.

'What do you want?' demanded Mrs Ttt.

'You are a *Martian*!' The man smiled. 'The word is not familiar to you certainly. It's an Earth expression.' He nodded at his men. 'We are from Earth. I'm Captain Williams. We've landed on Mars within the hour. Here we are, the *Second* Expedition! There was a First Expedition, but we don't know what happened to it. But here we are, anyway. And you are the first Martian we've met!'

'Martian?' Her eyebrows went up.

'What I mean to say is, you live on the fourth planet from the sun. Correct?'

'Elementary,' she snapped, eyeing them.

'And we' — he pressed his chubby pink hand to his chest — 'we are from Earth. Right, men?'

'Right, sir!' A chorus.

'This is the planet Tyrr,' she said, 'if you want to use the proper name.'

'Tyrr, Tyrr.' The captain laughed exhaustedly. 'What a *fine* name! But, my good woman, how is it you speak such perfect English?'

'I'm not speaking, I'm thinking,' she said. 'Telepathy! Good day!' And she slammed the door.

A moment later there was that dreadful man knocking again.

She whipped the door open. 'What now?' she wondered.

The man was still there, trying to smile, looking bewildered. He put out his hands. 'I don't think you *understand*—'

'What?' she snapped.

The man gazed at her in surprise. 'We're from *Earth*!'

'I haven't time,' she said. 'I've a lot of cooking today and there's cleaning and sewing and all. You evidently wish to see Mt Ttt; he's upstairs in his study.'

'Yes,' said the Earth Man confusedly, blinking. 'By all means, let us see Mr Ttt.'

'He's busy.' She slammed the door again.

This time the knock on the door was most impertinently loud.

'See here!' cried the man when the door was thrust open again. He jumped in as if to surprise her. 'This is no way to treat visitors!'

'All over my clean floor!' she cried. 'Mud! Get out! If you come in my house, wash your boots first.'

The man looked in dismay at his muddy boots. 'This,' he said, 'is no time for trivialities. I think,' he said, 'we should be celebrating.' He looked at her for a long time as if looking might make her understand.

'If you've made my crystal buns fall in the oven,' she exclaimed, 'I'll hit you with a piece of wood!' She peered into a little hot oven. She came back, red, steamy-faced. Her eyes were sharp yellow, her skin was soft brown, she was thin and quick as an insect. Her voice was metallic and sharp. 'Wait here. I'll see if I can let you have a moment with Mr Ttt. What was your business?'

The man swore luridly, as if she'd hit his hand with a hammer. 'Tell him we're from Earth and it's never been done before!'

'What hasn't?' She put her brown hand up. 'Never mind. I'll be back.'

The sound of her feet fluttered through the stone house.

Outside, the immense blue Martian sky was hot and still as warm deep sea-water. The Martian desert lay broiling like a prehistoric mud-pot, waves of heat rising and shimmering. There was a small rocket-ship reclining upon a hilltop nearby. Large footprints came from the rocket to the door of this stone house.

Now there was a sound of quarrelling voices upstairs. The men within the door stared at one another, shifting on their boots, twiddling their fingers, and holding on to their hip-belts. A mans voice shouted upstairs. The woman's voice replied. After fifteen minutes the Earth Men began walking in and out of the kitchen door, with nothing to do.

'Cigarette?' said one of the men.

Somebody got out a packet and they lit up. They puffed low streams of pale white smoke. They adjusted their uniforms, fixed their collars. The voices upstairs continued to mutter and chant. The leader of the men looked at his watch.

'Twenty-five minutes,' he said. 'I wonder what they're up to up there.' He went to a window and looked out.

'Hot day,' said one of the men.

'Yeah,' said someone else in the slow warm time of early afternoon. The voices had faded to a murmur and were now silent. There was not a sound in the house. All the men could hear was their own breathing.

An hour of silence passed. 'I hope we didn't cause any trouble,' said the captain. He went and peered into the living-room.

Mrs Ttt was there, watering some flowers that grew in the centre of the room.

'I knew I had forgotten something,' she said when she saw the captain. She walked out to the kitchen. 'I'm sorry.' She handed him a slip of paper. 'Mr Ttt is much too busy.' She turned to her cooking. 'Anyway, it's not Mr Ttt you want to see; it's Mr Aaa. Take that paper over to the next farm, by the blue canal, and Mr Aaa'll advise you about whatever it is you want to know.'

'We don't want to know anything,' objected the captain, pouting out his thick lips. 'We already know it.'

'You have the paper, what more do you want?' she asked him straight off. And she would say no more.

'Well,' said the captain, reluctant to go. He stood as if waiting for something. He looked like a child staring at an empty Christmas tree. 'Well,' he said again. 'Come on, men.'

The four men stepped out into the hot, silent day.

Half an hour later, Mr Aaa, seated in his library sipping a bit of electric fire from a metal cup, heard the voices outside in the stone causeway. He leaned over the windowsill and gazed at the four uniformed men who squinted up at him.

'Are you Mr Aaa?' they called.

'I am.'

'Mr Ttt sent us to see you!' shouted the captain.

'Why did he do that?' asked Mr Aaa.

'He was busy!'

'Well, that's a shame,' said Mr Aaa sarcastically. 'Does he think I have nothing else to do but entertain people he's too busy to bother with?'

'That's not the important thing, sir,' shouted the captain.

'Well, it is to me. I have much reading to do. Mr Ttt is inconsiderate. This is not the first time he has been this thoughtless of me. Stop waving your hands, sir, until I finish. And pay attention. People usually listen to me when I talk. And you'll listen courteously or I won't talk at all.'

Uneasily the four men in the court shifted and opened their mouths, and once the captain, the veins on his face bulging, showed a few little tears in his eyes.

'Now,' lectured Mr Aaa, 'do you think it fair of Mr Ttt to be so ill-mannered?'

The four men gazed up through the heat. The captain said, 'We're from Earth!'

'I think it very ungentlemanly of him,' brooded Mr Aaa.

'A *rocket* ship. We came in it. Over there!'

'Not the first time. Ttt's been unreasonable, you know.'

'All the way from Earth.'

'Why, for half a mind, I'd call him up and tell him off.'

'Just the four of us; myself and these three men, my crew.'

'I'll call him up; yes, that's what I'll do!'

'Earth. Rocket. Men. Trip. Space.'

'Call him and give him a good lashing!' cried Mr Aaa. He vanished like a puppet from a stage. For a minute there were angry voices back and forth over some weird mechanism or other. Below, the captain and his crew glanced longingly back at their pretty rocket ship lying on the hillside, so sweet and lovely and fine.

Mr Aaa jerked up in the window, wildly triumphant. 'Challenged him to a duel, by the gods! A duel!'

'Mr Aaa – ' the captain started all over again, quietly.

'I'll shoot him dead, do you hear!'

'Mr Aaa, I'd like to *tell* you. We came sixty million miles.'

Mr Aaa regarded the captain for the first time. 'Where'd you say you were from?'

The captain flashed a white smile. Aside to his men he whispered, '*Now* we're getting some place!' To Mr Aaa he called, 'We travelled sixty million miles. From Earth!'

Mr Aaa yawned. 'That's only *fifty* million miles this time of year.' He picked up a frightful-looking weapon. 'Well, I have to go now. Just take that silly note, though I don't know what good it'll do you, and go over that hill into the little town of Iopr and tell Mr Iii all about it. *He's* the man you want to see. Not Mr Ttt, he's an idiot; I'm going to kill him. Not me, because you're not in my line of work.'

'Line of work, line of work!' bleated the captain. 'Do you have to be in a certain line of work to welcome Earth Men?'

'Don't be silly, everyone knows *that*!' Mr Aaa rushed

downstairs. 'Good-bye!' And down the causeway he raced, like a pair of wild calipers.

The four travellers stood shocked. Finally the captain said, 'We'll find someone yet who'll listen to us.'

'Maybe we could go out and come in again,' said one of the men in a dreary voice. 'Maybe we should take off and land again. Give them time to organize a party.'

'That might be a good idea,' murmured the tired captain.

The little town was full of people drifting in and out of doors, saying hello to one another, wearing gold masks and blue masks and crimson masks for pleasant variety, masks with silver lips and bronze eyebrows, masks that smiled or masks that frowned, according to the owners' dispositions.

The four men, wet from their long walk, paused and asked a little girl where Mr Iii's house was.

'There,' The child nodded her head.

The captain got eagerly, carefully down on one knee, looking into her sweet young face. 'Little girl, I want to talk to you.'

He seated her on his knee and folded her small brown hands neatly in his own big ones, as if ready for a bedtime story which he was shaping in his mind slowly and with a great patient happiness in details.

'Well, here's how it is, little girl. Six months ago another rocket came to Mars. There was a man named York in it, and his assistant. Whatever happened to them, we don't know. Maybe they crashed. They came in a rocket. So did we. You should see it! A *big* rocket! So we're the *Second* Expedition, following up the First. And we came all the way from Earth . . .'

The little girl disengaged one hand without thinking about it, and clapped an expressionless golden mask over her face. Then she pulled forth a golden spider toy and dropped it to the ground while the captain talked on. The toy spider climbed back up to her knee obediently, while she speculated upon it coolly through the slits of her emotionless mask and the captain shook her gently and urged his story upon her.

'We're Earth Men,' he said. 'Do you believe me?'

'Yes.' The little girl peeped at the way she was wiggling her toes in the dust.

'Fine.' The captain pinched her arm, a little bit with joviality, a little bit with meanness to get her to look at him. 'We built our own rocket ship. Do you believe *that*?'

The little girl dug in her nose with a finger. 'Yes.'

'And — take your finger out of your nose, little girl — *I* am the captain, and—'

'Never before in history has anybody come across space in a big rocket ship,' recited the little creature, eyes shut.

'Wonderful! How did you know?'

'Oh, telepathy.' She wiped a casual finger on her knee.

'Well, aren't you just *ever* so excited? cried the captain. 'Aren't you glad?'

'You just better go see Mr Iii right away.' She dropped her toy to the ground. 'Mr Iii will like talking to you.' She ran off, with the toy spider scuttling obediently after her.

The captain squatted there looking after her with his hand out. His eyes were watery in his head. He looked at his empty hands. His mouth hung open. The other three men stood with their shadows under them. They spat on the stone street . . .

Mr Iii answered the door. He was on his way to a lecture, but he had a minute, if they would hurry inside and tell him what they desired . . .

'A little attention,' said the captain, red-eyed and tired. 'We're from Earth, we have a rocket, there are four of us, crew and captain, we're exhausted, we're hungry, we'd like a place to sleep. We'd like someone to give us the key to the city or something like that, and we'd like somebody to shake our hands and say "Hooray" and say "Congratulations, old man!" That about sums it up.'

Mr Iii was a tall, vaporous, thin man with thick blind blue

crystals over his yellowish eyes. He bent over his desk and brooded upon some papers, glancing now and again with extreme penetration at his guests.

'Well, I haven't the forms with me here, I don't *think*.' He rummaged through the desk drawers. 'Now where *did* I put the forms?' He mused. 'Somewhere. Somewhere. Oh, *here* we are! Now!' He handed the papers over crisply. 'You'll have to sign these papers, of course.'

'Do we have to go through all this rigmarole?'

Mr Iii gave him a thick glassy look. 'You say you're from Earth, don't you? Well, then there's nothing for it but you sign.'

The captain wrote his name. 'Do you want my crew to sign also?'

Mr Iii looked at the captain, looked at the three others, and burst into a shout of derision. '*Them* sign! Ho! How marvellous! Them, oh, *them* sign!' Tears sprang from his eyes. He slapped his knee and bent to let his laughter jerk out of his gaping mouth. He held himself up with the desk. '*Them* sign!'

The four men scowled. 'What's funny?'

'*Them* sign!' sighed Mr Iii, weak with hilarity. 'So very funny. I'll have to tell Mr Xxx about this!' He examined the filled-out form, still laughing. 'Everything seems to be in order.' He nodded. 'Even the agreement for euthanasia if final decision on such a step is necessary.' He chuckled.

'Agreement for *what*?'

'Don't talk. I have something for you. Here, Take this key.'

The captain flushed. 'It's a great honour.'

'Not the key to the city, you fool!' snapped Mr Iii. 'Just a key to the House. Go down that corridor, unlock the big door, and go inside and shut the door tight. You can spend the night there. In the morning I'll send Mr Xxx to see you.'

Dubiously the captain took the key in hand. He stood looking at the floor. His men did not move. They seemed to be emptied of all their blood and their rocket fever. They were drained dry.

'What is it? What's wrong?' inquired Mr Iii. 'What are you waiting for? What do you want?' He came and peered up into the captain's face, stooping. 'Out with it, you!'

'I don't suppose you could even—' suggested the captain. 'I mean, that is, try to, or think about . . .' He hesitated. 'We've worked hard, we've come a long way, and maybe you could just shake our hands and say "Well done!" do you — think?' His voice faded.

Mr Iii stuck out his hand stiffly. 'Congratulations!' He smiled a cold smile. 'Congratulations.' He turned away. 'I must go now. Use that key.'

Without noticing them again, as if they had melted down through the floor, Mr Iii moved about the room packing a little manuscript case with papers. He was in the room another five minutes but never again addressed the solemn quartet that stood with heads down, their heavy legs sagging, the light dwindling from their eyes. When Mr Iii went out of the door he was busy looking at his fingernails. . . .

They straggled along the corridor in the dull, silent afternoon light. They came to a large burnished silver door, and the silver key opened it. They entered, shut the door, and turned.

They were in a vast sunlit hall. Men and women sat at tables and stood in conversing groups. At the sound of the door they regarded the four uniformed men.

One Martian stepped forward, bowing. 'I am Mr Uuu,' he said.

'And I am Captain Jonathan Williams, of New York City, on Earth,' said the captain without emphasis.

Immediately the hall exploded!

The rafters trembled with shouts and cries. The people, rushing forward, waved and shrieked happily, knocking down tables, swarming, rollicking, seizing the four Earth Men, lifting them swiftly to their shoulders. They charged about the hall six times, six times making a full and wonderful circuit of the room, jumping, bounding, singing.

The Earth Men were so stunned that they rode the toppling shoulders for a full minute before they began to laugh and shout at each other:

'Hey! This is more *like* it!'

'This is the life! Boy! Yay! Yow! Whoopee!'

They winked tremendously at each other. They flung up their hands to clap the air. 'Hey!'

'Hooray!' said the crowd.

They set the Earth Men on a table. The shouting died. The captain almost broke into tears. 'Thank you. It's good, it's good.'

'Tell us about yourselves,' suggested Mr Uuu.

The captain cleared his throat.

The audience ohed and ahed as the captain talked. He introduced his crew; each made a small speech and was embarrassed by the thunderous applause.

Mr Uuu clapped the captain's shoulder. 'It's good to see another man from Earth. I am from Earth also.'

'How was that again?'

'There are many of us here from Earth.'

'You? From Earth?' The captain stared. 'But is that possible? Did you come by rocket? Has space travel been going on for centuries?' His voice was disappointed. 'What – what country are you from?'

'Tuiereol. I came by the spirit of my body, years ago.'

'Tuiereol.' The captain mouthed the word. 'I don't know that country. What's this about spirit of body?'

'And Miss Rrr over here, she's from Earth too, *aren't* you, Miss Rrr?'

Miss Rrr nodded and laughed strangely.

'And so is Mr Www and Mr Qqq and Mr Vvv!'

'I'm from Jupiter,' declared one man, preening himself.

'I'm from Saturn,' said another, eyes glinting slyly.

'Jupiter, Saturn,' murmured the captain, blinking.

It was very quiet now; the people stood around and sat at the tables, which were strangely empty for banquet tables. Their yellow eyes were glowing, and there were dark shadows under their cheekbones. The captain noticed for the first time that there were no windows; the light seemed to permeate the walls. There was only one door. The captain winced. 'This is confusing. Where on Earth is this Tuiereol? Is it near America?'

'What is America?'

'You never heard of America! You say you're from Earth and yet you don't know!'

Mr Uuu drew himself up angrily. 'Earth is a place of seas and nothing but seas. There is no land. I am from Earth, and know.'

'Wait a minute.' The captain sat back. 'You look like a regular Martian. Yellow eyes. Brown skin.'

'Earth is a place of all *jungle*,' said Miss Rrr proudly. 'I am from Orri, on Earth, a civilization built of silver!'

Now the captain turned his head from and then to Mr Uuu and then to Mr Www and Mr Zzz and Mr Nnn and Mr Hhh and Mr Bbb. He saw their yellow eyes waxing and waning in the light, focusing and unfocusing. He began to shiver. Finally he turned to his men and regarded them sombrely.

'Do you realize what this is?'

'What, sir?'

'This is no celebration,' replied the captain tiredly. 'This is no banquet. These aren't government representatives. This is no surprise party. Look at their eyes. Listen to them!'

Nobody breathed. There was only a soft white move of eyes in the close room.

'Now I understand' — the captain's voice was far away — 'why everyone gave us notes and passed us on, one from the other, until we met Mr Iii, who sent us down a corridor with a key to open a door and shut a door. And here we are . . .'

'Where are we, sir?'

The captain exhaled. 'In an insane asylum.'

It was night. The large hall lay quiet and dimly illuminated by hidden light sources in the transparent walls. The four Earth Men sat around a wooden table, their bleak heads bent over their whispers. On the floor, men and women lay huddled. There were little stirs in the dark corners, solitary men or women gesturing their hands. Every half-hour one of the captain's men would try the silver door and return to the table. 'Nothing doing, sir. We're locked in proper.'

'They think we're really insane, sir?'

'Quite. That's why there was no hullabaloo to welcome us. They merely tolerated what, to them, must be a constantly recurring psychotic condition.' He gestured at the dark sleeping shapes all about them. 'Paranoids, every single one! What a welcome they gave us! For a moment there' — a little fire rose and died in his eyes — 'I thought we were getting our true reception. All the yelling and singing and speeches. Pretty nice, wasn't it — while it lasted?'

'How long will they keep us here, sir?'

'Until we prove we're not psychotics.'

'That should be easy.'

'I *hope* so.'

'You don't sound very certain, sir.'

'I'm not. Look in that corner.'

A man squatted alone in darkness. Out of his mouth issued a blue flame which turned into the round shape of a small naked woman. It flourished on the air softly in vapours of cobalt light, whispering and sighing.

The captain nodded at another corner. A woman stood there, changing. First she was embedded in a crystal pillar, then she melted into a golden statue, finally a staff of polished cedar, and back to a woman.

All through the midnight hall people were juggling thin

violent flames, shifting, changing, for night-time was the time of change and affliction.

'Magicians, sorcerers,' whispered one of the Earth Men.

'No, hallucination. They pass their insanity over into us so that we see their hallucinations too. Telepathy. Autosuggestion and telepathy.'

'Is that what worries you, sir?'

'Yes. If hallucinations can appear this "real" to us, to anyone, if hallucinations are catching and almost believable, it's no wonder they mistook us for psychotics. If that man can produce little blue fire women and that woman there melt into a pillar, how natural if normal Martians think we produce our rocket ship with our minds'.

'Oh,' said his men in the shadows.

Around them, in the vast hall, flames leaped blue, flared, evaporated. Little demons of red sand ran between the teeth of sleeping men. Women became oily snakes. There was a smell of reptiles and animals.

In the morning everyone stood around looking fresh, happy, and normal. There were no flames or demons in the room. The captain and his men waited by the silver door, hoping it would open.

Mr Xxx arrived after about four hours. They had a suspicion that he had waited outside the door, peering in at them for at least three hours before he stepped in, beckoned, and led them to his small office.

He was a jovial, smiling man, if one could believe the mask he wore, for upon it was painted not one smile, but three. Behind it, his voice was the voice of a not so smiling psychologist. 'What seems to be the trouble?'

'You think we're insane, and we're not,' said the captain.

'Contrarily, I do not think *all* of you are insane.' The psychologist pointed a little wand at the captain. 'No. Just *you*, sir. The others are secondary hallucinations.'

The captain slapped his knee. 'So *that's* it! That's why

Mr Iii laughed when I suggested my men sign the papers too!'

'Yes, Mr Iii told me.' The psychologist laughed out of the carved, smiling mouth. 'A good joke. Where was I? Secondary hallucinations, yes. Women come to me with snakes crawling from their ears. When I cure them, the snakes vanish.'

'We'll be glad to be cured. Go right ahead.'

Mr Xxx seemed surprised. 'Unusual. Not many people want to be cured. The cure is drastic, you know.'

'Cure ahead! I'm confident you'll find we're all sane.'

'Let me check your papers to be sure they're in order for a "cure".' He checked a file. 'Yes. You know, such cases as yours need special "curing". The people in the hall are simpler forms. But once you've gone this far, I must point out, with primary, secondary, auditory, olfactory, and labial hallucinations, as well as tactile and optical fantasies, it is pretty bad business. We have to resort to euthanasia.'

The captain leaped up with a roar. 'Look here, we've stood quite enough! Test us, tap our knees, check our hearts, exercise us, ask questions!'

'You are free to speak.'

The captain raved for an hour. The psychologist listened.

'Incredible,' he mused. 'Most detailed dream fantasy I've ever heard.'

'God damn it, we'll show you the rocket ship!' screamed the captain.

'I'd like to see it. Can you manifest it in this room?'

'Oh, certainly. It's in that file of yours, under *R*.'

Mr Xxx peered seriously into his file. He went 'Tsk' and shut the file solemnly. 'Why did you tell me to look? The rocket isn't there.'

'Of course not, you idiot! I was joking. Does an insane man joke?'

'You find some odd senses of humour. Now, take me out to your rocket. I wish to see it.'

It was noon. The day was very hot when they reached the rocket.

'So.' The psychologist walked up to the ship and tapped it. It gonged softly. 'May I go inside?' he asked slyly.

'You may.'

Mr Xxx stepped in and was gone for a long time.

'Of all the silly, exasperating things.' The captain chewed a cigar as he waited. 'For two cents I'd go back home and tell people not to bother with Mars. What a suspicious bunch of louts.'

'I gather that a good number of their population are insane, sir. That seems to be their main reason for doubting.'

'Nevertheless, this is all so damned irritating.'

The psychologist emerged from the ship after half an hour of prowling, tapping, listening, smelling, tasting.

'*Now* do you believe!' shouted the captain, as if he were deaf.

The psychologist shut his eyes and scratched his nose. 'This is the most incredible example of sensual hallucination and hypnotic suggestion I've ever encountered. I went through your "rocket", as you call it.' He tapped the hull. 'I hear it. Auditory fantasy.' He drew a breath. 'I smell it. Olfactory hallucination, induced by sensual telepathy.' He kissed the ship. 'I taste it. Labial fantasy!'

He shook the captain's hand. 'May I congratulate you? You are a psychotic genius! You have done a most complete job! The task of projecting your psychotic image into the mind of another via telepathy and keeping the hallucinations from becoming sensually weaker is almost impossible. Those people in the House usually concentrate on visuals or, at the most, visuals and auditory fantasies combined. You have balanced the whole conglomeration! Your insanity is beautifully complete!'

'My insanity.' The captain was pale.

'Yes, yes, what a lovely insanity. Metal, rubber, gravitizers, foods, clothing, fuel, weapons, ladders, nuts, bolts, spoons. Ten thousand separate items I checked on your vessel. Never have I seen such a complexity. There were even *shadows* under the bunks and under *everything*! Such concentration of will! And everything, no matter how or when tested, had a smell, a solidity, a taste, a sound! Let me embrace you!'

He stood back at last. 'I'll write this into my greatest monograph! I'll speak of it at the Martian Academy next month! *Look* at you! Why, you've even changed your eye colour from yellow to blue, your skin to pink from brown. And those clothes, and your hands having five fingers instead of six! Biological metamorphosis through psychological imbalance! And your three friends—'

He took out a little gun. 'Incurable, of course. You poor, wonderful man. You will be happier dead. Have you any last words?'

'Stop, for God's sake! Don't shoot!'

'You sad creature. I shall put you out of your misery which has driven you to imagine this rocket and these three men. It will be most engrossing to watch your friends and your rocket vanish once I have killed you. I will write a neat paper on the dissolvement of neurotic images from what I perceive here today.'

'I'm from Earth! My name is Jonathan Williams, and these—'

'Yes, I know,' soothed Mr Xxx, and fired his gun.

The captain fell with a bullet in his heart. The other three men screamed.

Mr Xxx stared at them. 'You continue to exist? This is superb! Hallucinations with time and spatial persistence!' He pointed the gun at them. 'Well, I'll scare you into dissolving.'

'No!' cried the three men.

'An auditory appeal, even with the patient dead,' observed Mr Xxx as he shot the three men down.

They lay on the sand, intact, not moving.

He kicked them. Then he rapped on the ship.

'*It* persists! *They* persist!' He fired his gun again at the bodies. Then he stood back. The smiling mask dropped from his face.

Slowly the little psychologist's face changed. His jaw sagged. The gun dropped from his fingers. His eyes were dull and vacant. He put his hands up and turned in a blind circle. He fumbled at the bodies, saliva filling his mouth.

'Hallucinations,' he mumbled frantically. 'Taste. Sight. Smell. Sound. Feeling.' He waved his hands. His eyes bulged. His mouth began to give off a faint froth.

'Go away!' he shouted to the bodies. 'Go away!' he screamed at the ship. He examined his trembling hands. 'Contaminated,' he whimpered wildly. 'Carried over into me. Telepathy. Hypnosis. Now *I'm* insane. Now *I'm* contaminated. Hallucinations in all their sensual forms.' He stopped and searched around with his numb hands for the gun. 'Only one cure. Only one way to make them go away, vanish.'

A shot rang out. Mr Xxx fell.

The four bodies lay in the sun. Mr Xxx lay where he fell.

The rocket reclined on the little sunny hill and didn't vanish.

When the town people found the rocket at sunset they wondered what it was. Nobody knew, so it was sold to a junkman and hauled off to be broken up for scrap metal.

That night it rained all night. The next day was fair and warm.

# MARCH 2000

## *The Taxpayer*

He wanted to go to Mars on the rocket. He went down to the rocketfield in the early morning and yelled in through wire fence at the men in uniform that he wanted to go to Mars. He told them he was a taxpayer, his name was Pritchard, and he had a right to go to Mars. Wasn't he born right here in Ohio? Wasn't he a good citizen? Then why couldn't *he* go to Mars? He shook his fists at them and told them that he wanted to get away from Earth; anybody with any sense wanted to get away from Earth. There was going to be a big atomic war on Earth in about two years, and he didn't want to be here when it happened. He and thousands of others like him, if they had any sense, would go to Mars. See if they wouldn't! To get away from wars and censorship and statism and conscription and government control of this and that, of art and science! You could have Earth! He was offering his good right hand, his heart, his head, for the opportunity to go to Mars! What did you have to do, what did you have to sign, whom did you have to know, to get on the rocket?

They laughed out through the wire screen at him. He didn't want to go to Mars, they said. Didn't he know that the First and Second Expeditions had failed, had vanished; the men were probably dead?

But they couldn't prove it, they didn't know for *sure*, he said, clinging to the wire fence. Maybe it was a land of milk and honey up there, and Captain York and Captain Williams had just never bothered to come back. Now were they going to open the gate and let him in to board the Third Expeditionary Rocket, or was he going to have to kick it down?

They told him to shut up.

He saw the men walking out to the rocket.

'Wait for me!' he cried. 'Don't leave me here on this terrible world, I've got to get away; there's going to be an atom war! Don't leave me on Earth!'

They dragged him, struggling, away. They slammed the police wagon door and drove him off into the early morning, his face pressed to the rear window, and just before they sirened over a hill, he saw the red fire and heard the big sound and felt the huge tremor as the silver rocket shot up and left him behind on an ordinary Monday morning on the ordinary planet Earth.

# The Third Expedition

The ship came down from space. It came from the stars, and the black velocities, and the shining movements, and the silent gulfs of space. It was a new ship; it had fire in its body and men in its metal cells, and it moved with a clean silence, fiery and warm. In it were seventeen men, including a captain. The crowd at the Ohio field had shouted and waved their hands up into the sunlight, and the rocket had bloomed out great flowers of heat and colour and run away into space on the *third* voyage to Mars?

Now it was decelerating with metal efficiency in the upper Martian atmospheres. It was still a thing of beauty and strength. It had moved in the midnight waters of space like a pale sea leviathan; it had passed the ancient moon and thrown itself onward into one nothingness following another. The men within it had been battered, thrown about, sickened, made well again, each in his turn. One man had died, but now the remaining sixteen, with their eyes clear in their heads and their faces pressed to the thick glass ports, watched Mars swing up under them.

'Mars!' cried Navigator Lustig.

'Good old Mars!' said Samuel Hinkston, archaeologist.

'Well,' said Captain John Black.

The rocket landed on a lawn of green grass. Outside, upon this lawn, stood an iron deer. Farther up on the green stood a tall brown Victorian house, quiet in the sunlight, all covered with scrolls and rococo, its windows made of blue and pink and yellow and green coloured glass. Upon the porch were hairy geraniums and an old swing which was hooked into the porch ceiling and which now swung back and forth, back and forth, in a little breeze. At the summit of the house was a cupola with diamond leaded-glass windows and a dunce-cap roof! Through the front window you could see a piece of music titled 'Beautiful Ohio' sitting on the music-rest.

Around the rocket in four directions spread the little town, green and motionless in the Martian spring. There were white houses and red brick ones, and tall elm-trees blowing in the wind, and tall maples and horse-chestnuts. And church steeples with golden bells silent in them.

The rocket men looked out and saw this. Then they looked at one another and then they looked out again. They held to each other's elbows, suddenly unable to breathe, it seemed. Their faces grew pale.

'I'll be damned,' whispered Lustig, rubbing his face with his numb fingers. 'I'll be damned.'

'It just can't be,' said Samuel Hinkston.

'Lord,' said Captain John Black.

There was a call from the chemist. 'Sir, the atmosphere is thin for breathing. But there's enough oxygen. It's safe.'

'Then we'll go out,' said Lustig.

'Hold on,' said Captain John Black. 'How do we know what this is?'

'It's a small town with thin but breathable air in it, sir.'

'And it's a small town the like of Earth towns,' said Hinkston, the archaeologist. 'Incredible. It can't be, but it *is*.'

Captain John Black looked at him idly. 'Do you think that the civilizations of two planets can progress at the same rate and evolve in the same way, Hinkston?'

'I wouldn't have thought so, sir.'

Captain Black stood by the port. 'Look out there. The geraniums. A specialized plant. That specific variety has only been known on Earth for fifty years. Think of the thousands of years it takes to evolve plants. Then tell me if it is logical that the Martians should have: one, leaded-glass windows; two, cupolas; three, porch swings; four, an instrument that looks like a piano and probably *is* a piano; and five, if you look closely through this telescope lens here, is it logical that a Martian composer would have published a piece of music titled, strangely enough, "Beautiful Ohio"? All of which means that we have an Ohio River on Mars!'

'Captain Williams, of course!' cried Hinkston.

'What?'

'Captain Williams and his crew of three men! Or Nathaniel York and his partner. That would, explain it!'

'That would explain absolutely nothing. As far as we've been able to figure, the York expedition exploded the day it reached Mars, killing York and his partner. As for Williams and his three men, their ship exploded the second day after their arrival. At least the pulsations from their radios ceased at that time, so we figure that if the men were alive after that they'd have contacted us. And anyway, the York expedition was only a year ago, while Captain Williams and his men landed here some time during last August. Theorizing that they are still alive, could they, even with the help of a brilliant Martian race, have built such a town as this and *aged* it in so short a time? Look at that town out there; why it's been standing here for the last seventy years. Look at the wood on the porch newel; look at the trees, a century old, all of them! No, this isn't York's work or William's. It's something else. I don't like it. And I'm not leaving the ship until I know what it is.'

'For that matter,' said Lustig, nodding, 'Williams and his men, as well as York, landed on the *opposite* side of Mars. We were very careful to land on *this* side.'

'An excellent point. Just in case a hostile local tribe of Martians killed off York and Williams, we have instructions to land in a farther region, to forestall a recurrence of such a disaster. So here we are, as far as we know, in a land that Williams and York never saw.'

'Damn it,' said Hinkston, 'I want to get out into this town, sir, with your permission. It may be there *are* similar thought patterns, civilization graphs on every planet in our sun system. We may be on the threshold of the greatest psychological and metaphysical discovery of our age!'

'I'm willing to wait a moment,' said Captain John Black.

'It may be, sir, that we're looking upon a phenomenon that, for the first time, would absolutely prove the existence of God, sir.'

'There are many people who are of good faith without such proof, Mr Hinkston.'

'I'm one myself, sir. But certainly a town like this could not occur without divine intervention. The *detail*. It fills me with such feelings that I don't know whether to laugh or cry.'

'Do neither, then, until we know what we're up against.'

'Up against?' Lustig broke in. 'Against nothing, Captain. It's a good, quiet green town, a lot like the old fashioned one I was born in. I like the looks of it.'

'When were you born, Lustig?'

'Nineteen-fifty, sir.'

'And you, Hinkston?'

'Nineteen-fifty-five, sir. Grinnell, Iowa. And this looks like home to me.'

'Hinkston, Lustig, I could be either of your fathers. I'm just eighty years old. Born in 1920 in Illinois, and through the grace of God and a science that, in the last fifty years, knows how to make *some* old men young again, here I am on Mars, not any more tired than the rest of you, but infinitely more suspicious. This town out here looks very peaceful and cool, and so much like Green Bluff, Illinois, that it frightens me. It's too *much* like Green Bluff.' He turned to the radioman. 'Radio Earth. Tell them we've landed. That's all. Tell them we'll radio a full report tomorrow.'

'Yes, sir.'

Captain Black looked out the rocket port with his face

that should have been the face of a man of eighty but seemed like the face of a man in his fortieth year. 'Tell you what we'll do, Lustig; you and I and Hinkston'll look the town over. The other men'll stay aboard. If anything happens they can get the hell out. A loss of three men's better than a whole ship. If something bad happens, our crew can warn the next rocket. That's Captain Wilder's rocket, I think, due to be ready to take off next Christmas. If there's something hostile about Mars we certainly want the next rocket to be well armed.'

'So are we. We've got a regular arsenal with us.'

'Tell the men to stand by the guns, then. Come on, Lustig, Hinkston.'

The three men walked together down through the levels of the ship.

It was a beautiful spring day. A robin sat on a blossoming apple tree and sang continuously. Showers of petal snow sifted down when the wind touched the green branches, and the blossom scent drifted upon the air. Somewhere in the town someone was playing the piano, and the music came and went, came and went, softly, drowsily. The song was 'Beautiful Dreamer'. Somewhere else a phonograph, scratchy and faded, was hissing out a record of 'Roamin' through the Gloamin' ', sung by Harry Lauder.

The three men stood outside the ship. They sucked and gasped at the thin, thin air and moved slowly so as not to tire themselves.

Now the phonograph record being played was:

> 'Oh, give me a June night,
> The moonlight and you . . .'

Lustig began to tremble. Samuel Hinkston did likewise.

The sky was serene and quiet, and somewhere a stream of water ran through the cool caverns and tree shadings of a ravine. Somewhere a horse and wagon trotted and rolled by, bumping.

'Sir,' said Samuel Hinkston, 'it must be, it *has* to be, that rocket travel to Mars began in the years before the First World War!'

'No.'

'How else can you explain these houses, the iron deer, the pianos, the music?' Hinkston took the captain's elbow persuasively and looked into the captain's face. 'Say that there were people in the year 1905 who hated war and got together with some scientists in secret and built a rocket and came out here to Mars—'

'No, no, Hinkston.'

'Why not? The world was a different world in 1905; they could have kept it a secret much more easily.'

'But a complex thing like a rocket; no, you couldn't keep it secret.'

'And they came up here to live, and naturally the houses they built were similar to Earth houses because they brought the culture with them.'

'And they've lived here all these years?' said the captain.

'In peace and quiet, yes. Maybe they made a few trips, enough to bring enough people here for one small town, and then stopped for fear of being discovered. That's why this town seems so old-fashioned. I don't see a thing, myself, older than the year 1927, do you? Or maybe, sir, rocket travel is older than we think. Perhaps it started in some part of the world centuries ago and was kept secret by the small number of men who came to Mars with only occasional visits to Earth over the centuries.'

'You make it sound almost reasonable.'

'It has to be. We've the proof here before us; all we have to do is find some people and verify it.'

Their boots were deadened of all sound in the thick green grass. It smelled from a fresh mowing. In spite of himself, Captain John Black felt a great peace come over him. It had been thirty years since he had been in a small town, and the buzzing of spring bees on the air lulled and quieted him, and the fresh look of things was a balm to the soul.

They set foot upon the porch. Hollow echoes sounded from under the boards as they walked to the screen door. Inside they could see a bead curtain hung across the hall entry, and a crystal chandelier and a Maxfield Parrish painting framed on one wall over a comfortable Morris chair. The house smelled old, and of the attic, and infinitely comfortable. You could hear the tinkle of ice in a lemonade pitcher. In a distant kitchen, because of the heat of the day, someone was preparing a cold lunch. Someone was humming under her breath, high and sweet.

Captain John Black rang the bell.

Footsteps, dainty and thin, came along the hall, and a kind-faced lady of some forty years, dressed in the sort of dress you might expect in the year 1909, peered out at them.

'Can I help you?' she asked.

'Beg your pardon,' said Captain Black uncertainly. 'But we're looking for – that is, could you help us—' He stopped. She looked out at him with dark, wondering eyes.

'If you're selling something—' she began.

'No wait!' he cried. 'What town is this?'

She looked him up and down. 'What do you mean, what town is it? How could you be in a town and not know the name?'

The captain looked as if he wanted to go sit under a shady apple tree. 'We're strangers here. We want to know how this town got here and how you got here.'

'Are you census-takers?'

'No.'

'Everyone knows,' she said, 'this town was built in 1868. Is this a game?'

'No, not a game!' cried the captain. 'We're from Earth.'

'Out of the *ground*, do you mean?' she wondered.

'No, we came from the third planet, Earth, in a ship. And we've landed here on the fourth planet, Mars—'

'This,' explained the woman, as if she were addressing a child, 'is Green Bluff, Illinois, on the continent of America, surrounded by the Atlantic and Pacific oceans, on a place called the world, or, sometimes, the Earth. Go away now. Good-bye.'

She trotted down the hall, running her fingers through the beaded curtains.

The three men looked at one another.

'Let's knock the screen door in,' said Lustig.

'We can't do that. This is private property. Good God!'

They went to sit down on the porch step.

'Did it ever strike you, Hinkston, that perhaps we got ourselves somehow, in some way, off track, and by accident came back and landed on Earth?'

'How could we have done that?'

'I don't know, I don't know. Oh God, let me think!'

Hinkston said, 'But we checked every mile of the way. Our chronometers said so many miles. We went past the moon and out into space, and here we are. I'm *positive* we're on Mars.'

Lustig said, 'But suppose, by accident, in space, in time, we got lost in the dimensions and landed on an Earth that is thirty or forty years ago.'

'Oh, go away, Lustig!'

Lustig went to the door, rang the bell, and called into the cool dim rooms: 'What year is this?'

'Nineteen twenty-six, of course,' said the lady, sitting in a rocking-chair, taking a sip of her lemonade.

'Did you hear that?' Lustig turned wildly to the others. 'Nineteen twenty-six! We *have* gone back in time! This *is* Earth!'

Lustig sat down, and the three men let the wonder and terror of the thought afflict them. Their hands stirred fitfully on their knees. The captain said, 'I didn't ask for a thing like this. It scares the hell out of me. How can a thing like this happen? I wish we'd brought Einstein with us.'

'Will anyone in this town believe us?' said Hinkston. 'Are we playing with something dangerous? Time, I mean. Shouldn't we just take off and go home?'

'No. Not until we try another house.'

They walked three houses down to a little white cottage under an oak-tree. 'I like to be as logical as I can be,' said the captain. 'And I don't believe we've put our finger on it yet. Suppose, Hinkston, as you originally suggested, that rocket travel occurred years ago? And when the Earth people lived here a number of years they began to get homesick for Earth. First a mild neurosis about it, then a full-fledged psychosis. Then threatened insanity. What would you do as a psychiatrist if faced with such a problem?'

Hinkston thought. 'Well, I think I'd arrange the civilization on Mars so it resembled Earth more and more each day. If there was any way of reproducing every plant, every road, and every lake, and even an ocean, I'd do so. Then by some vast crowd hypnosis I'd convince everyone in a town this size that this really was Earth, not Mars at all.'

'Good enough, Hinkston. I think we're on the right track now. That woman in that house there just *thinks* she's living on Earth. It protects her sanity. She and all the others in this town are the patients of the greatest experiment in migration and hypnosis you will ever lay eyes on in your life.'

'That's *it*, sir!' cried Lustig.

'Right!' said Hinkston.

'Well.' The captain sighed. 'Now we've got somewhere I feel better. It's all a bit more logical. That talk about time and going back and forth and travelling through time turns my stomach upside down. But *this* way—' The captain smiled. 'Well, well, it looks as if we'll be fairly popular here.'

'Or will we?' said Lustig. 'After all, like the Pilgrims,

these people came here to escape Earth. Maybe they won't be too happy to see us. Maybe they'll try to drive us out or kill us.'

'We have superior weapons. This next house now. Up we go.'

But they had hardly crossed the lawn when Lustig stopped and looked off across the town, down the quiet, dreaming afternoon street. 'Sir,' he said.

'What is it, Lustig?'

'Oh, sir, *sir*, what I see—' said Lustig, and he began to cry. His fingers came up, twisting and shaking, and his face was all wonder and joy and incredulity. He sounded as if at any moment he might go quite insane with happiness. He looked down the street and began to run, stumbling awkwardly, falling, picking himself up, and running on. 'Look, look!'

'Don't let him get away!' The captain broke into a run.

Now Lustig was running swiftly, shouting. He turned into a yard half-way down the shady street and leaped up upon the porch of a large green house with an iron rooster on the roof.

He was beating at the door, hollering and crying, when Hinkston and the captain ran up behind him. They were all gasping and wheezing, exhausted from their run in the thin air. 'Grandma! Grandpa!' cried Lustig.

Two old people stood in the doorway.

'David!' their voices piped, and they rushed out to embrace and pat him on the back and move around him. 'David, oh, David, it's been so many years! How you've grown, boy; how big you are, boy! Oh, David boy, how are you?'

'Grandma, Grandpa!' sobbed David Lustig. 'You look fine, fine!' He held them, turned them, kissed them, hugged them, cried on them, held them out again, blinking at the little old people. The sun was in the sky, the wind blew, the grass was green, the screen door stood wide.

'Come in, boy, come in. There's iced tea for you, fresh; lots of it!'

'I've got friends here.' Lustig turned and waved at the captain and Hinkston frantically, laughing. 'Captain, come on up.'

'Howdy,' said the old people. 'Come in. Any friends of David's are our friends too. Don't stand there!'

In the living-room of the old house it was cool, and a grandfather clock ticked high and long and bronzed in one corner. There were soft pillows on large couches and walls filled with books and a rug cut in a thick rose pattern, and iced tea in the hand, sweating, and cool on the thirsty tongue.

'Here's to our health.' Grandma tipped her glass to her porcelain teeth.

'How long have you been here, Grandma?' said Lustig.

'Ever since we died,' she said tartly.

'Ever since you what?' Captain John Black set down his glass.

'Oh yes.' Lustig nodded. 'They've been dead thirty years.'

'And you sit there calmly!' shouted the captain.

'Tush.' The old woman winked glitteringly. 'Who are you to question what happens? Here we are. What's life, anyway? Who does what for why and where? All we know is here we are, alive again, and no questions asked. A second chance.' She toddled over and held out her thin wrist. 'Feel.' The captain felt. 'Solid, ain't it?' she asked. He nodded. 'Well, then,' she said triumphantly, 'why go around questioning?'

'Well,' said the captain, 'it's simply that we never thought we'd find a thing like this on Mars.'

'And now you've found it. I dare say there's lots on every planet that'll show you God's infinite ways.'

'Is this Heaven?' asked Hinkston.

'Nonsense, no. It's a world and we get a second chance. Nobody told us why. But then nobody told us why we were on Earth, either. That other Earth, I mean. The one you came from. How do we know there wasn't *another* before *that* one?'

'A good question,' said the captain.

Lustig kept smiling at his grandparents. 'Gosh. it's good to see you. Gosh, it's good.'

The captain stood up and slapped his hand on his leg in a casual fashion. 'We've got to be going. Thank you for the drinks.'

'You'll be back, of course,' said the old people. 'For supper tonight?'

'We'll try to make it, thanks. There's so much to be done. My men are waiting for me back at the rocket and—'

He stopped. He looked towards the door, startled.

Far away in the sunlight there was a sound of voices, a shouting and a great hello.

'What's that?' asked Hinkston.

'We'll soon find out.' And Captain John Black was out of the front door abruptly, running across the green lawn into the street of the Martian town.

He stood looking at the rocket. The ports were open and his crew was streaming out, waving their hands. A crowd of people had gathered, and in and through and among these people the members of the crew were hurrying, talking, laughing, shaking hands. People did little dances. People swarmed. The rocket lay empty and abandoned.

A brass band exploded in the sunlight, flinging off a gay tune from upraised tubas and trumpets. There was a bang of drums and a shrill of fifes. Little girls with golden hair jumped up and down. Little boys shouted, 'Hooray!' Fat men passed around ten-cent cigars. The town mayor made a speech. Then each member of the crew, with a mother on one arm, a father or sister on the other, was spirited off down the street into little cottages or big mansions.

'Stop!' cried Captain Black.

The doors slammed shut.

The heat rose in the clear spring sky, and all was silent. The brass band banged off around a corner, leaving the rocket to shine and dazzle alone in the sunlight.

'Abandoned!' said the captain. 'They abandoned the ship, they did! I'll have their skins, by God! They had orders!'

'Sir,' said Lustig, 'don't be too hard on them. Those were all old relatives and friends.'

'That's no excuse!'

'Think how they felt, Captain, seeing familiar faces outside the ship!'

'They had their orders, damn it!'

'But how would you have felt, Captain?'

'I would have obeyed orders—' The captain's mouth remained open.

Striding along the sidewalk under the Martian sun, tall, smiling, eyes amazingly clear and blue, came a young man of some twenty-six years. 'John!' the man called out, and broke into a trot.

'What?' Captain John Black swayed.

'John, you old son of a bitch!'

The man ran up and gripped his hand and slapped him on the back.

'It's you,' said Captain Black.

'Of course, who'd you *think* it was?'

'Edward!' The captain appealed now to Lustig and Hinkston, holding the stranger's hand. 'This is my brother Edward. Ed, meet my men, Lustig, Hinkston! My brother!'

They tugged at each other's hands and arms and then finally embraced. 'Ed!' 'John, you bum, you!' 'You're looking fine, Ed; but, Ed, what *is* this? You haven't changed over the years. You died, I remember, when you were twenty-six and I was nineteen. Good God! so many years ago, and here you are and, Lord, what goes on?'

'Mom's waiting,' said Edward Black, grinning.

'Mom?'

'And Dad too.'

'Dad?' The captain almost fell as if he had been hit by a mighty weapon. He walked stiffly and without co-ordination. 'Mom and Dad alive? Where?'

'At the old house on Oak Knoll Avenue.'

'The old house.' The captain stared in delighted amaze. 'Did you hear that, Lustig, Hinkston?'

Hinkston was gone. He had seen his own house down the street and was running for it. Lustig was laughing. 'You see, Captain, what happened to everyone on the rocket? They couldn't help themselves.'

'Yes. Yes.' The captain shut his eyes. 'When I open my eyes you'll be gone.' He blinked. 'You're still there. God, Ed, but you look *fine*!'

'Come on; lunch's waiting. I told Mom.'

Lustig said, 'Sir, I'll be with my grandfolks if you need me.'

'What? Oh, fine, Lustig. Later, then.'

Edward seized his arm and marched him. 'There's the house. Remember it?'

'Hell! Bet I can beat you to the front porch!'

They ran. The trees roared over Captain Black's head; the earth roared under his feet. He saw the golden figure of Edward Black pull ahead of him in the amazing dream of reality. He saw the house rush forward, the screen door swing wide.

'Beat you!' cried Edward.

'I'm an old man,' panted the captain, 'and you're still young. But then, you *always* beat me, I remember!'

In the doorway, Mom, pink, plump, and bright. Behind her, pepper-grey, Dad, his pipe in his hand.

'Mom, Dad!'

He ran up the steps like a child to meet them.

It was a fine long afternoon. They finished a late lunch and they sat in the parlour and he told them all about his rocket and they nodded and smiled upon him and Mother was just the same and Dad bit the end off a cigar and lighted it thoughtfully in his old fashion. There was a big turkey dinner at night and time flowing on. When the drumsticks were sucked clean and lay brittle upon the plates, the captain leaned back and exhaled his deep satisfaction. Night was in all the trees and colouring the sky, and the lamps were halos of pink light in the gentle house. From all the other houses down the street came sounds of music, pianos playing, doors slamming.

Mom put a record on the victrola, and she and Captain John Black had a dance. She was wearing the same perfume he remembered from the summer when she and Dad had been killed in the train accident. She was very real in his arms as they danced lightly to the music. 'It's not every day,' she said, 'you get a second chance to live.'

'I'll wake in the morning,' said the captain. 'And I'll be in my rocket, in space, and all this will be gone.'

'No, don't think that,' she cried softly. 'Don't question. God's good to us. Let's be happy.'

'Sorry, Mom.'

The record ended in a circular hissing.

'You're tired, Son.' Dad pointed with his pipe. 'Your old bedroom's waiting for you, brass bed and all.'

'But I should report my men in.'

'Why?'

'Why? Well, I don't know. No reason, I guess. No, none at all. They're all eating or in bed. A good night's sleep won't hurt them.'

'Good night, Son.' Mom kissed his cheek. 'It's good to have you home.'

'It's good to *be* home.'

He left the land of cigar-smoke and perfume and books and gentle light and ascended the stairs, talking, talking with Edward. Edward pushed a door open, and there was the yellow brass bed and the old semaphore banners from college and a very musty racoon coat which he stroked with muted affection. 'It's too much,' said the captain. 'I'm numb and I'm tired. Too much has happened today. I feel as if I'd been out in a pounding rain for forty-eight hours without an umbrella or a coat. I'm soaked to the skin with emotion.'

Edward slapped wide the snowy linens and flounced the pillows. He slid the window up and let the night-blooming jasmine float in. There was moonlight and the sound of distant dancing and whispering.

'So this is Mars,' said the captain, undressing.

'This is it.' Edward undressed in idle, leisurely moves, drawing his shirt off over his head, revealing golden shoulders and the good muscular neck.

The lights were out; they were in bed, side by side, as in the days how many decades ago? The captain lolled and was nourished by the scent of jasmine pushing the lace curtains out upon the dark air of the room. Among the trees, upon a lawn, someone had cranked up a portable phonograph and now it was playing softly, 'Always'.

The thought of Marilyn came to his mind.

'Is Marilyn here?'

His brother, lying straight out in the moonlight from the window, waited and then said, 'Yes. She's out of town. But she'll be here in the morning.'

The captain shut his eyes. 'I want to see Marilyn very much.'

The room was square and quiet except for their breathing.

'Good night, Ed.'

A pause. 'Good night, John.'

He lay peacefully, letting his thoughts float. For the first time the stress of the day was moved aside; he could think logically now. It had all been emotion. The bands playing, the familiar faces. But now . . .

How? he wondered. How was all this made? And why? For what purpose? Out of the goodness of some divine intervention? Was God, then, really that thoughtful of his children? How and why and what for?

He considered the various theories advanced in the first heat of the afternoon by Hinkston and Lustig. He let all kinds of new theories drop in lazy pebbles down through his mind, turning, throwing out dull flashes of light. Mom. Dad. Edward. Mars. Earth. Mars. Martians.

Who had lived here a thousand years ago on Mars? Martians? Or had this always been the way it was today?

Martians. He repeated the word idly, inwardly.

He laughed out loud almost. He had the most ridiculous theory quite suddenly. It gave him a kind of chill. It was really nothing to consider, of course. Highly improbable. Silly. Forget it. Ridiculous.

But, he thought, just *suppose* . . . Just suppose, now, that there were Martians living on Mars and they saw our ship coming and saw us inside our ship and hated us. Suppose, now, just for the hell of it, that they wanted to destroy us, as invaders, as unwanted ones, and they wanted to do it in a very clever way, so that we would be taken off guard. Well, what would the best weapon be that a Martian could use against Earth Men with atomic weapons?

The answer was interesting. Telepathy, hypnosis, memory, and imagination.

Suppose all of these houses aren't real at all, this bed not real, but only figments of my own imagination, given substance by telepathy and hypnosis through the Martians, thought Captain John Black. Suppose these houses are really some *other* shape, a Martian shape, but, by playing on my desires and wants, these Martians have made this seem like my old home town, my old house, to lull me out of my suspicions. What better way to fool a man, using his own mother and father as bait?

And this town, so old, from the year 1926, long before any of my men were born. From a year when I was six years old and there *were* records of Harry Lauder, and Maxfield

Parrish paintings *still* hanging, and bead curtains, and 'Beautiful Ohio', and turn-of-the-century architecture. What if the Martians took the memories of a town *exclusively* from *my* mind? They say childhood memories are the clearest. And after they built the town from *my* mind, they populated it with the most loved people from all the minds of the people on the rocket!

And suppose those two people in the next room, asleep, are not my mother and father at all. But two Martians, incredibly brilliant, with the ability to keep me under hypnosis all of the time.

And that brass band today? What a startlingly wonderful plan it would be! First, fool Lustig, then Hinkston, then gather a crowd; and all the men in the rocket, seeing mothers, aunts, uncles, sweethearts, dead ten, twenty years ago, naturally, disregarding orders, rush out and abandon ship. What more natural? What more unsuspecting? What more simple? A man doesn't ask too many questions when his mother is suddenly brought back to life; he's much too happy. And here we all are tonight, in various houses, in various beds, with no weapons to protect us, and the rocket lies in the moonlight, empty. And wouldn't it be horrible and terrifying to discover that all of this was part of some great clever plan by the Martians to divide and conquer us, and kill us? Sometime during the night, perhaps, my brother here on this bed will change form, melt, shift, and become another thing, a terrible thing, a Martian. It would be very simple for him just to turn over in bed and put a knife into my heart. And in all those other houses down the street, a dozen other brothers or fathers suddenly melting away and taking knives and doing things to the unsuspecting, sleeping men of Earth . . .

His hands were shaking under the covers. His body was cold. Suddenly it was not a theory. Suddenly he was very afraid.

He lifted himself in bed and listened. The night was very

quiet. The music had stopped. The wind had died. His brother lay sleeping beside him.

Carefully he lifted the covers, rolled them back. He slipped from the bed and was walking softly across the room when his brother's voice said, 'Where are you going?'

'What?'

His brother's voice was quite cold. 'I said, where do you think you're going?'

'For a drink of water.'

'But you're not thirsty.'

'Yes, yes, I am.'

'No, you're not.'

Captain John Black broke and ran across the room. He screamed. He screamed twice.

He never reached the door.

In the morning the brass band played a mournful dirge. From every house in the street came little solemn processions bearing long boxes, and along the sun-filled street, weeping, came the grandmas and mothers and sisters and brothers and uncles and fathers, walking to the churchyard, where there were new holes freshly dug and new tombstones installed. Sixteen holes in all, and sixteen tombstones.

The mayor made a little speech, his face sometimes looking like the mayor, sometimes looking like something else.

Mother and Father Black were there, with Brother Edward, and they cried, their faces melting now from a familiar face into something else.

Grandpa and Grandma Lustig were there, weeping, their faces shifting like wax, shimmering as all things shimmer on a hot day.

The coffins were lowered. Someone murmured about 'the unexpected and sudden deaths of sixteen fine men during the night—'

Earth pounded down on the coffin lids.

The brass band, playing 'Columbia, the Gem of the Ocean', marched and slammed back into town, and everyone took the day off.

# – and the Moon be Still as Bright

It was so cold when they first came from the rocket into the night that Spender began to gather the dry Martian wood and build a small fire. He didn't say anything about a celebration; he merely gathered the wood, set fire to it, and watched it burn.

In the flare that lighted the thin air of this dried-up sea of Mars he looked over his shoulder and saw the rocket that had brought them all, Captain Wilder and Cheroke and Hathaway and Sam Parkhill and himself, across a silent black space of stars to land upon a dead, dreaming world.

Jeff Spender waited for the noise. He watched the other men and waited for them to jump around and shout. It would happen as soon as the numbness of being the 'first' men to Mars wore off. None of them said anything, but many of them were hoping, perhaps, that the other expeditions had failed and that this, the Fourth, would be *the* one. They meant nothing evil by it. But they stood thinking it, nevertheless, thinking of the honour and fame, while their lungs became accustomed to the thinness of the atmosphere, which almost made you drunk if you moved too quickly.

Gibbs walked over to the freshly ignited fire and said, 'Why don't we use the ship chemical fire instead of that wood?'

'Never mind,' said Spender, not looking up.

It wouldn't be right, the first night on Mars, to make a loud noise, to introduce a strange, silly bright thing like a stove. It would be a kind of imported blasphemy. There'd be time for that later; time to throw condensed-milk cans in the proud Martian canals; time for copies of the New

York *Times* to blow and caper and rustle across the lone grey Martian sea-bottoms; time for banana-peels and picnic papers in the fluted, delicate ruins of the old Martian valley towns. Plenty of time for that. And he gave a small inward shiver at the thought.

He fed the fire by hand, and it was like an offering to a dead giant. They had landed on an immense tomb. Here a civilization had died. It was only simple courtesy that the first night be spent quietly.

'This isn't my idea of a celebration.' Gibbs turned to Captain Wilder. 'Sir, I thought we might break our rations of gin and meat and whoop it up a bit.'

Captain Wilder looked off towards a dead city a mile away. 'We're all tired,' he said remotely, as if his whole attention was on the city and his men forgotten. 'Tomorrow night, perhaps. Tonight we should be glad we got across all that space without getting a meteor in our bulkhead or having one man of us die.'

The men shifted around. There were twenty of them, holding to each other's shoulders or adjusting their belts. Spender watched them. They were not satisfied. They had risked their lives to do a big thing. Now they wanted to be shouting drunk, firing off guns to show how wonderful they were to have kicked a hole in space and ridden a rocket all the way to Mars.

But nobody was yelling.

The captain gave a quiet order. One of the men ran into the ship and brought forth food-tins, which were opened and dished out without much noise. The men were beginning to talk now. The captain sat down and recounted the trip to them. They already knew it all, but it was good to hear about it, as something over and done and safely put away. They would not talk about the return trip. Someone brought that up, but they told him to keep quiet. The spoons moved in the double moonlight; the food tasted good and the wine was even better.

There was a touch of fire across the sky, and an instant later the auxiliary rocket landed beyond the camp. Spender watched as the small port opened and Hathaway, the physician-geologist – they were all men of twofold ability, to conserve space on the trip – stepped out. He walked slowly over to the captain.

'Well?' said Captain Wilder.

Hathaway gazed out at the distant cities twinkling in the starlight. After swallowing and focusing his eyes he said, 'That city there, Captain, is dead and has been dead a good many thousand years. That applies to those three cities in the hills also. But that fifth city, two hundred miles over, sir—'

'What about it?'

'People were living in it last week, sir.'

Spender got to his feet.

'Martians,' said Hathaway.

'Where are they now?'

'Dead,' said Hathaway. 'I went into a house on one street. I thought that it, like the other towns and houses, had been dead for centuries. My God, there were bodies there. It was like walking in a pile of autumn leaves. Like sticks and pieces of burnt newspaper, that's all. And *fresh*. They'd been dead ten days at the outside.

'Did you check other towns? Did you see *anything* alive?'

'Nothing whatever. So I went out to check the other towns. Four out of five have been empty for thousands of years. What happened to the original inhabitants I haven't the faintest idea. But the fifth city always contained the same thing. Bodies. Thousands of bodies.'

'What did they die of?' Spender moved forward.

'You won't believe it.'

'What killed them?'

Hathaway said simply, 'Chicken-pox.'

'My God, no!'

'Yes. I made tests. Chicken-pox. It did things to the

Martians it never did to Earth Men. Their metabolism reacted differently, I suppose. Burnt them black and dried them out to brittle flakes. But it's chicken-pox, nevertheless. So York and Captain Williams and Captain Black must have got through to Mars, all three expeditions. God knows what happened to them. But we at least know what *they* unintentionally did to the Martians.'

'You saw no other life?'

'Chances are a few of the Martians, if they were smart, escaped to the mountains. But there ain't enough, I'll lay you money, to be a native problem. This planet is through.'

Spender turned and went to sit at the fire, looking into it. Chicken-pox, God, chicken-pox, think of it! A race builds itself for a million years, refines itself, erects cities like those out there, does everything it can to give itself respect and beauty, and then it dies. Part of it dies slowly, in its own time, before our age, with dignity. But the rest! Does the rest of Mars die of a disease with a fine name or a terrifying name or a majestic name? No, in the name of all that's holy, it has to be chicken-pox, a child's disease, a disease that doesn't even kill *children* on Earth. It's not right and it's not fair. It's like saying the Greeks died of mumps, or the proud Romans died on their beautiful hills of athlete's foot! If only we'd given the Martians time to arrange their death-robes, lie down, look fit, and think up some *other* excuse for dying. It can't be a dirty, silly thing like chicken-pox. It doesn't fit the architecture; it doesn't fit this entire world!

'All right, Hathaway, get yourself some food.'

'Thank you, Captain.'

And as quickly as that it was forgotten. The men talked among themselves.

Spender did not take his eyes off them. He left his food on his plate under his hands. He felt the land getting colder. The stars drew closer, very clear.

When anyone talked too loudly the captain would reply in a low voice that made them talk quietly from imitation.

The air smelled clean and new. Spender sat for a long time just enjoying the way it was made. It had a lot of things in it he couldn't identify: flowers, chemistries, dusts, winds.

'Then there was that time in New York when I got that blonde, what's her name? — Ginnie!' cried Biggs. '*That* was it!'

Spender tightened in. His hand began to quiver. His eyes moved behind the thin, sparse lids.

'And Ginnie said to me—' cried Biggs.

The men roared.

'So I smacked her!' shouted Biggs, with a bottle in his hand.

Spender set down his plate. He listened to the wind over his ears, cool and whispering. He looked at the cool ice of the white Martian buildings over there on the empty sea lands.

'What a woman, what a woman!' Biggs emptied his bottle in his wide mouth. 'Of all the women I ever knew!'

The smell of Biggs's sweating body was on the air. Spender let the fire die. 'Hey, dick her up there, Spender!' said Biggs, glancing at him for a moment, then back to his bottle. 'Well, one night Ginnie and me—'

A man named Schoenke got out his accordion, and did a kicking dance, the dust springing up around him.

'Ahoo — I'm alive!' he shouted.

'Yay!' roared the men. They threw down their empty plates. Three of them lined up and kicked like chorus-maidens, joking loudly. The others, clapping hands, yelled for something to happen. Cheroke pulled off his shirt and showed his naked chest, sweating as he whirled about. The moonlight shone on his crew-cut hair and his young, clean-shaven cheeks.

In the sea bottom the wind stirred along faint vapours, and from the mountains great stone visages looked upon the silvery rocket and the small fire.

The noise got louder, more men jumped up, someone sucked on a mouth-organ, someone else blew on a tissue-papered comb. Twenty more bottles were opened and drunk. Biggs staggered about, wagging his arms to direct the dancing men.

'Come on, sir!' cried Cheroke to the captain, wailing a song.

The captain had to join the dance. He didn't want to. His face was solemn. Spender watched, thinking: You poor man, what a night this is! They don't know what they're doing. They should have had an orientation programme before they came to Mars to tell them how to look and how to walk around and be good for a few days.

'That does it.' The captain begged off and sat down, saying he was exhausted. Spender looked at the captain's chest. It wasn't moving up and down very fast. His face wasn't sweaty, either.

Accordion, harmonica, wine, shout, dance, wail, roundabout, clash of pan, laughter.

Biggs weaved to the rim of the Martian canal. He carried six empty bottles and dropped them one by one into the deep blue canal waters. They made empty, hollow, drowning sounds as they sank.

'I christen thee, I christen thee, I christen thee—' said Biggs thickly. 'I christen thee Biggs, Biggs, Biggs, Canal—'

Spender was on his feet, over the fire, and alongside Biggs before anyone moved. He hit Biggs once in the teeth and once in the ear. Biggs toppled and fell down into the canal water. After the splash Spender waited silently for Biggs to climb back up on to the stone bank. By that time the men were holding Spender.

'Hey, what's eating you, Spender? Hey?' they asked.

Biggs climbed up and stood dripping. He saw the men holding Spender. 'Well,' he said and started forward.

'That's enough,' snapped Captain Wilder. The men broke away from Spender. Biggs stopped and glanced at the captain.

'All right, Biggs, get some dry clothes. You men, carry on your party! Spender, come with me!'

The men took up the party. Wilder moved off some distance and confronted Spender. 'Suppose you explain what just happened,' he said.

Spender looked at the canal. 'I don't know. I was ashamed. Of Biggs and us and the noise. Christ, what a spectacle!'

'It's been a long trip. They've got to have their fling.'

'Where's their respect, sir? Where's their sense of the right thing?'

'You're tired, and you've a different way of seeing things, Spender. That's a fifty-dollar fine for you.'

'Yes, sir. It was just the idea of Them watching us make fools of ourselves.'

'Them?'

'The Martians, whether they're dead or not.'

'Most certainly dead,' said the captain. 'Do you think They know we're here?'

'Doesn't an old thing always know when a new thing comes?'

'I suppose so. You sound as if you believe in spirits.'

'I believe in the things that were done, and there are evidences of many things done on Mars. There are streets and houses, and there are books, I imagine, and big canals and clocks and places for stabling, if not horses, well, then some domestic animal, perhaps with twelve legs, who knows? Everywhere I look I see things that were used. They were touched and handled for centuries.

'Ask me, then, if I believe in the spirit of the things as they were used, and I'll say yes. They're all here. All the things which had uses. All the mountains which had names. And we'll never be able to use them without feeling uncomfortable. And somehow the mountains will never sound right to us; we'll give them new names, but the old names are there, somewhere in time, and the mountains were shaped and seen under those names. The names we'll give to the canals and mountains and cities will fall like so much water on the back of a mallard. No matter how we touch Mars, we'll never touch it. And then we'll get mad at it, and you know what we'll do? We'll rip it up, rip the skin off, and change it to fit ourselves.'

'We won't ruin Mars,' said the captain. 'It's too big and too good.'

'You think not? We Earth Men have a talent for ruining big, beautiful things. The only reason we didn't set up hot-dog stands in the midst of the Egyptian temple of Karnak is because it was out of the way and served no large commercial purpose. And Egypt is a small part of Earth. But here, this whole thing is ancient and different, and we have to set down somewhere and start fouling it up. We'll call the canal the Rockefeller Canal and the mountain King George Mountain and the sea the Dupont Sea, and there'll be Roosevelt and Lincoln and Coolidge cities, and it won't ever be right, when there are the *proper* names for these places.'

'That'll be your job, as archaeologist, to find out the old names, and we'll use them.'

'A few men like us against all the commercial interests.' Spender looked at the iron mountains. '*They* know we're here tonight, to spit in their wine, and I imagine they hate us.'

The captain shook his head. 'There's no hatred here.' He listened to the wind. 'From the look of their cities, they were a graceful, beautiful and philosophical people. They accepted what came to them. They acceded to racial death, that much we know, and without a last-moment war of frustration to tumble down their cities. Every town we've seen so far has been flawlessly intact. They probably don't mind us being here any more than they'd mind children playing on the lawn, knowing and understanding children for what they are. And, anyway, perhaps all this will change us for the better.

'Did you notice the peculiar quiet of the men, Spender, until Biggs forced them to get happy? They looked pretty humble and frightened. Looking at all this, we know we're not so hot; we're kids in rompers, shouting with our play rockets and atoms, loud and alive. But one day Earth will be as Mars is today. This will sober us. It's an object lesson in civilizations. We'll learn from Mars. Now suck in your chin. Let's go back and play happy. That fifty-dollar fine still goes.'

The party was not going well. The wind kept coming in off the dead sea. It moved around the men and it moved around the captain and Jeff Spender as they returned to the group. The wind pulled at the dust and the shining rocket and pulled at the accordion, and the dust got into the vamped harmonica. The dust got in their eyes and the wind made a high singing sound in the air. As suddenly as it had come the wind died.

But the party had died too.

The men stood upright against the dark, cold sky.

'Come on gents, come on!' Biggs bounced from the ship in a fresh uniform, not looking at Spender even once. His voice was like someone in an empty auditorium. It was alone. 'Come on!'

Nobody moved.

'Come one, Whitie, your harmonica!'

Whitie blew a chord. It sounded funny and wrong. Whitie knocked the moisture from his harmonica and put it away.

'What kinda party *is* this?' Biggs wanted to know.

Someone hugged the accordion. It gave a sound like a dying animal. That was all.

'Okay, me and my bottle will go have our own party.' Biggs squatted against the rocket, drinking from a flask.

Spender watched him. Spender did not move for a long time. Then his fingers crawled up along his trembling leg to his holstered pistol, very quietly, and stroked and tapped the leather sheath.

'All those who want to can come into the city with me,' announced the captain. 'We'll post a guard here at the rocket and go armed, just in case.'

The men counted off. Fourteen of them wanted to go, including Biggs, who laughingly counted himself in, waving his bottle. Six others stayed behind.

'Here we go!' Biggs shouted.

The party moved out into the moonlight silently. They made their way to the outer rim of the dreaming dead city in the light of the racing twin moons. Their shadows, under them, were double shadows. They did not breathe, or seemed not to, perhaps, for several minutes. They were waiting for something to stir in the dead city, some grey form to rise, some ancient, ancestral shape to come galloping across the vacant sea bottom on an ancient, armoured steed of impossible lineage, of unbelievable derivation.

Spender filled the streets with his eyes and his mind. People moved like blue vapour lights on the cobbled avenues; and there were faint murmurs of sound, and odd animals scurrying across the grey-red sands. Each window was given a person who leaned from it and waved slowly, as if under a timeless water, at some moving form in the fathoms of space below the moon-silvered towers. Music was played on some inner ear, and Spender imagined the shape of such instruments to evoke such music. The land was haunted.

'Hey!' shouted Biggs, standing tall, his hands around his open mouth. 'Hey, you people in the city there, you!'

'Biggs!' said the captain.

Biggs quieted.

They walked forward on a tiled avenue. They were all whispering now, for it was like entering a vast open library or a mausoleum in which the wind lived and over which the stars shone. The captain spoke quietly. He wondered where the people had gone, and what they had been, and who their kings were, and how they had died. And he wondered, quietly aloud, how they had built this city to last the ages through, and had they ever come to Earth? Were they ancestors of Earth Men ten thousand years removed? And had they loved and hated similar loves and hates, and done similar silly things when silly things were done?

Nobody moved. The moons held and froze them; the wind beat slowly around them.

'Lord Byron,' said Jeff Spender.

'Lord who?' The captain turned and regarded him.

'Lord Byron, a nineteenth-century poet. He wrote a poem a long time ago that fits this city and how the Martians must feel, if there's anything left of them to feel. It might have been written by the last Martian poet.'

The men stood motionless, their shadows under them.

The captain said, 'How does the poem go, Spender?'

Spender shifted, put out his hand to remember, squinted silently a moment; then remembering, his slow quiet voice repeated the words and the men listened to everything he said:

> 'So we'll go no more a-roving
>     So late into the night,
> Though the heart be still as loving,
>     And the moon be still as bright.'

The city was grey and high and motionless. The men's faces were turned in the light.

> 'For the sword outwears its sheath,
>     And the soul wears out the breast,
> And the heart must pause to breathe,
>     And love itself have rest.
>
> 'Though the night was made for loving,
>     And the day returns too soon,
> Yet we'll go no more a-roving
>     By the light of the moon.'

Without a word the Earth Men stood in the centre of the city. It was a clear night. There was not a sound except the wind. At their feet lay a tile court worked into the shapes of ancient animals and peoples. They looked down upon it.

Biggs made a sick noise in his throat. His eyes were dull. His hands went to his mouth; he choked, shut his eyes, bent, and a thick rush of fluid filled his mouth, spilled out, fell to splash on the tiles, covering the designs. Biggs did this twice. A sharp winy stench filled the cool air.

No one moved to help Biggs. He went on being sick.

Spender stared for a moment, then turned and walked off into the avenues of the city, alone in the moonlight. Never once did he pause to look back at the gathered men there.

They turned in at four in the morning. They lay upon blankets and shut their eyes and breathed the quiet air. Captain Wilder sat feeding little sticks into the fire.

McClure opened his eyes two hours later. 'Aren't you sleeping, sir?'

'I'm waiting for Spender.' The captain smiled faintly.

McClure thought it over. 'You know, sir, I don't think he'll ever come back. I don't know how I know, but that's the way I feel about him, sir; he'll never come back.'

McClure rolled over into sleep. The fire crackled and died.

Spender did not return in the following week. The captain sent searching parties, but they came back saying they didn't know where Spender could have gone. He would be back when he got good and ready. He was a sorehead, they said. To the devil with him!

The captain said nothing but wrote it down in his log . . .

It was a morning that might have been a Monday or a Tuesday or any day on Mars. Biggs was on the canal rim; his feet hung down into the cool water, soaking while he took the sun on his face.

A man walked along the bank of the canal. The man threw a shadow down upon Biggs. Biggs glanced up.

'Well, I'll be damned!' said Biggs.

'I'm the last Martian,' said the man, taking out a gun.

'What did you say?' said Biggs.

'I'm going to kill you.'

'Cut it. What kind of joke's that, Spender?'

'Stand up and take it in the stomach.'

'For Christ's sake, put that gun away.'

Spender pulled the trigger only once. Biggs sat on the edge of the canal for a moment before he leaned forward and fell into the water. The gun had made only a whispering hum. The body drifted with slow unconcern under the slow canal tides. It made a hollow bubbling sound that ceased after a moment.

Spender shoved his gun into its holster and walked soundlessly away. The sun was shining down upon Mars. He felt it burn his hands and slide over the sides of his tight face. He did not run; he walked as if nothing were new except the daylight. He walked down to the rocket, and some of the men were eating a freshly cooked breakfast under a shelter built by Cookie.

'Here comes The Lonely One,' someone said.

'Hello, Spender! Long time no see!'

The four men at the table regarded the silent man who stood looking back at them.

'You and them goddamn ruins,' laughed Cookie, stirring a black substance in a crock. 'You're like a dog in a bone yard.'

'Maybe,' said Spender. 'I've been finding out things. What would you say if I said I'd found a Martian prowling around?'

The four men laid down their forks.

'Did you? Where?

'Never mind. Let me ask you a question. How would you

feel if you were a Martian and people came to your land and started tearing it up?'

'I know exactly how I'd feel,' said Cheroke. 'I've got some Cherokee blood in me. My grandfather told me lots of things about Oklahoma Territory. If there's a Martian around, I'm all for him.'

'What about you other men?' asked Spender carefully.

Nobody answered; their silence was talk enough. Catch as catch can, finder's keepers, if the other fellow turns his cheek slap it hard, etc. . . .

'Well,' said Spender, 'I've found a Martian.'

The men squinted at him.

'Up in a dead town. I didn't think I'd find him. I didn't intend looking him up. I don't know what he was doing there. I've been living in a little valley town for about a week, learning how to read the ancient books and looking at their old art forms. And one day I saw this Martian. He stood there for a moment and then he was gone. He didn't come back for another day. I sat around learning how to read the old writing, and the Martian came back, each time a little nearer, until on the day I learned how to decipher the Martian's language — it's amazingly simple and there are picturegraphs to help you — the Martian appeared before me and said, "Give me your boots." And I gave him my boots and he said, "Give me your uniform and all the rest of your apparel." And I gave him all of that, and then he said, "Give me your gun," and I gave him my gun. Then he said, "Now come along and watch what happens." And the Martian walked down into camp and he's here now.'

'I don't see any Martian,' said Cheroke.

'I'm sorry.'

Spender took out his gun. It hummed softly. The first bullet got the man on the left; the second and third bullets took the men on the right and the centre of the table. Cookie turned in horror from the fire to receive the fourth bullet.

He fell back into the fire and lay there while his clothes caught fire.

The rocket lay in the sun. Three men sat at breakfast, their hands on the table, not moving, their food getting cold in front of them. Cheroke, untouched, sat alone, staring in numb disbelief at Spender.

'You can come with me,' said Spender.

Cheroke said nothing.

'You can be with me on this.' Spender waited.

Finally Cheroke was able to speak. 'You killed them,' he said, daring to look at the men around him.

'They deserved it.'

'You're crazy!'

'Maybe I am. But you can come with me.'

'Come with you, for what?' cried Cheroke, the colour gone from his face, his eyes watering. 'Go on, get out!'

Spender's face hardened. 'Of all of them, I thought you would understand.'

'Get out!' Cheroke reached for his gun.

Spender fired one last time. Cheroke stopped moving.

Now Spender swayed. He put his hand to his sweating face. He glanced at the rocket and suddenly began to shake all over. He almost fell, the physical reaction was so overwhelming. His face held an expression of one awakening from hypnosis, from a dream. He sat down for a moment and told the shaking to go away.

'Stop it, stop it!' he commanded of his body. Every fibre of him was quivering and shaking. 'Stop it!' He crushed his body with his mind until all the shaking was squeezed out of it. His hands lay calmly now upon his silent knees.

He arose and strapped a portable storage locker on his back with quiet efficiency. His hand began to tremble again, just for a breath of an instant, but he said, 'No!' very firmly, and the trembling passed. Then, walking stiffly, he moved out between the hot red hills of the land, alone.

*

The sun burned farther up the sky. An hour later the captain climbed down out of the rocket to get some ham and eggs. He was just saying hello to the four men sitting there when he stopped and noticed a faint smell of gun-fumes on the air. He saw the cook lying on the ground, with the campfire under him. The four men sat before food that was now cold.

A moment later Parkhill and two others climbed down. The captain stood in their way, fascinated by the silent men and the way they sat at their breakfast.

'Call the men, all of them,' said the captain.

Parkhill hurried off down the canal rim.

The captain touched Cheroke. Cheroke twisted quietly and fell from his chair. Sunlight burned in his bristled short hair and on his high cheekbones.

The men came in.

'Who's missing?'

'It's still Spender, sir. We found Biggs floating in the canal.'

'Spender!'

The captain saw the hills rising in the daylight. The sun showed his teeth in a grimace. 'Damn him,' he said tiredly. 'Why didn't he come and talk to me?'

'He should've talked to *me*,' cried Parkhill, eyes blazing. 'I'd have shot his bloody brains out, that's what I'd have done, by God!'

Captain Wilder nodded at two of his men. 'Get shovels,' he said.

It was hot digging the graves. A warm wind came from over the vacant sea and blew the dust into their faces as the captain turned the Bible pages. When the captain closed the book someone began shovelling slow streams of sand down upon the wrapped figures.

They walked back to the rocket, clicked the mechanisms of their rifles, put thick grenade packets on their backs, and checked the free play of pistols in their holsters. They were each assigned a certain part of the hills. The captain directed them without raising his voice or moving his hands where they hung at his sides.

'Let's go,' he said.

Spender saw the thin dust rising in several places in the valley and he knew the pursuit was organized and ready. He put down the thin silver book that he had been reading as he sat easily on a flat boulder. The book's pages were tissue-thin, pure silver, hand-painted in black and gold. It was a book of philosophy at least ten thousand years old he had found in one of the villas of a Martian valley town. He was reluctant to lay it aside.

For a time he had thought, What's the use? I'll sit here reading until they come along and shoot me.

The first reaction to his killing the six men this morning had caused a period of stunned blankness, then sickness, and now, a strange peace. But the peace was passing, too, for he saw the dust billowing from the trails of the hunting men, and he experienced the return of resentment.

He took a drink of cool water from his hip canteen. Then he stood up, stretched, yawned, and listened to the peaceful wonder of the valley around him. How very fine if he and a few others he knew on Earth could be here, live out their lives here, without a sound or a worry.

He carried the book with him in one hand, the pistol ready in his other. There was a little swift-running stream filled with white pebbles and rocks where he undressed and waded in for a brief washing. He took all the time he wanted before dressing and picking up his gun again.

The firing began about three in the afternoon. By then Spender was high in the hills. They followed him through three small Martian hill towns. Above the towns, scattered like pebbles, were single villas where ancient families had found a brook, a green spot, and laid out a tile pool, a library, and a court with a pulsing fountain. Spender took half an hour, swimming in one of the pools which was filled with seasonal rain, waiting for the pursuers to catch up with him.

Shots rang out as he was leaving the little villa. Tile chipped up some twenty feet behind him, exploded. He broke into a trot, moved behind a series of small bluffs, turned and with his first shot dropped one of the men dead in his tracks.

They would form a net, a circle; Spender knew that. They would go around and close in and they would get him. It was a strange thing that the grenades were not used. Captain Wilder could easily order the grenades tossed.

But I'm much too nice to be blown to bits, thought Spender. That's what the captain thinks. He wants me with only one hole in me. Isn't that odd? He wants my death to be clean. Nothing messy. Why? Because he understands me. And because he understands, he's willing to risk good men to give me a clean shot in the head. Isn't that it?

Nine, ten shots broke out in a rattle. Rocks around him jumped up. Spender fired steadily, sometimes while glancing at the silver book he carried in his hand.

The captain ran in the hot sunlight with a rifle in his hands. Spender followed him in his pistol sights but did not fire. Instead he shifted and blew the top off a rock where Whitie lay, and heard an angry shout.

Suddenly the captain stood up. He had a white handkerchief in his hands. He said something to his men and came walking up the mountain after putting aside his rifle. Spender lay there, then got to his feet, his pistol ready.

The captain came up and sat down on a warm boulder, not looking at Spender for a moment.

The captain reached into his blouse pocket. Spender's fingers tightened on the pistol.

The captain said, 'Cigarette?'

'Thanks.' Spender took one.

'Light?'

'Got my own.'

They took one or two puffs in silence.

'Warm,' said the captain.

'Is it?'

'You comfortable up here?'

'Quite.'

'How long do you think you can hold out?'

'About twelve men's worth.'

'Why didn't you kill all of us this morning when you had the chance? You could have, you know.'

'I know. I got sick. When you want to do a thing badly enough you lie to yourself. You say the other people are all wrong. Well, soon after I started killing people I realized they were just fools and I shouldn't be killing them. But it was too late. I couldn't go on with it then, so I came up here where I could lie to myself some more and get angry, to build it all up again.'

'Is it built up?'

'Not very high. Enough.'

The captain considered his cigarette. 'Why did you do it?'

Spender quietly laid the pistol at his feet. 'Because I've seen that what these Martians had was just as good as anything we'll ever hope to have. They stopped where we should have stopped a hundred years ago. I've walked in their cities and I know these people and I'd be glad to call them my ancestors.'

'They have a beautiful city there.' The captain nodded at one of several places.

'It's not that alone. Yes, their cities are good. They knew how to blend art into their living. It's always been a thing apart for Americans. Art was something you kept in the crazy son's room upstairs. Art was something you took in Sunday doses, mixed with religion, perhaps. Well, these Martians have art and religion and everything.'

'You think they knew what it was all about, do you?'

'For my money.'

'And for that reason you started shooting people.'

'When I was a kid my folks took me to visit Mexico City. I'll always remember the way my father acted — loud and big. And my mother didn't like the people because they were dark and didn't wash enough. And my sister wouldn't talk to most of them. I was the only one really liked it. And I can see my mother and father coming to Mars and acting the same way here.

'Anything that's strange is no good to the average American. If it doesn't have Chicago plumbing, it's nonsense. The thought of that! Oh God, the thought of that! And then — the war. You heard congressional speeches before we left. If things work out they hope to establish three atomic research and atom bomb depots on Mars. That means Mars is finished; all this wonderful stuff gone. How would you feel if a Martian vomited stale liquor on the White House floor?'

The captain said nothing, but listened.

Spender continued: 'And then the other power interests coming up. The mineral men and the travel men. Do you remember what happened to Mexico when Cortez and his very fine good friends arrived from Spain? A whole civilization destroyed by greedy, righteous bigots. History will never forgive Cortez.'

'You haven't acted ethically yourself today,' observed the captain.

'What could I do? Argue with you? It's simply me against the whole crooked grinding greedy set-up on Earth. They'll be flopping their filthy atom bombs up here, fighting for bases to have wars. Isn't it enough they've ruined one planet, without ruining another? Do they have to foul someone else's manger? The simple-minded windbags. When I got up here I felt I was not only free of their so-called culture, I felt I was free of their ethics and their customs. I'm out of their frame of reference, I thought. All I have to do is kill you off and live my own life.'

'But it didn't work out,' said the captain.

'No. After the fifth killing at breakfast, I discovered I wasn't all new, all Martian, after all. I couldn't throw away everything I had learned on Earth so easily. But now I'm feeling steady again. I'll kill you all off. That'll delay the next trip in a rocket for a good five years. There's no other rocket in existence today, save this one. The people on Earth will wait a year, two years, and then when they hear nothing from us, they'll be very afraid to build a new rocket. They'll take twice as long and make a hundred extra experimental models to insure themselves against another failure.'

'You're correct.'

'A good report from you, on the other hand, if you returned, would hasten the whole invasion of Mars. If I'm lucky I'll live to be sixty years old. Every expedition that lands on Mars will be met by me. There won't be more than one ship at a time coming up, one every year or so, and never more than twenty men in the crew. After I've made friends with them and explained that our rocket exploded one day – I intend to blow it up after I finish my job this week – I'll kill them off, every one of them. Mars will be untouched for the next half-century. After a while, perhaps the Earth people will give up trying. Remember how they grew leery of the idea of building Zeppelins that were always going down in flames?'

'You've got it all planned,' admitted the captain.

'I have.'

'Yet you're outnumbered. In an hour we'll have you surrounded. In an hour you'll be dead.'

'I've found some underground passages and a place to live you'll never find. I'll withdraw there to live for a few weeks. Until you're off guard. I'll come out then to pick you off, one by one.'

The captain nodded. 'Tell me about your civilization here,' he said, waving his hand at the mountain towns.

'They knew how to live with nature and get along with nature. They didn't try too hard to be all man and no animal. That's the mistake we made when Darwin showed up. We embraced him and Huxley and Freud, all smiles. And then we discovered that Darwin and our religions didn't mix. Or at least we didn't think they did. We were fools. We tried to budge Darwin and Huxley and Freud. They wouldn't move very well. So, like idiots, we tried knocking down religion.

'We succeeded pretty well. We lost our faith and went around wondering what life was for. If art was no more than a frustrated outflinging of desire, if religion was no more than self-delusion, what good was life? Faith had always given us answers to all things. But it all went down the drain with Freud and Darwin. We were and still are a lost people.'

'And these Martians are a *found* people?' inquired the captain.

'Yes. They knew how to combine science and religion so the two worked side by side, neither denying the other, each enriching the other.'

'That sounds ideal.'

'It was. I'd like to show you how the Martians did it.'

'My men are waiting.'

'We'll be gone half an hour. Tell them that, sir.'

The captain hesitated, then rose and called an order down the hill.

Spender led him over into a little Martian village built all of cool perfect marble. There were great friezes of beautiful animals, white-limbed cat things and yellow-limbed sun symbols, and statues of bull-like creatures and statues of men and women and huge fine-featured dogs.

'There's your answer, Captain.'

'I don't see.'

'The Martians discovered the secret of life among animals. The animal does not question life. It lives. Its very reason for living *is* life; it enjoys and relishes life. You see — the statuary, the animal symbols, again and again.'

'It looks pagan.'

'On the contrary, those are God symbols, symbols of life.

Man had become too much man and not enough animal on Mars too. And the men of Mars realized that in order to survive they would have to forgo asking that one question any longer: *Why live?* Life was its own answer. Life was the propagation of more life and the living of as good a life as possible. The Martians realized that they asked the question "Why live at all?" at the height of some period of war and despair, when there was no answer. But once the civilization calmed, quieted, and wars ceased, the question became senseless in a new way. Life was now good and needed no arguments.'

'It sounds as if the Martians were quite naive.'

'Only when it paid to be naive. They quit trying too hard to destroy everything, to humble everything. They blended religion and art and science because, at base, science is no more than an investigation of a miracle we can never explain, and art is an interpretation of that miracle. They never let science crush the aesthetic and the beautiful. It's all simply a matter of degree. An Earth Man thinks: "In that picture, colour does not exist, really. A scientist can prove that colour is only the way the cells are placed in a certain material to reflect light. Therefore, colour is not really an actual part of things I happen to see." A Martian, far cleverer, would say: "This is a fine picture. It came from the hand and the mind of a man inspired. Its idea and its colour are from life. This thing is good." '

There was a pause. Sitting in the afternoon sun, the captain looked curiously around at the little silent cool town.

'I'd like to live here,' he said.

'You may if you want.'

'You ask *me* that?'

'Will any of those men under you ever really understand all this? They're professional cynics, and it's too late for them. Why do you want to go back with them? So you can keep up with the Joneses? To buy a gyro just like Smith has? To listen to music with your pocket-book instead of your glands? There's a little patio down here with a reel of Martian music in it at least fifty thousand years old. It still plays. Music you'll never hear in your life. You could hear it. There are books. I've gotten on well in reading them already. You could sit and read.'

'It all sounds quite wonderful, Spender.'

'But you won't stay?'

'No. Thanks, anyway.'

'And you certainly won't let me stay without trouble. I'll have to kill you all.'

'You're optimistic.'

'I have something to fight for and live for; that makes me a better killer. I've got what amounts to a religion, now. It's learning how to breathe all over again. And how to lie in the sun getting a tan, letting the sun work into you. And how to hear music and how to read a book. What does your civilization offer?'

The captain shifted his feet. He shook his head. 'I'm sorry this is happening. I'm sorry about it all.'

'I am too. I guess I'd better take you back now so you can start the attack.'

'I guess so.'

'Captain, I won't kill you. When it's all over, you'll still be alive.'

'What?'

'I decided when I started that you'd be untouched.'

'Well . . .'

'I'll save you out from the rest. When they're dead, perhaps you'll change your mind.'

'No,' said the captain. 'There's too much Earth blood in me. I'll have to keep after you.'

'Even when you have a chance to stay here?'

'It's funny, but yes, even with that. I don't know why. I've never asked myself. Well, here we are.' They had returned to their meeting-place now. 'Will you come quietly, Spender? This is my last offer.'

'Thanks, no.' Spender put out his hand. 'One last thing. If you win, do me a favour. See what can be done to restrict tearing this planet apart, at least for fifty years, until the archaeologists have had a decent chance, will you?'

'Right.'

'And last — if it helps any, just think of me a very crazy fellow who went berserk one summer day and never was right again. It'll be a little easier on you that way.'

'I'll think it over. So long, Spender. Good luck.'

'You're an odd one,' said Spender as the captain walked back down the trail in the warm-blowing wind.

The captain returned like something lost to his dusty men. He kept squinting at the sun and breathing hard.

'Is there a drink?' he said. He felt a bottle put cool into his hand. 'Thanks.' He drank. He wiped his mouth.

'All right,' he said. 'Be careful. We have all the time we want. I don't want any more lost. You'll have to kill him. He won't come down. Make it a clean shot if you can. Don't mess him. Get it over with.'

'I'll blow his damned brains out,' said Sam Parkhill.

'No, through the chest,' said the captain. He could see Spender's strong, clearly determined face.

'His bloody brains,' said Parkhill.

The captain handed him the bottle jerkily. 'You heard what I said. Through the chest.'

Parkhill muttered to himself.

'Now,' said the captain.

They spread again, walking and then running, and then walking on the hot hillside places where there would be sudden cool grottos that smelled of moss, and sudden open blasting-places that smelled of sun on stone.

I hate being clever, thought the captain, when you don't really feel clever and don't want to _be_ clever. To sneak around and make plans and feel big about making them.

I hate this feeling of thinking I'm doing right when I'm not really certain I am. Who are we, anyway? The majority? Is that the answer? The majority is always holy, is it not? Always, always; just never wrong for one little insignificant tiny moment, is it? Never ever wrong in ten million years? He thought: What is this majority and who are in it? And what do they think and how did they get that way and will they ever change and how the devil did I get caught in this rotten majority? I don't feel comfortable. Is it claustrophobia, fear of crowds, or common sense? Can one man be right, while all the world thinks they are right? Let's not think about it. Let's crawl around and act exciting and pull the trigger. There, and *there*!

The men ran and ducked and ran and squatted in shadows and showed their teeth, gasping, for the air was thin, not meant for running; the air was thin and they had to sit for five minutes at a time, wheezing and seeing black lights in their eyes, eating at the thin air and wanting more, tightening their eyes, and at last getting up, lifting their guns to tear holes in that thin summer air, holes of sound and heat.

Spender remained where he was, firing only on occasion.

'Damned brains all over!' Parkhill yelled, running uphill.

The captain aimed his gun at Sam Parkhill. He put it down and stared at it in horror. 'What were you doing?' he asked of his limp hand and the gun.

He had almost shot Parkhill in the back.

'God help me.'

He saw Parkhill still running, then falling to lie safe.

Spender was being gathered in by a loose, running net of men. At the hilltop, behind two rocks, Spender lay, grinning with exhaustion from the thin atmosphere, great islands of sweat under each arm. The captain saw the two rocks. There was an interval between them of some four inches, giving free access to Spender's chest.

'Hey, you!' cried Parkhill. 'Here's a slug for your head!'

Captain Wilder waited. Go on, Spender, he thought. Get out, like you said you would. You've only a few minutes to escape. Get out and come back later. Go on. You said you would. Go down in the tunnels you said you found, and lie there and live for months and years, reading your fine books and bathing in your temple pools. Go on, now, man, before it's too late.

Spender did not move from his position.

'What's wrong with him?' the captain asked himself.

The captain picked up his gun. He watched the running, hiding men. He looked at the towers of the little clean Martian village, like sharply carved chess-pieces lying in the afternoon. He saw the rocks and the interval between where Spender's chest was revealed.

Parkhill was charging up, screaming in fury.

'No, Parkhill,' said the captain. 'I can't let you do it. Nor the others. No, none of you. Only me.' He raised the gun and sighted it.

Will I be clean after this? he thought. Is it right that it's me who does it? Yes, it is. I know what I'm doing for what reason and it's right, because I think I'm the right person. I hope and pray I can live up to this.

He nodded his head at Spender. 'Go on,' he called in a loud whisper which no one heard. 'I'll give you thirty seconds more to get away. Thirty seconds!'

The watch ticked on his wrist. The captain watched it tick. The men were running. Spender did not move. The watch ticked for a long time, very loudly in the captain's ear. 'Go on, Spender, go on, get away!'

The thirty seconds were up.

The gun was sighted. The captain drew a deep breath. 'Spender,' he said, exhaling.

He pulled the trigger.

All that happened was that a faint powdering of rock went up in the sunlight. The echoes of the report faded.

*

The captain arose and called to his men: 'He's dead.'

The other men did not believe it. Their angles had prevented their seeing that particular fissure in the rocks. They saw their captain run up the hill, alone, and thought him either very brave or insane.

The men came after him a few minutes later.

They gathered around the body and someone said, 'In the chest?'

The captain looked down. 'In the chest,' he said. He saw how the rocks had changed colour under Spender. 'I wonder why he waited. I wonder why he didn't escape as he planned. I wonder why he stayed on and got himself killed.'

'Who knows?' someone said.

Spender lay there, his hands clasped, one around the gun, the other around the silver book that glittered in the sun.

Was it because of me? thought the captain. Was it because I refused to give in myself? Did Spender hate the idea of killing me? Am I any different from these others here? Is that what did it? Did he figure he could trust me? What other answer is there?

None. He squatted by the silent body.

I've got to live up to this, he thought. I can't let him down now. If he figured there was something in me that was like himself and couldn't kill me because of it, then what a job I have ahead of me! That's it, yes, that's it. I'm Spender all over again, but I think before I shoot. I don't shoot at all, I don't kill. I do things with people. And he couldn't kill me because I was himself under a slightly different condition.

The captain felt the sunlight on the back of his neck. He heard himself talking: 'If only he had come to me and talked it over before he shot anybody, we could have worked it out somehow.'

'Worked what out?' said Parkhill. 'What could we have worked out with *his* likes?'

There was a singing of heat in the land, off the rocks and

off the blue sky. 'I guess you're right,' said the captain. 'We could never have got together. Spender and myself, perhaps. But Spender and you and the others, no, never. He's better off now. Let me have a drink from that canteen.'

It was the captain who suggested the empty sarcophagus for Spender. They had found an ancient Martian tomb-yard. They put Spender into a silver case with waxes and wines which were ten thousand years old, his hands folded on his chest. The last they saw of him was his peaceful face.

They stood for a moment in the ancient vault. 'I think it would be a good idea for you to think of Spender from time to time,' said the captain.

They walked from the vault and shut the marble door.

The next afternoon Parkhill did some target practice in one of the dead cities, shooting out the crystal windows and blowing the tops off the fragile towers. The captain caught Parkhill and knocked his teeth out.

# The Settlers

The men of Earth came to Mars.

They came because they were afraid or unafraid, because they were happy or unhappy, because they felt like Pilgrims or did not feel like Pilgrims. There was a reason for each man. They were leaving bad wives or bad jobs or bad towns; they were coming to find something or leave something or get something, to dig up something or bury something or leave something alone. They were coming with small dreams or large dreams or none at all. But a government finger pointed from four-colour posters in many towns: THERE'S WORK FOR YOU IN THE SKY: SEE MARS! and the men shuffled forward, only a few at first, a double-score, for most men felt the great illness in them even before the rocket fired into space. And this disease was called The Loneliness, because when you saw your home town dwindle to the size of your fist and then lemon-size and then pin-size and vanish in the fire-wake, you felt you had never been born, there was no town, you were nowhere, with space all around, nothing familiar, only other strange men. And when the state of Illinois, Iowa, Missouri, or Montana vanished into cloud seas. and, doubly, when the United States shrank to a misted island and the entire planet Earth became a muddy baseball tossed away, then you were alone, wandering in the meadows of space, on your way to a place you couldn't imagine.

So it was not unusual that the first men were few. The number grew steadily in proportion to the census of Earth Men already on Mars. There was comfort in numbers. But the first Lonely Ones had to stand by themselves . . .

# The Green Morning

When the sun set he crouched by the path and cooked a small supper and listened to the fire crack while he put the food in his mouth and chewed thoughtfully. It had been a day not unlike thirty others, with many neat holes dug in the dawn hours, seeds dropped in, and water brought from the bright canals. Now, with an iron weariness in his slight body, he lay and watched the sky colour from one darkness to another.

His name was Benjamin Driscoll, and he was thirty-one years old. And the thing that he wanted was Mars grown green and tall with trees and foliage, producing air, more air, growing larger with each season; trees to cool the towns in the boiling summer, trees to hold back the winter winds. There were so many things a tree could do: add colour, provide shade, drop fruit, or become a children's playground, a whole sky universe to climb and hang from; an architecture of food and pleasure, that was a tree. But most of all the trees would distil an icy air for the lungs, and a gentle rustling for the ear when you lay nights in your snowy bed and were gentled to sleep by the sound.

He lay listening to the dark earth gather itself, waiting for the sun, for the rains that hadn't come yet. His ear to the ground, he could hear the feet of the years ahead moving at a distance, and he imagined the seeds he had placed today sprouting up with green and taking hold on the sky, pushing out branch after branch, until Mars was an afternoon forest, Mars was a shining orchard.

In the early morning, with the small sun lifting faintly among the folded hills, he would be up and finished with a smoky breakfast in a few minutes and, treading out the fire ashes, be on his way with knapsacks, testing, digging, placing seed or sprout, tamping lightly, watering, going on, whistling, looking at the clear sky brightening towards a warm noon.

'You need the air,' he told the night fire. The fire was a ruddy, lively companion that snapped back at you, that slept close by with drowsy pink eyes warm through the chilly night. 'We all need the air. It's thin air here on Mars. You get tired so soon. It's like living in the Andes, in South America, high. You inhale and don't get anything. It doesn't satisfy.'

He felt his rib-case. In thirty days, how it had grown. To take in more air, they would all have to build their lungs. Or plant more trees.

'That's what I'm here for,' he said. The fire popped. 'In school they told a story about Johnny Appleseed walking across America planting apple trees. Well, I'm doing more. I'm planting oaks, elms, and maples, every kind of tree, aspens and deodars and chestnuts. Instead of making just fruit for the stomach, I'm making air for the lungs. When those trees grow up some year, *think* of the oxygen they'll make!'

He remembered his arrival on Mars. Like a thousand others, he had gazed upon a still morning and thought, How do I fit here? What will I do? Is there a job for me?

Then he had fainted.

Someone pushed a vial of ammonia to his nose and, coughing, he came round.

'You'll be all right,' said the doctor.

'What happened?'

'The air's pretty thin. Some can't take it. I think you'll have to go back to Earth.'

'No!' He sat up, and almost immediately felt his eyes darken and Mars revolve twice around under him. His nostrils dilated and he forced his lungs to drink in deep nothingnesses. 'I'll be all right. I've got to stay here!'

They let him lie gasping in horrid fish-like motions. And he thought, Air, air, air. They're sending me back because of air. And he turned his head to look across the Martian fields and hills. He brought them to focus, and the first thing he noticed was that there were no trees, no trees at all, as far as you could look in any direction. The land was down upon itself, a land of black loam, but nothing on it, not even grass. Air, he thought, the thin stuff whistling in his nostrils. Air, air. And on top of hills, or in their shadows, or even by little creeks, not a tree and not a single green blade of grass. Of course! He felt the answer came not from his mind, but his lungs and his throat. And the thought was a sudden gust of pure oxygen, raising him up. Trees and grass. He looked down at his hands and turned them over. He would plant trees and grass. That would be his job, to fight against the very thing that might prevent his staying here. He would have a private horticultural war with Mars. There lay the old soil, and the plants of it so ancient they had worn themselves out. But what if new forms were introduced? Earth trees, great mimosas and weeping willows and magnolias and magnificent eucalyptus. What then? There was no guessing what mineral wealth hid in the soil, untapped because the old ferns, flowers, bushes, and trees had tired themselves to death.

'Let me up!' he shouted. 'I've got to see the Co-ordinator!'

He and the Co-ordinator had talked an entire morning about things that grew and were green. It would be months, if not years, before organized planting began. So far, frosted food was brought from Earth in flying icicles; a few community gardens were greening up in hydroponic plants.

'Meanwhile,' said the Co-ordinator, 'it's your job. We'll get what seed we can for you, a little equipment. Space on the rockets is mighty precious now. I'm afraid, since these first towns are mining communities, there won't be much sympathy for your tree-planting—'

'But you'll let me do it?'

They let him do it. Provided with a single motor-cycle, its bin full of rich seeds and sprouts, he had parked his vehicle in the valley wilderness and struck out on foot over the land.

That had been thirty days ago, and he had never glanced back. For looking back would have been sickening to the heart. The weather was excessively dry; it was doubtful if any seeds had sprouted yet. Perhaps his entire campaign, his four weeks of bending and scooping were lost. He kept his eyes only ahead of him, going on down this wide, shallow valley under the sun, away from First Town, waiting for the rains to come.

Clouds were gathering over the dry mountains now as he drew his blanket over his shoulders. Mars was a place as unpredictable as time. He felt the baked hills simmering down into frosty night, and he thought of the rich, inky soil, a soil so black and shiny it almost crawled and stirred in your fist, a rank soil from which might sprout gigantic beanstalks from which, with bone-shaking concussion, might drop screaming giants.

The fire fluttered into sleepy ash. The air tremored to the distant roll of a cart-wheel. Thunder. A sudden odour of water. Tonight, he thought, and put his hand out to feel for rain. Tonight.

He awoke to a tap on his brow.

Water ran down his nose into his lips. Another drop hit his eye, blurring it. Another splashed his chin.

The rain.

Raw, gentle, and easy, it mizzled out of the high air, a special elixir, tasting of spells and stars and air, carrying a peppery dust in it, and moving like a rare light sherry on his tongue.

Rain.

He sat up. He let the blanket fall and his blue denim shirt

spot, while the rain took on more solid drops. The fire looked as though an invisible animal were dancing on it, crushing it, until it was angry smoke. The rain fell. The great black lid of sky cracked in six powdery blue chips, like a marvellous crackled glaze, and rushed down. He saw ten billion rain crystals, hesitating long enough to be photographed by the electrical display. Then darkness and water.

He was drenched to the skin, but he held his face up and let the water hit his eyelids, laughing. He clapped his hands together and stepped up and walked around his little camp, and it was one o'clock in the morning.

It rained steadily for two hours and then stopped. The stars came out, freshly washed and clearer than ever.

Changing into dry clothes from his cellophane pack, Mr Benjamin Driscoll lay down and went happily to sleep.

The sun rose slowly among the hills. It broke out upon the land quietly and wakened Mr Driscoll where he lay.

He waited a moment before arising. He had worked and waited a long hot month, and now, standing up, he turned at last and faced the direction from which he had come.

It was a green morning.

As far as he could see, the trees were standing up against the sky. Not one tree, not two, not a dozen, but the thousands he had planted in seed and sprout. And not little trees, no, not saplings, not little tender shoots, but great trees, huge trees, trees as tall as ten men, green and green and huge and round and full, trees shimmering their metallic leaves, trees whispering, trees in a line over hills, lemon-trees, lime-trees, redwoods and mimosas and oaks and elms and aspens, cherry, maple, ash, apple, orange, eucalyptus, stung by a tumultuous rain, nourished by alien and magical soil and, even as he watched, throwing out new branches, popping open new buds.

'Impossible!' cried Mr Benjamin Driscoll.

But the valley and the morning were green.

And the air!

All about, like a moving current, a mountain river, came the new air, the oxygen blowing from the green trees. You could see it shimmer high in crystal billows. Oxygen, fresh, pure, green, cold oxygen turning the valley into a river delta. In a moment the town doors would flip wide, people would run through the new miracle of oxygen, sniffing, gusting in lungfuls of it, cheeks pinking with it, noses frozen with it, lungs revivified, hearts leaping, and worn bodies lifted into a dance.

Mr Benjamin Driscoll took one long deep drink of green water air and fainted.

Before he woke again five thousand new trees had climbed up into the yellow sun.

FEBRUARY 2002

# *The Locusts*

The rockets set the bony meadows afire, turned rock to lava, turned wood to charcoal, transmuted water to steam, made sand and silica into green grass which lay like shattered mirrors reflecting the invasion, all about. The rockets came like drums, beating in the night. The rockets came like locusts, swarming and settling in blooms of rosy smoke. And from the rockets ran men with hammers in their hands to beat the strange world into a shape that was familiar to the eye, to bludgeon away all the strangeness, their mouths fringed with nails so they resembled steel-toothed carnivores, spitting them into their swift hands as they hammered up frame cottages and scuttled over roofs with shingles to blot out the eerie stars, and fit green shades to pull against the night. And when the carpenters had hurried on, the women came in with flower-pots and chintz and pans and set up a kitchen clamour to cover the silence that Mars made waiting outside the door and the shaded window.

In six months a dozen small towns had been laid down upon the naked planet, filled with sizzling neon tubes and yellow electric bulbs. In all, some ninety thousand people came to Mars, and more, on Earth, were packing their grips . . .

# Night Meeting

Before going on up into the blue hills, Tomás Gomez stopped for gasoline at the lonely station.

'Kind of alone out here, aren't you, Pop?' said Tomás.

The old man wiped off the windshield of the small truck. 'Not bad.'

'How do you like Mars, Pop?'

'Fine. Always something new. I made up my mind when I came here last year I wouldn't expect nothing, nor ask nothing, nor be surprised at nothing. We've got to forget Earth and how things were. We've got to look at what we're in here, and how *different* it is. I get a hell of a lot of fun out of just the weather here. It's *Martian* weather. Hot as hell daytime, cold as hell nights. I get a big kick out of the different flowers and different rain. I came to Mars to retire, and I wanted to retire in a place where everything is different. An old man needs to have things different. Young people don't want to talk to him, other old people bore hell out of him. So I thought the best thing for me is a place so different that all you got to do is open your eyes and you're entertained. I got this gas-station. If business picks up too much, I'll move on back to some other old highway that's not so busy, where I can earn just enough to live on and still have time to feel the *different* things here.'

'You got the right idea, Pop,' said Tomás, his brown hands idly on the wheel. He was feeling good. He had been working in one of the new colonies for ten days straight, and now he had two days off and was on his way to a party.

'I'm not surprised at anything any more,' said the old man. 'I'm just looking. I'm just experiencing. If you can't take Mars for what she is, you might as well go back to

Earth. Everything's crazy up here, the soil, the air, the canals, the natives (I never saw any yet, but I can hear they're around), the clocks. Even my clock acts funny. Even *time* is crazy up here. Sometimes I feel I'm here all by myself, no one else on the whole damn planet. I'd take bets on it. Sometimes I feel about eight years old, my body squeezed up and everything else tall. Jesus, it's just the place for an old man. Keeps me alert and keeps me happy. You know what Mars is? It's like a thing I got for Christmas seventy years ago — don't know if you ever had one — they called them kaleidoscopes: bits of crystal and cloth and bead and pretty junk. You held it up to the sunlight and looked in through at it, and it took your breath away. All the patterns! Well, that's Mars. Enjoy it. Don't ask it to be nothing else but what it is. Jesus, you know the highway right there, built by the Martians, is over sixteen centuries old and still in good condition? That's one dollar and fifty cents, thanks and good night.'

Tomás drove off down the ancient highway, laughing quietly.

It was a long road going into darkness and hills, and he held to the wheel, now and again reaching into his lunch-bucket and taking out a piece of candy. He had been driving steadily for an hour, with no other car on the road, no light, just the road going under, the hum, the roar, and Mars out there, so quiet. Mars was always quiet, but quieter tonight than any other. The deserts and empty seas swung by him, and the mountains against the stars.

There was a smell of Time in the air tonight. He smiled and turned the fancy in his mind. There was a thought. What did Time smell like? Like dust and clocks and people. And if you wondered what Time sounded like it sounded like water running in a dark cave and voices crying and dirt dropping down upon hollow box-lids, and rain. And, going farther, what did Time *look* like? Time looked like snow dropping silently into a black room or it looked like a silent film in an ancient theatre, one hundred billion faces falling like those New Year balloons, down and down into nothing. That was how Time swelled and looked and sounded. And tonight — Tomás shoved a hand into the wind outside the truck — tonight you could almost *touch* Time.

He drove the truck between the hills of Time. His neck prickled and he sat up, watching ahead.

He pulled into a little dead Martian town, stopped the engine, and let the silence come in around him. He sat, not breathing, looking out at the white buildings in the moonlight. Uninhabited for centuries. Perfect, faultless, in ruins, yes, but perfect, nevertheless.

He started the engine and drove on another mile or more before stopping again, climbing out, carrying his lunch bucket, and walking to a little promontory where he could look back at that dusty city. He opened his thermos and poured himself a cup of coffee. A night bird flew by. He felt very good, very much at peace.

Perhaps five minutes later there was a sound. Off in the hills, where the ancient highway curved, there was a motion, a dim light, and then a murmur.

Tomás turned slowly with the coffee-cup in his hand.

And out of the hills came a strange thing.

It was a machine like a jade-green insect, a praying mantis, delicately rushing through the cold air, indistinct, countless green diamonds winking over its body, and red jewels that glittered with multifaceted eyes. Its six legs fell upon the ancient highway with the sounds of a sparse rain which dwindled away, and from the back of the machine a Martian with melted gold for eyes looked down at Tomás as if he were looking into a well.

Tomás raised his hand and thought Hello! automatically, but did not move his lips, for this *was* a Martian. But Tomás had swum in blue rivers on Earth, with strangers passing on the road, and eaten in strange houses with strange people, and his weapon had always been his smile. He did not carry a gun. And he did not feel the need of one now, even with the little fear that gathered about his heart at this moment.

The Martian's hands were empty too. For a moment they looked across the cool air at each other.

It was Tomás who moved first.

'Hello!' he called.

'Hello!' called the Martian in his own language.

They did not understand each other.

'Did you say hello?' they both asked.

'What did you say?' they said, each in a different tongue.

They scowled.

'Who are you?' said Tomás in English.

'What are you doing here?' In Martian; the stranger's lips moved.

'Where are you going?' they said, and looked bewildered.

'I'm Tomás Gomez.'

'I'm Muhe Ca.'

Neither understood, but they tapped their chests with the words, and then it became clear.

And then the Martian laughed. 'Wait!' Tomás felt his head touched, but no hand had touched him. 'There!' said the Martian in English. 'That is better!'

'You learned my language, so quick!'

'Nothing at all!'

They looked, embarrassed with a new silence, at the steaming coffee he had in one hand.

'Something different?' said the Martian, eyeing him and the coffee, referring to them both, perhaps.

'May I offer you a drink?' said Tomás.

'Please.'

The Martian slid down from his machine.

A second cup was produced and filled, steaming. Tomás held it out.

Their hands met and — like mist — fell through each other.

'Jesus Christ!' cried Tomás, and dropped the cup.

'Name of the Gods!' said the Martian in his own tongue.

'Did you see what happened?' they both whispered.

They were very cold and terrified.

The Martian bent to touch the cup, but could not touch it.

'Jesus!' said Tomás.

'Indeed.' The Martian tried again and again to get hold of the cup, but could not. He stood up and thought for moment, then took a knife from his belt. 'Hey!' cried Tomás. 'You misunderstand, catch!' said the Martian, and tossed it. Tomás cupped his hands. The knife fell through his flesh. It hit the ground. Tomás bent to pick it up, but could not touch it, and he recoiled, shivering.

Now he looked at the Martian against the sky.

'The stars!' he said.

'The stars!' said the Martian, looking, in turn, at Tomás.

The stars were white and sharp beyond the flesh of the Martian, and they were sewn into his flesh like scintillas swallowed into the thin, phosphorous membrane of a gelatinous sea-fish. You could see stars flickering like violet eyes in the Martian's stomach and chest, and through his wrists, like jewellery.

'I can see through you!' said Tomás.

'And I through you!' said the Martian, stepping back.

Tomás felt his own body and, feeling the warmth, was reassured. *I* am real, he thought.

The Martian touched his own nose and lips. '*I* have flesh,' he said, half aloud. '*I* am alive.'

Tomás stared at the stranger. 'And if *I* am real, then *you* must be dead.'

'No, you!'

'A ghost'

'A phantom!'

They pointed at each other, with starlight burning in their limbs like daggers and icicles and fireflies, and then fell to judging their limbs again, each finding himself intact, hot, excited, stunned, awed, and the other, ah yes, that other over there, unreal, a ghostly prism flashing the accumulated light of distant worlds.

I'm drunk, thought Tomás. I won't tell anyone of this tomorrow, no, no.

They stood there on the ancient highway, neither of them moving.

'Where are you from?' asked the Martian at last.

'Earth.'

'What is that?'

'There.' Tomás nodded to the sky.

'When?'

'We landed over a year ago, remember?'

'No.'

'And all of you were dead, all but a few. You're rare, don't you *know* that?'

'That's not true.'

'Yes, dead. I saw the bodies. Black, in the rooms, in the houses, dead. Thousands of them.'

'That's ridiculous. We're *alive*!'

'Mister, you're invaded, only you don't know it. You must have escaped.'

'I haven't escaped; there was nothing to escape. What do you mean? I'm on my way to a festival now at the canal, near the Eniall Mountains. I was there last night. Don't you see the city there?' The Martian pointed.

Tomás looked and saw the ruins. 'Why, that city's been dead thousands of years.'

The Martian laughed. 'Dead. I slept there yesterday!'

'And I was in it a week ago and the week before that, and I just drove through it now, and it's a heap. See the broken pillars?'

'Broken? Why, I see them perfectly. The moonlight helps. And the pillars are upright.'

'There's dust in the streets,' said Tomás.

'The streets are clean!'

'The canals are empty right there.'

'The canals are full of lavender wine!'

'It's dead.'

'It's alive!' protested the Martian, laughing more now. 'Oh, you're quite wrong. See all the carnival lights? There are beautiful boats as slim as women, beautiful women as slim as boats, women the colour of sand, women with fire-flowers in their hands. I can see them, small, running in the streets there. That's where I'm going now, to the festival; we'll float on the waters all night long; we'll sing, we'll drink, we'll make love. Can't you see it?'

'Mister, that city is dead as a dried lizard. As any of our party. Me, I'm on my way to Green City tonight; that's the new colony we just raised over near Illinois Highway. You're mixed up. We brought in a million board feet of Oregon lumber and a couple dozen tons of good steel nails and hammered together two of the nicest little villages you ever saw. Tonight we're warming one of them. A couple rockets are coming in from Earth, bringing our wives and girl friends. There'll be barn dances and whisky—'

The Martian was now disquieted. 'You say it is over *that* way?'

'There are the rockets.' Tomás walked him to the edge of the hill and pointed down. 'See?'

'No.'

'Damn it, there they *are*! Those long silver things.'

'No.'

Now Tomás laughed. 'You're blind!'

'I see very well. You are the one who does not see.'

'But you see the new *town*, don't you?'

'I see nothing but an ocean, and water at low tide.'

'Mister, that water's been evaporated for forty centuries.'

'Ah, now, now, that *is* enough.'

'It's true, I tell you.'

The Martian grew very serious. 'Tell me again. You do not see the city the way I describe it? The pillars very white, the boats very slender, the festival lights — oh, I see them *clearly*! And listen! I can hear them singing. It's no space away at all.'

Tomás listened and shook his head. 'No.'

'And I, on the other hand,' said the Martian, 'cannot see what you describe. Well.'

Again they were cold. An ice was in their flesh.

'Can it be . . .?'

'What?'

'You say "from the sky"?'

'Earth.'

'Earth, a name, nothing,' said the Martian. '*But* . . . as I came up the pass an hour ago . . .' He touched the back of his neck. 'I felt . . .'

'Cold?'

'Yes.'

'And now?'

'Cold again. Oddly. There was a thing in the light, to the hills, the road,' said the Martian. 'I felt the strangeness, the road, the light, and for a moment I felt as if I were the last man alive on this world . . .'

'So did I!' said Tomás, and it was like talking to an old and dear friend, confiding, growing warm with the topic.

The Martian closed his eyes and opened them again. 'This can only mean one thing. It has to do with Time. Yes. You are a figment of the Past!'

'No, you are from the Past,' said the Earth Man, having had time to think of it now.

'You are so *certain*. How can you prove who is from the Past, who from the Future? What year is it?'

'Two thousand and two!'

'What does that mean to *me*?'

Tomás considered and shrugged. 'Nothing.'

'It is as if I told you that it is the year 4462853 S.E.C. It is nothing and more than nothing! Where is the clock to show us how the stars stand?'

'But the ruins prove it! They prove that *I* am the Future, *I* am alive, *you* are dead!'

'Everything in me denies this. My heart beats, my stomach hungers, my mouth thirsts. No, no, not dead, not alive, either of us. More alive than anything else. Caught between is more like it. Two strangers passing in the night, that is it. Two strangers passing. Ruins, you say!'

'Yes. You're afraid!'

'Who wants to see the Future, who ever does? A man can face the Past, but think — the pillars *crumbled*, you say? And the sea empty, and the canals dry, and the maidens dead, and the flowers withered?' The Martian was silent, but then he looked on ahead. 'But there they are. I see them. Isn't that enough for me? They wait for me now, no matter *what* you say.'

And for Tomás the rockets, far away, waiting for *him*, and the town and the women from Earth. 'We can never agree,' he said.

'Let us agree to disagree,' said the Martian. 'What does it matter who is Past or Future, if we are both alive, for what follows will follow, tomorrow or in ten thousand years. How do you know that those temples are not the temples of your own civilization one hundred centuries from now, tumbled and broken? You do not know. Then don't ask. But the night is very short. There go the festival fires in the sky, and the birds.'

Tomás put out his hand. The Martian did likewise in imitation.

Their hands did not touch; they melted through each other.

'Will we meet again?'

'Who knows? Perhaps some other night.'

'I'd like to go with you to that festival.'

'And I wish I might come to your new town, to see this ship you speak of, to see these men, to hear all that has happened.'

'Good-bye,' said Tomás.

'Good-night.'

The Martian rode his green-metal vehicle quietly away into the hills. The Earth Man turned his truck and drove it silently in the opposite direction.

'Good Lord! what a dream that was,' sighed Tomás, his hands on the wheel, thinking of the rockets, the women, the raw whisky, the Virginia reels, the party.

How strange a vision was that, thought the Martian, rushing on, thinking of the festival, the canals, the boats, the women with golden eyes, and the songs.

The night was dark. The moons had gone down. Starlight twinkled on the empty highway where now there was not a sound, no car, no person, nothing. And it remained that way all the rest of the cool, dark night.

## *The Shore*

Mars was a distant shore, and the men spread upon it in waves. Each wave was different, and each wave stronger. The first wave carried with it men accustomed to spaces and coldness and being alone, the coyote and cattle-men, with no fat on them, with faces the years had worn the flesh off, with eyes like nailheads, and hands like the material of old gloves, ready to touch anything. Mars could do nothing for them, for they were bred to plains and prairies as open as the Martian fields. They came and made things a little less empty, so that others would find courage to follow. They put panes in hollow windows and lights behind the panes.

They were the first men.

Everyone knew who the first women would be.

The second men should have travelled from other countries with other accents and other ideas. But the rockets were American and the men were American and it stayed that way, while Europe and Asia and South America and Australia and the islands watched the Roman candles leave them behind. The rest of the world was buried in war or the thoughts of war.

So the second men were Americans also. And they came from the cabbage tenements and subways, and they found much rest and vacation in the company of the silent men from the tumble-weed states who knew how to use silences so they filled you up with peace after long years crushed in tubes, tins, and boxes in New York.

And among the second men were men who looked, by their eyes, as if they were on their way to God . . .

# The Fire Balloons

Fire exploded over summer night lawns. You saw sparkling faces of uncles and aunts. Sky-rockets fell up in the brown shining eyes of cousins on the porch, and the cold charred sticks thumped down in dry meadows far away.

The Most Reverend Father Joseph Daniel Peregrine opened his eyes. What a dream: he and his cousins with their fiery play at his grandfather's ancient Ohio home so many years ago!

He lay listening to the great hollow of the church, the other cells where other Fathers lay. Had they, too, on the eve of the flight of the rocket *Crucifix*, lain with memories of the Fourth of July? Yes. This was like those breathless Independence dawns when you waited for the first concussion and rushed out on the dewy sidewalks, your hands full of loud miracles.

So here they were, the Episcopal Fathers, in the breathing dawn before they pin-wheeled off to Mars, leaving their incense through the velvet cathedral of space.

'Should we go at all?' whispered Father Peregrine. 'Shouldn't we solve our own sins on Earth? Aren't we running from our lives here?'

He arose, his fleshy body, with its rich look of strawberries, milk, and steak, moving heavily.

'Or is it sloth?' he wondered. 'Do I dread the journey?'

He stepped into the needle-spray shower.

'But I shall take you to Mars, body.' He addressed himself. 'Leaving old sins here. And on to Mars to find new sins?' A delightful thought almost. Sins no one had ever thought of. Oh, he himself had written a little book: *The Problem of Sin on Other Worlds*, ignored as somehow not serious enough by his Episcopal brethren.

Only last night, over a final cigar, he and Father Stone had talked of it.

'On Mars sin might appear as virtue. We must guard against virtuous acts there that, later, might be found to be sins!' said Father Peregrine, beaming. 'How exciting! It's been centuries since so much adventure has accompanied the prospect of being a missionary!'

'*I* will recognize sin,' said Father Stone bluntly, '*even* on Mars.'

'Oh, we priests pride ourselves on being litmus paper, changing colour in sin's presence,' retorted Father Peregrine, 'but what if Martian chemistry is such we do not colour *at all*! If there are new senses on Mars, you must admit the possibility of unrecognizable sin.'

'If there is no malice aforethought, there is no sin or punishment for same — the Lord assures us that,' Father Stone replied.

'On Earth, yes. But perhaps a Martian sin might inform the subconscious of its evil, telepathically, leaving the conscious mind of man free to act, seemingly without malice! What *then*?'

'What *could* there be in the way of new sins?'

Father Peregrine leaned heavily forward. 'Adam *alone* did not sin. Add Eve and you add temptation. Add a second man and you make adultery possible. With the addition of sex or people, you add sin. If men were armless they could not strangle with their hands. You would not have that particular sin of murder. Add arms, and you add the possibility of a new violence. Amoebas cannot sin because they reproduce by fission. They do not covet wives or murder each other. Add sex to amoebas, add arms and legs, and you would have murder and adultery. Add an arm or leg or person, or take away each, and you add or subtract possible evil. On Mars, what if there are five new senses, organs, invisible limbs we can't conceive of — then mightn't there be five new *sins*?'

Father Stone gasped. 'I think you *enjoy* this sort of thing!'

'I keep my mind alive, Father; just alive, is all.'

'Your mind's always juggling, isn't it? — mirrors, torches, plates.'

'Yes. Because sometimes the Church seems like those posed circus tableaux where the curtain lifts and men, white, zinc-oxide, talcum-powder statues, freeze to represent abstract Beauty. Very wonderful. But I hope there will always be room for me to dart about among the statues, don't you, Father Stone?'

Father Stone had moved away. 'I think we'd better go to bed. In a few hours we'll be jumping up to see your *new* sins, Father Peregrine.'

The rocket stood ready for the firing.

The Fathers walked from their devotions in the chilly morning, many a fine priest from New York or Chicago or Los Angeles — the Church was sending its best — walking across town to the frosty field. Walking, Father Peregrine remembered the Bishop's words:

'Father Peregrine, you will captain the missionaries, with Father Stone at your side. Having chosen you for this serious task, I find my reasons deplorably obscure, Father, but your pamphlet on planetary sin did not go unread. You are a flexible man. And Mars is like that uncleaned closet we have neglected for millennia. Sin has collected there like bric-à-brac. Mars is twice Earth's age and has had double the number of Saturday nights, liquor-baths, and eye-poppings at women as naked as white seals. When we open that closet door, things will fall on us. We need a quick, flexible man — one whose mind can dodge. Anyone a little dogmatic might break in two. I feel you'll be resilient. Father, the job is yours.'

The Bishop and the Fathers knelt.

The blessing was said and the rocket given a little shower of holy water. Arising, the Bishop addressed them:

'I know you will go with God, to prepare the Martians for the reception of His Truth. I wish you all a *thoughtful* journey.'

They filed past the Bishop, twenty men, robes whispering, to deliver their hands into his kind hands before passing into the cleansed projectile.

'I wonder,' said Father Peregrine, at the last moment, 'if Mars is Hell? Only waiting for our arrival before it bursts into brimstone and fire.'

'Lord be with us,' said Father Stone.

The rocket moved.

Coming out of space was like coming out of the most beautiful cathedral they had ever seen. Touching Mars was like touching the ordinary pavement outside the church five minutes after having *really* known your love for God.

The Fathers stepped gingerly from the steaming rocket and knelt upon Martian sand while Father Peregrine gave thanks.

'Lord, we thank Thee for the journey through Thy rooms. And, Lord, we have reached a new land, so we must have new eyes. We shall hear new sounds, and must needs have new ears. And there will be new sins, for which we ask the gift of better and firmer and purer hearts. Amen.'

They arose.

And here was Mars like a sea under which they trudged in the guise of submarine biologists, seeking life. Here the territory of hidden sin. Oh, how carefully they must all balance, like grey feathers, in this new element, afraid that walking *itself* might be sinful; or breathing, or simple fasting!

And here was the mayor of First Town come to meet them with outstretched hand. 'What can I do for you, Father Peregrine?'

'We'd like to know about the Martians. For only if we know about them can we plan our church intelligently. Are they ten feet tall? We will build large doors. Are their skins blue or red or green? We must know when we put human figures in the stained glass so we may use the right skin colour. Are they heavy? We will build sturdy seats for them.'

'Father,' said the mayor, 'I don't think you should worry about the Martians. There are two races. One of them is pretty well dead. A few are in hiding. And the second race – well, they're not quite human.'

'Oh?' Father Peregrine's heart quickened.

'They're round luminous globes of light, Father, living in those hills. Man or beast, who can say? But they act intelligently, I hear.' The mayor shrugged. 'Of course, they're not men, so I don't think you'll care—'

'On the contrary,' said Father Peregrine swiftly. 'Intelligent, you say?'

'There's a story. A prospector broke his leg in those hills and would have died there. The blue spheres of light came at him. When he woke, he was down on a highway and didn't know he got there.'

'Drunk,' said Father Stone.

'That's the story,' said the mayor. 'Father Peregrine, with most of the Martians dead, and only those blue spheres, I frankly think you'd be better off in First City. Mars is opening up. It's a frontier now, like in the old days on Earth, out West, and in Alaska. Men are pouring up here. There're a couple thousand black Irish mechanics and miners and day labourers in First Town who need saving, because there're too many wicked women came with them, and too much ten-century-old Martian wine—'

Father Peregrine was gazing into the soft blue hills.

Father Stone cleared his throat. 'Well, Father?'

Father Peregrine did not hear. 'Spheres of blue *fire*?'

'Yes, Father.'

'Ah,' Father Peregrine sighed.

'Blue balloons.' Father Stone shook his head. 'A circus!'

Father Peregrine felt his wrists pounding. He saw the little frontier town with raw, fresh-built sin, and he saw the hills, old with the oldest and yet perhaps an even newer (to him) sin.

'Mayor, could your black Irish labourers cook one more day in hellfire?'

'I'd turn and baste them for you, Father.'

Father Peregrine nodded to the hills. 'Then that's where we'll go.'

There was a murmur from everyone.

'It would be so simple,' explained Father Peregrine, 'to go into town. I prefer to think that if the Lord walked here and people said, "Here is the beaten path," He would reply, "Show me the weeds. I will *make* a path." '

'But—'

'Father Stone, think how it would weigh upon us if we passed sinners by and did not extend our hands.'

'But globes of fire!'

'I imagine man looked funny to other animals when we first appeared. Yet he has a soul, for all his homeliness. Until we prove otherwise, let us assume that these fiery spheres have souls.'

'All right,' agreed the mayor, 'but you'll be back to town.'

'We'll see. First, some breakfast. Then you and I, Father Stone, will walk alone into the hills. I don't want to frighten those fiery Martians with machines or crowds. Shall we have breakfast?'

The Fathers ate in silence.

At nightfall Father Peregrine and Father Stone were high in the hills. They stopped and sat upon a rock to enjoy a moment of relaxation and waiting. The Martians had not as yet appeared, and they both felt vaguely disappointed.

'I wonder—' Father Peregrine mopped his face. 'Do you think if we called "Hello!" they might answer?'

'Father Peregrine, won't you ever be serious?'

'Not until the good Lord is. Oh, don't look so terribly

shocked, please. The Lord is not serious. In fact, it is a little hard to know just what else He is except loving. And love has to do with humour, doesn't it? For you cannot love someone unless you put up with him, can you? And you cannot put up with someone constantly unless you can laugh at him. Isn't that true? And certainly we are ridiculous little animals wallowing in the fudge-bowl, and God must love us all the more because we appeal to his humour.'

'*I* never thought of God as humorous,' said Father Stone.

'The Creator of the platypus, the camel, the ostrich, and man? Oh, come now!' Father Peregrine laughed.

But at this instant, from among the twilight hills, like a series of blue lamps lit to guide their way, came the Martians.

Father Stone saw them first. 'Look!'

Father Peregrine turned, and the laughter stopped in his mouth.

The round blue globes of fire hovered among the twinkling stars, distantly trembling.

'Monsters!' Father Stone leaped up.

But Father Peregrine caught him. 'Wait!'

'We should've gone to town!'

'No, listen, look!' pleaded Father Peregrine.

'I'm afraid!'

'Don't be. This is God's work!'

'The devil's!'

'No, now, quiet!' Father Peregrine gentled him and they crouched with the soft blue light on their upturned faces as the fiery orbs drew near.

And again, Independence Night, thought Father Peregrine, tremoring. He felt like a child back in those July Fourth evenings, the sky blowing apart, breaking into powdery stars and burning sound, the concussions jingling house-windows like the ice on a thousand thin ponds. The aunts, uncles, cousins crying, 'Ah!' as to some celestial physician. The summer sky colours. And the Fire Balloons, lit by an indulgent grandfather, steadied in his massively tender hands. Oh, the memory of those lovely Fire Balloons, softly lighted, warmly billowed bits of tissue, like insect wings, lying like folded wasps in boxes and, last of all, after the day of riot and fury, at long last from their boxes, delicately unfolded, blue, red, white, patriotic — the Fire Balloons! He saw the dim faces of dear relatives long dead and mantled with moss as Grandfather lit the tiny candle and let the warm air breathe up to form the balloon plumply luminous in his hands, a shining vision which they held, reluctant to let it go; for, once released, it was yet another year gone from life, another Fourth, another bit of Beauty vanished. And then up, up, still up through the warm summer night constellations, the Fire Balloons had drifted, while red-white-and-blue eyes followed them, wordless, from family porches. Away into deep Illinois country, over night rivers and sleeping mansions the Fire Balloons dwindled, forever gone . . .

Father Peregrine felt tears in his eyes. Above him the Martians, not one but a *thousand* whispering Fire Balloons, it seemed, hovered. Any moment he might find his long-dead and blessed grandfather at his elbow, staring up at Beauty.

But it was Father Stone.

'Let's go, please, Father!'

'I must speak to them.' Father Peregrine rustled forward, not knowing what to say, for what had he ever said to the Fire Balloons of time past except with his mind: *you are beautiful, you are beautiful*, and that was not enough now, He could only lift his heavy arms and call upward, as he had often wished to call after the enchanted Fire Balloons, 'Hello!'

But the fiery spheres only burned like images in a dark mirror. They seemed fixed, gaseous, miraculous, forever.

'We come with God,' said Father Peregrine to the sky.

'Silly, silly, silly.' Father Stone chewed the back of his hand. 'In the name of God, Father Peregrine, stop!'

But now the phosphorescent spheres blew away into the hills. In a moment they were gone.

Father Peregrine called again, and the echo of his last cry shook the hills above. Turning, he saw an avalanche shake out dust, pause, and then, with a thunder of stone wheels, crash down the mountain upon them.

'Look what you've done!' cried Father Stone.

Father Peregrine was almost fascinated, then horrified. He turned, knowing they could run only a few feet before the rocks crushed them into ruins. He had time to whisper, *Oh, Lord!* and the rocks fell!

'Father!'

They were separated like chaff from wheat. There was a blue shimmering of globes, a shift of cold stars, a roar, and then they stood upon a ledge two hundred feet away watching the spot where their bodies should have been buried under tons of stone.

The blue light evaporated.

The two Fathers clutched each other. 'What happened?'

'The blue fires lifted us!'

'We ran, *that* was it!'

'No, the globes saved us.'

'They couldn't!'

'They *did*.'

The sky was empty. There was a feel as if a great bell had just stopped tolling. Reverberations lingered in their teeth and marrows.

'Let's get away from here. You'll have us killed.'

'I haven't feared death for a good many years, Father Stone.'

'We've proved nothing. Those blue lights ran off at the first cry. It's useless.'

'No.' Father Peregrine was suffused with a stubborn wonder. 'Somehow, they saved us. That proves they have souls.'

'It proves only that they *might* have saved us. Everything was confused. We might have escaped, ourselves.'

'They are not animals, Father Stone. Animals do not save

lives, especially of strangers. There is mercy and compassion here. Perhaps, tomorrow, we may prove more.'

'Prove what? How?' Father Stone was immensely tired now; the outrage to his mind and body showed on his stiff face. 'Follow them in helicopters, reading chapter and verse? They're not human. They haven't eyes or ears or bodies like ours.'

'But I feel something about them,' replied Father Peregrine. 'I know a great revelation is at hand. They saved us. They *think*. They had a choice; let us live or die. That proves free will!'

Father Stone set to work building a fire, glaring at the sticks in his hands, choking on the grey smoke. 'I myself will open a convent for nursling geese, a monastery for sainted swine, and I shall build a miniature apse in a microscope so that paramecium can attend services and tell their beads with their flagella.'

'Oh, Father Stone.'

'I'm sorry.' Father Stone blinked redly across the fire. 'But this is like blessing a crocodile before he chews you up. You're risking the entire missionary expedition. We belong in First Town, washing liquor from men's throats and perfume off their hands!'

'Can't you recognize the human in the inhuman?'

'I'd much rather recognize the inhuman in the human.'

'But if I prove these things sin, know sin, know a moral life, have free will and intellect, Father Stone?'

'That will take much convincing.'

The night grew rapidly cold and they peered into the fire to find their wildest thoughts, while eating biscuits and berries, and soon they were bundled for sleep under the chiming stars. And just before turning over one last time Father Stone, who had been thinking for many minutes to find something to bother Father Peregrine about, stared into the soft pink charcoal bed and said, 'Not Adam and Eve on Mars. No original sin. Maybe the Martians live in a state of God's grace. Then we can go back down to town and start work on the Earth Men.'

Father Peregrine reminded himself to say a little prayer for Father Stone, who got so mad and who was now being vindictive, God help him. 'Yes, Father Stone, but the Martians killed some of our settlers. That's sinful. There must have been an Original Sin and a Martian Adam and Eve. We'll find them. Men are men, unfortunately, no matter what their shape, and inclined to sin.'

But Father Stone was pretending sleep.

Father Peregrine did not shut his eyes.

Of course they couldn't let these Martians go to hell, could they? With a compromise to their consciences, could they go back to the new colonial towns, those towns so full of sinful gullets and women with scintilla eyes and white oyster bodies rollicking in beds and with lonely labourers? Wasn't that the place for the Fathers? Wasn't this trek into the hills merely a personal whim? Was he really thinking of God's Church, or was he quenching the thirst of a sponge-like curiosity? Those blue round globes of St Anthony's fire – how they burned in his mind! What a challenge, to find the man behind the mask, the human behind the inhuman. Wouldn't he be proud if he could say, even to his secret self, that he had converted a rolling huge pool-table full of fiery spheres! What a sin of pride! Worth doing penance for! But then one did many prideful things out of Love, and he loved the Lord so much and was so happy at it that he wanted everyone else to be happy too.

The last thing he saw before sleep was the return of the blue fires, like a flight of burning angels silently singing him to his worried rest.

The blue round dreams were still there in the sky when Father Peregrine awoke in the early morning.

Father Stone slept like a stiff bundle, quietly. Father Peregrine watched the Martians floating and watching him.

They were human — he *knew* it. But he must prove it or face a dry-mouthed, dry-eyed Bishop telling him kindly to step aside.

But how to prove humanity if they hid in the high vaults of the sky? How to bring them nearer and provide answers to the many questions?

'They saved us from the avalanche.'

Father Peregrine arose, moved off among the rocks, and began to climb the nearest hill until he came to a place where a cliff dropped sheerly to a floor two hundred feet below. He was choking from his vigorous climb in the frosty air. He stood, getting his breath.

'If I fell from here, it would surely kill me.'

He let a pebble drop. Moments later it clicked on the rocks below.

'The Lord would never forgive me.'

He tossed another pebble.

'It wouldn't be suicide, would it, if I did it out of Love . . .'

He lifted his gaze to the blue spheres. 'But first, another try.' He called to them: 'Hello, hello!'

The echoes tumbled upon each other, but the blue fires did not blink or move.

He talked to them for five minutes. When he stopped, he peered down and saw Father Stone, still indignantly asleep, below in the little camp.

'I must prove everything.' Father Peregrine stepped to the cliff rim. 'I am an old man. I am not afraid. Surely the Lord will understand that I am only doing this for Him?'

He drew a deep breath. All his life swam through his eyes, and he thought, In a moment shall I die? I am afraid that I love living much too much. But I love things more.

And, thinking thus, he stepped off the cliff.

He fell.

'Fool!' he cried. He tumbled end over end. 'You were wrong! The rocks rushed up at him, and he saw himself dashed on them and sent to glory. 'Why did I do this thing?' But he knew the answer, and an instant later was calm as he fell. The wind roared around him and the rocks hurtled to meet him.

And then there was a shift of stars, a glimmering of blue light, and he felt himself surrounded by blueness and suspended. A moment later he was deposited, with a gentle bump, upon the rocks, where he sat a full moment, alive, and touching himself, and looking up at those blue lights that had withdrawn instantly.

'You saved me!' he whispered. 'You wouldn't let me die. You knew it was wrong.'

He rushed over to Father Stone, who still lay quietly asleep. 'Father, Father, wake up!' He shook him and brought him round. 'Father, they saved me!'

'Who saved you?' Father Stone blinked and sat up.

Father Peregrine related his experience.

'A dream, a nightmare; go back to sleep,' said Father Stone irritably. 'You and you circus balloons.'

'But I was awake!'

'Now, now, Father, calm yourself. There now.'

'You don't believe me? Have you a gun? Yes, there, let me have it.'

'What are you going to do?' Father Stone handed over the small pistol they had brought along for protection against snakes or other similar and unpredictable animals.

Father Peregrine seized the pistol. 'I'll prove it!'

He pointed the pistol at his own hand and fired.

'Stop!'

There was a shimmer of light, and before their eyes the bullet stood upon the air, poised an inch from his open palm. It hung for a moment, surrounded by a blue phosphorescence. Then it fell, hissing, into the dust.

Father Peregrine fired the gun three times – at his hand, at his leg, at his body. The three bullets hovered, glittering, and, like dead insects, fell at their feet.

'You see?' said Father Peregrine, letting his arm fall, and allowing the pistol to drop after the bullets. 'They know. They understand. They are not animals. They think and judge and live in a moral climate. What animal would save me from myself like this? There is no animal would do that. Only another man, Father. Now, do you believe?'

Father Stone was watching the sky and the blue lights, and now, silently, he dropped to one knee and picked up the warm bullets and cupped them in his hand. He closed his hand tight.

The sun was rising behind them.

'I think we had better go down to the others and tell them of this and bring them back up here,' said Father Peregrine.

By the time the sun was up, they were well on their way back to the rocket.

Father Peregrine drew the round circle in the centre of the blackboard.

'This is Christ, the son of the Father.'

He pretended not to hear the other Father's sharp intake of breath.

'This is Christ, in all his Glory,' he continued.

'It looks like a geometry problem,' observed Father Stone.

'A fortunate comparison, for we deal with symbols here. Christ is no less Christ, you must admit, in being represented by a circle or a square. For centuries the cross has symbolized his love and agony. So this circle will be the Martian Christ. This is how we shall bring Him to Mars.'

The Fathers stirred fretfully and looked at each other.

'You, Brother Mathias, will create, in glass, a replica of this circle, a globe, filled with bright fire. It will stand upon the altar.'

'A cheap magic trick,' muttered Father Stone.

Father Peregrine went on patiently: 'On the contrary. We are giving them God in an understandable image. If Christ had come to us on Earth as an octopus, would we have accepted him readily?' He spread his hands. 'Was it then a cheap magic trick of the Lord's to bring us Christ through Jesus, in man's shape? After we bless the church we build here and sanctify its altar and this symbol, do you think Christ would refuse to inhabit the shape before us? You know in your hearts he would not refuse.'

'But the body of a soulless animal!' said Brother Mathias.

'We've already gone over that, many times since we returned this morning, Brother Mathias. These creatures saved us from the avalanche. They realized that self-destruction was sinful, and prevented it, time after time. Therefore we must build a church in the hills, live with them, to find their own special ways of sinning, the alien ways, and help them to discover God.'

The Fathers did not seem pleased at the prospect.

'Is it because they are so odd to the eye?' wondered Father Peregrine. 'But what is a shape? Only a cup for the blazing soul that God provides us all. If tomorrow I found that sea-lions suddenly possessed free will, intellect, knew when not to sin, knew what life was and tempered justice with mercy and life with love, then I would build an undersea cathedral. And if the sparrows should, miraculously, with God's will, gain everlasting souls tomorrow, I would freight a church with helium and take after them, for all souls, in any shape, if they have free will and are aware of their sins, will burn in hell unless given their rightful communions. I would not let a Martian sphere burn in hell, either, for it is a sphere only in mine eyes. When I close my eyes it stands before me, an intelligence, a love, a soul — and I must not deny it.'

'But that glass globe you wish placed on the altar,' protested Father Stone.

'Consider the Chinese,' replied Father Peregrine imperturbably. 'What sort of Christ do Christian Chinese worship? An oriental Christ, naturally. You've all seen oriental Nativity scenes. How is Christ dressed? In Eastern robes. Where does he walk? In Chinese settings of bamboo and misty mountain and crooked tree. His eyelids taper, his cheekbones rise. Each country, each race adds something to our Lord. I am reminded of the Virgin of Guadalupe, to whom all Mexico pays its love. Her skin? Have you noticed the paintings of her? A dark skin, like that of her worshippers. Is this blasphemy? Not at all. It is not logical that men should accept a God, no matter how real, of another colour. I often wonder why our missionaries do well in Africa, with a snow-white Christ. Perhaps because white is a sacred colour, in albino, or any other form, to the African tribes. Given time, mightn't Christ darken there too? The form does not matter. Content is everything. We cannot expect these Martians to accept an alien form. We shall give them Christ in their own image.'

'There's a flaw in your reasoning, Father,' said Father Stone. 'Won't the Martians suspect us of hypocrisy? They will realize that we don't worship a round, globular Christ, but a man with limbs and a head. How do we explain the difference?'

'By showing there is none. Christ will fill any vessel that is offered. Bodies or globes, he is there, and each will worship the same thing in a different guise. What is more, we must *believe* in this globe we give the Martians. We must believe in a shape which is meaningless to us as to form. This spheroid *will* be Christ. And we must remember that we ourselves, and the shape of our Earth Christ, would be meaningless, ridiculous, a squander of material to these Martians.'

Father Peregrine laid aside his chalk. 'Now let us go into the hills and build our church.'

The Fathers began to pack their equipment.

The church was not a church, but an area cleared of rocks, a plateau on one of the low mountains, its soil smoothed and brushed, and an altar established whereon Brother Mathias placed the fiery globe he had constructed.

At the end of the six days of the work the 'church' was ready.

'What shall we do with this?' Father Stone tapped an iron bell they had brought along. 'What does a bell mean to *them*?'

'I imagine I brought it for our own comfort,' admitted Father Peregrine. 'We need a few familiarities. This church seems so little like a church. And we feel somewhat absurd here — even I; for it is something new, this business of converting the creatures of another world. I feel like a ridiculous play-actor at times. And then I pray to God to lend me strength.'

'Many of the Fathers are unhappy. Some of them joke about all this, Father Peregrine.'

'I know. We'll put this bell in a small tower, for their comfort, anyway.'

'What about the organ?'

'We'll play it at the first service, tomorrow.'

'But, the Martians—'

'I know. But again, I suppose, for our own comfort, our own music. Later we may discover theirs.'

They arose very early on Sunday morning and moved through the coldness like pale phantoms, rime tinkling on their habits; covered with chimes they were, shaking down showers of silver water.

'I wonder if it *is* Sunday here on Mars?' mused Father Peregrine, but seeing Father Stone wince, he hastened on. 'It might be Tuesday or Thursday — who knows? But no matter. My idle fancy. It's Sunday to us. Come.'

The Fathers walked into the flat, wide area of the 'church' and knelt, shivering and blue-lipped.

Father Peregrine said a little prayer and put his cold fingers to the organ keys. The music went up like a flight of pretty birds. He touched the keys like a man moving his hands among the weeds of a wild garden, startling up great soarings of beauty into the hills.

The music calmed the air. It smelled the fresh smell of morning. The music drifted into the mountains and shook down mineral powders in a dusty rain.

The Fathers waited.

'Well, Father Peregrine.' Father Stone eyed the empty sky where the sun was rising, furnace-red. 'I don't see our friends.'

'Let me try again.' Father Peregrine was perspiring.

He built an architecture of Bach, stone by exquisite stone, raising a music cathedral so vast that its farthest chancels were in Nineveh, its farthest dome at St Peter's left hand. The music stayed and did not crash in ruin when it was over, but partook of a series of white clouds and was carried away among other lands.

The sky was still empty.

'They'll come!' But Father Peregrine felt the panic in his chest, very small, growing. 'Let us pray. Let us ask them to come. They read minds; they *know*.'

The Fathers lowered themselves yet again, in rustlings and whispers. They prayed.

And to the East, out of the icy mountains of seven o'clock on Sunday morning or perhaps Thursday morning or maybe Monday morning on Mars, came the soft fiery globes.

They hovered and sank and filled the area around the shivering priests. 'Thank you; oh, thank you, Lord.' Father Peregrine shut his eyes tight and played the music, and when it was done he turned and gazed upon his wondrous congregation.

And a voice touched his mind, and the voice said:

'We have come for a little while.'

'You may stay,' said Father Peregrine.

'For a little while only,' said the voice quietly. 'We have come to tell you certain things. We should have spoken sooner. But we had hoped that you might go on your way if left alone.'

Father Peregrine started to speak, but the voice hushed him.

'We are the Old Ones,' the voice said, and it entered him like a blue gaseous flare and burned in the chambers of his head. 'We are the old Martians, who left our marble cities and went into the hills, forsaking the material life we had lived. So very long ago we became these things that we are now. Once we were men, with bodies and legs and arms such as yours. The legend has it that one of us, a good man, discovered a way to free man's soul and intellect, to free him of ills and melancholies, of deaths and transfigurations, of ill humours and senilities, and so we took on the look of lightning and blue fire and have lived in the winds and skies and hills forever after that, neither prideful nor arrogant, neither rich nor poor, passionate nor cold. We have lived apart from those we left behind, those other men of this world, and how we came to be has been forgotten, the process lost; but we shall never die, nor do harm. We have put away the sins of the body and live in God's grace. We covet no other property; we have no property. We do not steal, nor kill, nor lust, nor hate. We live in happiness. We cannot reproduce; we do not eat or drink or make war. All the sensualities and childishness and sins of the body were stripped away when our bodies were put aside. We have left sin behind, Father Peregrine, and it is burned like the leaves in the autumn wicker, and it is gone like the soiled snow of an evil winter, and it is gone like the sexual flowers of a red-and-yellow spring, and it is gone like the panting nights of hottest summer, and our season is temperate and our clime is rich in thought.'

Father Peregrine was standing now, for the voice touched him at such a pitch that it almost shook him from his senses. It was an ecstasy and a fire washing through him.

'We wish to tell you that we appreciate you building this place for us, but we have no need of it, for each of us is a temple unto himself and we need no place wherein to cleanse ourselves. Forgive us for not coming to you sooner, but we are separate and apart and have talked to no one for ten thousand years, nor have we interfered in any way with the life of this planet. It has come into your mind now that we are the lilies of the field; we toil not, neither do we spin. You are right. And so we suggest that you take the parts of this temple into your own cities and there cleanse them. For, rest assured, we are happy, and at peace.'

The Fathers were on their knees in the vast blue light, and Father Peregrine was down, too, and they were weeping, and it did not matter that their time had been wasted; it did not matter to them at all.

The blue spheres murmured and began to rise once more, on a breath of cold air.

'May I' — cried Father Peregrine, not daring to ask, eyes closed — 'may I come again, someday, that I may learn from you?'

The blue fires blazed. The air trembled.

Yes. Someday he might come again. Someday.

And then the Fire Balloons blew away and were gone, and he was like a child, on his knees, tears streaming from his eyes, crying to himself. 'Come back, come back!' And at any moment Grandfather might lift him and carry him upstairs to his bedroom in a long-gone Ohio town . . .

They filed down out of the hills at sunset. Looking back, Father Peregrine saw the blue fires burning. No, he thought, we couldn't build a church for the likes of you. You're Beauty itself. What church could compete with the fireworks of the pure soul?

Father Stone moved in silence beside him. And at last he spoke:

'The way I see it is there's a Truth on every planet. All parts of the Big Truth. On a certain day they'll all fit together like the pieces of a jigsaw. This has been a shaking experience. I'll never doubt again, Father Peregrine. For this

Truth here is as true as Earth's Truth, and they lie side by side. And we'll go on to other worlds, adding the sum of the parts of the Truth until one day the whole Total will stand before us like the light of a new day.'

'That's a lot, coming from you, Father Stone.'

'I'm sorry now, in a way, we're going down to the town to handle our own kind. Those blue lights now. When they settled about us, and that *voice* . . .' Father Stone shivered.

Father Peregrine reached out to take the other's arm. They walked together.

'And you know,' said Father Stone finally, fixing his eyes on Brother Mathias, who strode ahead with the glass sphere tenderly carried in his arms, that glass sphere with the blue phosphorous light glowing forever inside it, 'you know, Father Peregrine, that globe there—'

'Yes?'

'It's Him. It *is* Him, after all.'

Father Peregrine smiled, and they walked down out of the hills towards the new town.

# Interim

They brought in fifteen thousand lumber feet of Oregon pine to build Tenth City, and seventy-nine thousand feet of California redwood, and they hammered together a clean, neat little town by the edge of the stone canals. On Sunday nights you could see red, blue, and green stained-glass light in the churches and hear the voices singing the numbered hymns. 'We will now sing 79. We will now sing 94.' And in certain houses you heard the hard clatter of a typewriter, the novelist at work; or the scratch of a pen, the poet at work; or no sound at all, the former beachcomber at work. It was as if, in many ways, a great earthquake had shaken loose the roots and cellars of an Iowa town, and then, in an instant, a whirlwind twister of Oz-like proportions had carried the entire town off to Mars to set it down without a bump . . .

# The Musicians

The boys would hike far out into the Martian country. They carried odorous paper bags into which from time to time upon the long walk they would insert their noses to inhale the rich smell of the ham and mayonnaised pickles, and to listen to the liquid gurgle of the orange-soda in the warming bottles. Swinging their grocery bags full of clean watery green onions and odorous liverwurst and red catsup and white bread, they would dare each other on past the limits set by their stern mothers. They would run, yelling:

'First one there gets to kick!'

They hiked in summer, autumn, or winter. Autumn was most fun, because then they imagined, like on Earth, they were scuttering through autumn leaves.

They would come like a scatter of jackstones on the marble flats beside the canals, the candy-cheeked boys with blue-agate eyes, panting onion-tainted commands to each other. For now that they had reached the dead, forbidden town it was no longer a matter of 'Last one there's a girl!' or 'First one gets to play Musician!' Now the dead town's doors lay wide and they thought they could hear the faintest crackle, like autumn leaves, from inside. They would hush themselves forward, by each other's elbows, carrying sticks, remembering their parents had told them, 'Not there! No, to none of the old towns! Watch where you hike. You'll get the beating of your life when you come home. We'll check your shoes!'

And there they stood in the dead city, a heap of boys, their hiking lunches half devoured, daring each other in shrieky whispers.

'Here goes nothing!' And suddenly one of them took off,

into the nearest stone house, through the door, across the living-room, and into the bedroom, where, without half looking, he would kick about, thrash his feet, and the black leaves would fly through the air, brittle, thin as tissue cut from midnight sky. Behind him would race six others, and the first boy there would be the Musician, playing the white xylophone bones beneath the outer covering of black flakes. A great skull would roll to view, like a snowball; they shouted! Ribs, like spider legs, plangent as a dull harp, and then the black flakes of mortality blowing all about them in their scuffling dance; the boys pushed and heaved and fell in the leaves, in the death that had turned the dead to flakes and dryness, into a game played by boys whose stomachs gurgled with orange pop.

And then out of one house into another, into seventeen houses, mindful that each of the towns in its turn was being burned clean of its horrors by the Firemen, antiseptic warriors with shovels and bins, shovelling away at the ebony tatters and peppermint-stick bones, slowly but assuredly separating the terrible from the normal; so they must play very hard, these boys, the Firemen would soon be here!

Then, luminous with sweat, they gnashed at their last sandwiches. With a final kick, a final marimba concert, a final autumnal lunge through leaf-stacks, they went home.

Their mothers examined their shoes for black flakelets which, when discovered, resulted in scalding baths and fatherly beatings.

By the year's end the Firemen had raked the autumn leaves and white xylophones away, and it was no more fun.

# Way up in the Middle of the Air

'Did you hear about it?'

'About what?'

'The niggers, the niggers!'

'What about 'em?'

'Them leaving, pulling out, going away; did you hear?'

'What do you mean, pulling out? How can they do that?'

'They can, they will, they are.'

'Just a couple?'

'Every single one here in the South!'

'No.'

'Yes!'

'I got to see that. I don't believe it. Where they going —
Africa?'

A silence.

'Mars.'

'You mean the *planet* Mars?'

'That's right.'

The men stood up in the hot shade of the hardware porch.
Someone quit lighting a pipe. Somebody else spat out into
the hot dust of noon.

'They can't leave, they can't do that.'

'They're doing it, anyways.'

'Where'd you hear this?'

'It's everywhere, on the radio a minute ago, just come
through.'

Like a series of dusty statues, the men came to life.

Samuel Teece, the hardware proprietor, laughed uneasily.
'I *wondered* what happened to Silly. I sent him on my bike
an hour ago. He ain't come back from Mrs Bordman's yet.
You think that black fool just pedalled off to Mars?'

The men snorted.

'All I say is, he better bring back my bike. I don't take stealing from no one, by God.'

'Listen!'

The men collided irritably with each other, turning.

Far up the street the levee seemed to have broken. The black, warm waters descended and engulfed the town. Between the blazing white banks of the town stores, among the tree silences, a black tide flowed. Like a kind of summer molasses, it poured turgidly forth upon the cinnamon-dusty road. It surged slow, slow, and it was men and women and horses and barking dogs, and it was little boys and girls. And from the mouths of the people partaking of this tide came the sound of a river. A summer-day river going somewhere, murmuring and irrevocable. And in that slow, steady channel of darkness that cut across the white glare of day were touches of alert white, the eyes, the ivory eyes staring ahead, glancing aside, as the river, the long and endless river, took itself from old channels into a new one. From various and uncountable tributaries, in creeks and brooks of colour and motion, the parts of this river had joined, become one mother current, and flowed on. And brimming the swell were things carried by the river: grandfather clocks chiming, kitchen clocks ticking, caged hens screaming, babies wailing; and swimming among the thickened eddies were mules and; cats, and sudden excursions of burst mattress springs floating by, insane hair stuffing sticking out, and boxes and crates and pictures of dark grandfathers in oak frames — the river flowing it on while the men sat like nervous hounds on the hardware porch, too late to mend the levee, their hands empty.

Samuel Teece wouldn't believe it. 'Why, hell, where'd they get the transportation? How they goin' to *get* to Mars?'

'Rockets,' said Grandpa Quartermain.

'All the damn-fool things. Where'd they get rockets?'

'Saved their money and built them.'

'I never heard about it.'

'Seems these niggers kept it secret, worked on the rockets all themselves, don't know where — in Africa, maybe.'

'Could they *do* that?' demanded Samuel Teece, pacing about the porch. 'Ain't there a law?'

'It ain't as if they declarin' war,' said Grandpa quietly.

'Where do they get off, God damn it, workin' in secret, plottin'?' shouted Teece.

'Schedule is for all this town's niggers to gather out by Loon Lake. Rockets be there at one o'clock, pick 'em up, take 'em to Mars.'

'Telephone the governor, call out the militia,' cried Teece. 'They should've given notice!'

'Here comes your woman, Teece.'

The men turned again.

As they watched, down the hot road in the windless light first one white woman and then another arrived, all of them with stunned faces, all of them rustling like ancient papers. Some of them were crying, some were stern. All came to find their husbands. They pushed through bar-room swing doors, vanishing. They entered cool, quiet groceries. They went in at drug-shops and garages. And one of them, Mrs Clara Teece, came to stand in the dust by the hardware porch, blinking up at her stiff and angry husband as the black river flowed behind her.

'It's Lucinda, Pa; you got to come home!'

'I'm not comin' home for no damn darkie!'

'She's leaving. What'll I do without her?'

'Fetch for yourself, maybe. I won't get down on my knees to stop her.'

'But she's like a family member,' Mrs Teece moaned.

'Don't shout! I won't have you blubberin' in public this way about no goddamn—'

His wife's small sob stopped him. She dabbed at her eyes. 'I kept telling her, "Lucinda," I said, "you stay on and I raise your pay and you get *two* nights off a week, if you want,'' but she just looked set! I never seen her so set, and I said, ''Don't you *love* me, Lucinda?'' and she said yes, but she had to go because that's the way it was, is all. She cleaned the house and dusted it and put luncheon on the table and then she went to the parlour door and — and stood there with two bundles, one by each foot, and shook my hand and said, ''Good-bye, Mrs Teece.'' And she went out the door. And there was her luncheon on the table, and all of us too upset to even eat it. It's still there now, I know; last time I looked it was getting cold.'

Teece almost struck her. 'God damn it, Mrs Teece, you get the hell home. Standin' there makin' a sight of yourself!'

'But, Pa . . .'

He strode away into the hot dimness of the store. He came back out a few seconds later with a silver pistol in his hand.

His wife was gone.

The river flowed black between the buildings, with a rustle and a creak and a constant whispering shuffle. It was a very quiet thing, with a great certainty to it; no laughter, no wildness, just a steady, decided, and ceaseless flow.

Teece sat on the edge of his hardwood chair. 'If one of 'em so much as laughs, by Christ, I'll kill 'em.'

The men waited.

The river passed quietly in the dreamland noon.

'Looks like you goin' to have to hoe your own turnips, Sam,' Grandpa chuckled.

'I'm not bad at shootin' white folks neither.' Teece didn't look at Grandpa. Grandpa turned his head away and shut up his mouth.

'Hold on there!' Samuel Teece leaped off the porch. He reached up and seized the reins of a horse ridden by a tall Negro man. 'You Belter, come down off there!'

'Yes, sir.' Belter slid down.

Teece looked him over. 'Now, just what you think you're doin'?'

'Well, Mr Teece . . .'

'I reckon you think you're goin', just like that song —
what's the words? "Way up in the middle of the air"; ain't
*that* it?'

'Yes, sir.' The Negro waited.

'You recollect you owe me fifty dollars, Belter?'

'Yes, sir.'

'You tryin' to sneak out? By God, I'll horse-whip you!'

'All the excitement, and it slipped my mind, sir.'

'It slipped his mind.' Teece gave a vicious wink at his men
on the hardware porch. 'God damn mister, you know what
you're goin' to do?'

'No, sir.'

'You're stayin' here to work out that fifty bucks, or my
name ain't Samuel W. Teece.' He turned again to smile
confidently at the men in the shade.

Belter looked at the river going along the street, that dark
river flowing between the ships, the dark river on wheels
and horses and in dusty shoes, the dark river from which
he had been snatched on his journey. He began to shiver.
'Let me go, Mr Teece. I'll send your money from up there,
I promise!'

'Listen, Belter.' Teece grasped the man's braces like two
harp-strings, playing them now and again, contemptuously,
snorting at the sky, pointing one bony finger straight at God.
'Belter, you know anything about what's up there?'

'What they tells me.'

'What they tells him! Christ! Hear that? What they tells
him!' He swung the man's weight by his braces, idly, ever
so casual, flicking a finger in the black face. 'Belter, you
fly up and up like a July Fourth rocket and bang! There
you are, cinders, spread all over space. Them crackpot
scientists, they don't know nothin', they kill you all off!'

'I don't care.'

'Glad to hear that. Because you know what's up on that
planet Mars? There's monsters with big raw eyes like
mushrooms! You seen them pictures on those future

magazines you buy at the drug-store for a dime, ain't you? Well! Them monsters jump up and suck marrow from your bones!'

'I don't care, don't care at all, don't care.' Belter watched the parade slide by, leaving him. Sweat lay on his dark brow. He seemed about to collapse.

'And it's cold up there; no air, you fall down, jerk like a fish, gaspin', dyin', stranglin', stranglin' and dyin'. You *like* that?'

'Lots of things I don't like, sir. Please, sir, let me go. I'm late.'

'I'll let you go when I'm *ready* to let you go. We'll just talk here polite and until I say you can leave, and you know it damn well. You want to travel, do you? Well, Mister Way up in the Middle of the Air, you get the hell home and work out that fifty bucks you owe me! Take you two months to do that!'

'But if I work it out, I'll miss the rocket, sir!'

'Ain't that a shame now?' Teece tried to look sad.

'I give you my horse, sir.'

'Horse ain't legal tender. You don't move until I get my money.' Teece laughed inside. He felt very warm and good.

A small crowd of dark people had gathered to hear all this. Now as Belter stood, head down, trembling, an old man stepped forward.

'Mister?'

Teece flashed him a quick look. 'Well?'

'How much this man owe you, mister?'

'None of your damn business!'

The old man looked at Belter. 'How much, son?'

'Fifty dollars.'

The old man put out his black hands at the people around him. 'There's twenty-five of you. Each give two dollars; quick now, this no time for argument.'

'Here, now!' cried Teece, stiffening up, tall, tall.

The money appeared. The old man fingered it into his

hat and gave the hat to Belter. 'Son,' he said, 'you ain't missin' no rocket.'

Belter smiled into the hat. 'No, sir, I guess I ain't.'

Teece shouted: 'You give that money back to them!'

Belter bowed respectfully, handing the money over, and when Teece would not touch it he set it down in the dust at Teece's feet. 'There's your money, sir,' he said. 'Thank you kindly.' Smiling, he gained the saddle of his horse and whipped his horse along, thanking the old man, who rode with him now until they were out of sight and hearing.

'Son of a bitch,' whispered Teece, staring blind at the sun. 'Son of a bitch.'

'Pick up the money, Samuel,' said someone from the porch.

It was happening all along the way. Little white boys, barefoot, dashed up with the news. 'Them that has helps them that hasn't! And that way they *all* get free! Seen a rich man give a poor man two hundred bucks to pay off some'un! Seen some'un else give some'un else ten bucks, five bucks, sixteen, lots of that, all over, everybody!'

The white men sat with sour water in their mouths. Their eyes were almost puffed shut, as if they had been struck in their faces by wind and sand and heat.

The rage was in Samuel Teece. He climbed up on the porch and glared at the passing swarms. He waved his gun. And after a while when he had to do something, he began to shout at anyone, any Negro who looked up at him. 'Bang! There's another rocket out in space!' he shouted so all could hear. 'Bang! By God!' The dark heads didn't flicker or pretend to hear but their eyes slid swiftly over and back. 'Crash! All of them rockets fallin'! Screamin', dyin'! Bang! God Almighty, I'm glad *I'm* right here on old terra firma. As they says in that old joke, the more firma, the less terra! Ha, ha!'

Horses clopped along, shuffling up dust. Wagons bumbled on ruined springs.

'Bang!' His voice was lonely in the heat, trying to terrify the dust and the blazing sun sky. 'Wham! Niggers all over space! Jerked outa rockets like so many minnows hit by a meteor, by God! Space fulla meteors. You know that? Sure! Thick as buckshot; powie! Shoot down them tin-can rockets like so many ducks, so many clay pipes! Ole sardine-cans full of black cod! Bangin' like a stringa lady-fingers, bang, bang, bang! Ten thousand dead here, ten thousand there. Floatin' in space, around and around earth, ever and ever, cold and way out, Lord! You hear that, *you* there!'

Silence. The river was broad and continuous. Having entered all cotton shacks during the hour, having flooded all the valuables out, it was now carrying the clocks and the washboards, the silk bolts and curtain rods on down to some distant black sea.

High tide passed. It was two o'clock. Low tide came. Soon the river was dried up, the town silent, the dust settling in a film on the stores, the seated men, the tall hot trees.

Silence.

The men on the porch listened.

Hearing nothing, they extended their thoughts and their imaginations out and out into the surrounding meadows. In the early morning the land had been filled with its usual concoctions of sounds. Here and there, with stubborn persistence to custom, there had been voices singing, the honey laughter under the mimosa branches, the piccaninnies rushing in clear water laughter at the creek, movements and bendings in the fields, jokes and shouts of amusement from the shingle shacks covered with fresh green vine.

Now it was as if a great wind had washed the land clean of sounds. There was nothing. Skeleton doors hung open on leather hinges. Rubber-tyre swings hung in the silent air, uninhibited. The washing rocks at the river were empty, and the water-melon patches, if any, were left alone to heat their hidden liquors in the sun. Spiders started building new webs in abandoned huts; dust started to sift in from unpatched roofs in golden spicules. Here and there a fire, forgotten in the last rush, lingered and in a sudden access of strength fed upon the dry bones of some littered shack. The sound of a gentle feeding burn went up through the silenced air.

The men sat on the hardware porch, not blinking or swallowing.

'I can't figure why they left *now*. With things lookin' up. I mean, every day they got more rights. What they *want*, anyway? Here's the poll tax gone, and more and more states passin' anti-lynchin' bills, and all kinds of equal rights. What *more* they want? They make almost as good money as a white man, but there they go.'

Far down the empty street a bicycle came.

'I'll be god-damned, Teece, here comes your Silly now.'

The bicycle pulled up before the porch, a seventeen-year-old coloured boy on it, all arms and feet and long legs and round water-melon head. He looked up at Samuel Teece and smiled.

'So you got a guilty conscience and came back,' said Teece.

'No, sir, I just brought the bicycle.'

'What's wrong, couldn't get it on the rocket?'

'That wasn't it, sir.'

'Don't tell me what it was! Get off, you're not goin' to steal my property!' He gave the boy a push. The bicycle fell. 'Get inside and start cleaning the brass.'

'Beg pardon?' The boy's eyes widened.

'You heard what I said. There's guns need unpacking there, and a crate of nails just come from Natchez—'

'Mr Teece.'

'And a box of hammers need fixin'—'

'Mr Teece, sir?'

'You *still* standin' there!' Teece glared.

'Mr Teece, you don't mind I take the day off,' he said apologetically.

'And tomorrow and the day after tomorrow and the day after the day after that,' said Teece.

'I'm afraid so, sir.'

'You *should* be afraid, boy. Come here.' He marched the boy across the porch and drew a paper out of a desk. 'Remember this?'

'Sir?'

'It's your workin' paper. You signed it, there's your X right there, ain't it? Answer me.'

'I didn't sign that, Mr Teece.' The boy trembled. 'Anyone can make an X.'

'Listen to this, Silly. Contract: "I will work for Mr Samuel Teece two years, starting July 15, 2001, and if intending to leave will give four weeks' notice and continue working until my position is filled." There.' Teece slapped the paper, his eyes glittering. 'You cause trouble, we'll take it to court.'

'I can't do that,' wailed the boy, tears starting to roll down his face. 'If I don't go today, I don't go.'

'I know just how you feel, Silly; yes, sir, I sympathize with you, boy. But we'll treat you good and give you good food, boy. Now you just get inside and start working and forget all about that nonsense, 'eh, Silly? Sure.' Teece grinned and patted the boy's shoulder.

The boy turned and looked at the old men sitting on the porch. He could hardly see now for his tears. 'Maybe — maybe one of these gentlemen here . . .' The men looked up in the hot, uneasy shadows, looking first at the boy and then at Teece.

'You meanin' to say you think a *white man* should take your place, boy?' asked Teece coldly.

Grandpa Quartermain took his red hands off his knees. He looked out at the horizon thoughtfully and said, 'Teece, what about me?'

'What?'

'I'll take Silly's job.'

The porch was silent.

Teece balanced himself in the air. 'Grandpa,' he said warningly.

'Let the boy go. I'll clean the brass.'

'Would you, would you, really?' Silly ran over to Grandpa, laughing, tears on his cheeks, unbelieving.

'Sure.'

'Grandpa,' said Teece, 'keep your damn trap outa this.'

'Give the kid a break, Teece.'

Teece walked over and seized the boy's arm. 'He's mine. I'm lockin' him in the back room until tonight.'

'Don't, Mr Teece!'

The boy began to sob now. His crying filled the air of the porch. His eyes were tight. Far down the street an old tin Ford was choking along, approaching, a last load of coloured people in it. 'Here comes my family, Mr Teece, oh please, oh God, please!'

'Teece,' said one of the other men on the porch, getting up, 'let him go.'

Another man rose also. 'That goes for me too.'

'And me,' said another.

'What's the use?' The men all talked now. 'Cut it out, Teece.'

'Let him go.'

Teece felt for his gun in his pocket. He saw the men's faces. He took his hand away and left the gun in his pocket and said, 'So that's how it is?'

'That's how it is,' someone said.

Teece let the boy go. 'All right. Get out.' He jerked his hand back in the store. 'But I hope you don't think you're gonna leave any trash behind to clutter my store.'

'No, sir!'

'You clean everything outa your shed in back; burn it.'

Silly shook his head. 'I'll take it with.'

'They won't let you put it on that damn rocket.'

'I'll take it with,' insisted the boy softly.

He rushed back through the hardware store. There were sounds of sweeping and cleaning out, and a moment later he appeared, his hands full of tops and marbles and old dusty kites and junk collected through the years. Just then the old tin Ford drove up and Silly climbed in and the door slammed. Teece stood on the porch with a bitter smile.

'What you goin' to do *up there*?'

'Startin' new,' said Silly. 'Gonna have my *own* hardware.'

'God damn it, you been learnin' my trade so you could run off and use it!'

'No, sir, I never thought one day *this'd* happen, sir, but it did. I can't help it if I learned, Mr Teece.'

'I suppose you got names for your rockets?'

They looked at their one clock on the dashboard of the car. 'Yes, sir.'

'Like Elijah and the Chariot, The Big Wheel and The Little Wheel, Faith, Hope and Charity, eh?'

'We got names for the ships, Mr Teece.'

'God the Son and the Holy Ghost, I wouldn't wonder? Say, boy, you got one named the First Baptist church?'

'We got to leave now, Mr Teece.'

Teece laughed. 'You got one named Swing Low, and another named Sweet Chariot?'

The car started up. 'Good-bye, Mr Teece.'

'You got one named Roll Dem Bones?'

'Good-bye, mister!'

'And another called Over Jordan! Ha! Well, tote that rocket, boy, lift that rocket, boy, go on, get blown up, see if *I* care!'

The car churned off into the dust. The boy rose and cupped his hands to his mouth and shouted one last time at Teece: 'Mr Teece, Mr Teece, what *you* goin' to do nights from now on? What you goin' to *do* nights, Mr Teece?'

Silence. The car faded down the road. It was gone. 'What in hell did he mean?' mused Teece. 'What am I goin' to *do* nights?'

He watched the dust settle, and it suddenly came to him.

He remembered nights when men drove to his house, their knees sticking up sharp and their shot-guns sticking up sharper, like a carful of cranes under the night trees of summer, their eyes mean. Honking the horn and him slamming his door, a gun in his hand, laughing to himself, his heart racing like a ten-year-old's, driving off down the summer-night road, a ring of hemp rope coiled on the car floor, fresh shell-boxes making every man's coat look bunchy. How many nights over the years, how many nights of the wind rushing in the car, flopping their hair over their mean eyes, roaring, as they picked a tree, a good strong tree, and rapped on a shanty door!

'So *that's* what the son of a bitch meant?' Teece leaped out into the sunlight. 'Come back, you bastard! What am I goin' to do nights? Why, that lousy, insolent son of a . . .'

It was a good question. He sickened and was empty. Yes. What *will* we do nights? he thought. Now *they're* gone, what? He was absolutely empty and numb.

He pulled the pistol from his pocket, checked its load.

'What you goin' to do, Sam?' someone asked.

'Kill that son of a bitch.'

Grandpa said, 'Don't get yourself heated.'

But Samuel Teece was gone around behind the store. A moment later he drove out of the drive in his open-top car. 'Anyone comin' with me?'

'I'd like a drive,' said Grandpa, and got up.

'Anyone else?'

Nobody replied.

Grandpa got in and slammed the door. Samuel Teece gutted the car out in a great whorl of dust. They didn't speak as they rushed down the road under the bright sky. The heat from the dry meadows was shimmering.

They stopped at a crossroad. 'Which way'd they go, Grandpa?'

Grandpa squinted. 'Straight on ahead, I figure.'

They went on. Under the summer trees their car made a lonely sound. The road was empty, and as they drove along they began to notice something. Teece slowed the car and bent out, his yellow eyes fierce.

'God damn it, Grandpa, you see what them bastards did?'

'What?' asked Grandpa, and looked.

Where they had been carefully set down and left, in neat bundles every few feet along the empty country road, were old roller skates, a bandanna full of knick-knacks, some old shoes, a cartwheel, stacks of pants and coats and ancient hats, bits of oriental crystal that had once tinkled in the wind, tin cans of pink geraniums, dishes of waxed fruit, cartons of Confederate money, washtubs, scrub-boards, wash-lines, soap, somebody's tricycle, someone else's hedge shears, a toy wagon, a jack-in-the-box, a stained-glass window from the Negro Baptist Church, a whole set of brake-rims, inner tubes, mattresses, couches, rocking-chairs, jars of cold cream, hand mirrors. None of it flung down, no, but deposited gently and with feeling, with decorum, upon the dusty edges of the road, as if a whole city had walked here with hands full, at which time a great bronze trumpet had sounded, the articles had been relinquished to the quiet dust, and one and all, the inhabitants of the earth had fled straight up into the blue heavens.

'Wouldn't burn them, they said,' cried Teece angrily. 'No, wouldn't burn them like I said, but had to take them along and leave them where they could see them for the last time, on the road, all together and whole. Them niggers think they're smart.'

He veered the car wildly, mile after mile, down the road, tumbling, smashing, breaking, scattering bundles of paper, jewel boxes, mirrors, chairs. 'There, by damn, and *there*!'

The front tyre gave a whistling cry. The car spilled crazily off the road into a ditch, flinging Teece against the glass.

'Son of a bitch!' He dusted himself off and stood out of the car, almost crying with rage.

He looked at the silent, empty road. 'We'll never catch them now, never, never.' As far as he could see there was nothing but bundles and stacks and more bundles neatly placed like little abandoned shrines in the late day, in the warm-blowing wind.

Teece and Grandpa came walking tiredly back to the hardware store an hour later. The men were still sitting there, listening and watching the sky. Just as Teece sat down and eased his tight shoes off someone cried, 'Look!'

'I'll be *damned* if I will,' said Teece.

But the others looked. And they saw the golden bobbins rising in the sky far away. Leaving flame behind, they vanished.

In the cotton-fields the wind blew idly among the snow-clusters. In still farther meadows the water-melons lay, unfingerprinted, striped like tortoise cats lying in the sun.

The men on the porch sat down, looked at each other, looked at the yellow rope piled neat on the store shelves, glanced at the gun-shells glinting shiny brass in their cartons, saw the silver pistols and long black metal shotguns hung high and quiet in the shadows. Somebody put a straw in his mouth. Someone else drew a figure in the dust.

Finally Samuel Teece held his empty shoe up in triumph, turned it over, stared at it, and said, 'Did you notice? Right up to the very last, by God, he said "Mister"!'

# The Naming of Names

They came to the strange blue lands and put their names upon the lands. Here was Hinkston Creek and Lustig Corners and Black River and Driscoll Forest and Peregrine Mountain and Wilder Town, all the names of people and the things that the people did. Here was the place where Martians killed the first Earth Men, and it was Red Town and had to do with blood. And here where the second expedition was destroyed, and it was named Second Try, and each of the other places where the rocket men had set down their fiery cauldrons to burn the land, the names were left like cinders, and of course there was a Spender Hill and Nathaniel York Town . . .

The old Martian names were names of water and air and hills. They were the names of snows that emptied south in stone canals to fill the empty seas. And the names of sealed and buried sorcerers and towers and obelisks. And the rockets struck at the names like hammers, breaking away the marble into shale, shattering the crockery milestones that named the old towns, in the rubble of which great pylons were plunged with new names: IRON TOWN, STEEL TOWN, ALUMINIUM CITY, ELECTRIC VILLAGE, CORN TOWN, GRAIN VILLA, DETROIT II, all the mechanical names and the metal names from Earth.

And after the towns were built and named, the graveyards were built and named too: Green Hill, Moss Town, Boot Hill, Bide a Wee; and the first dead went into their graves . . .

## *The Old Ones*

And what more natural than that, at last, the old people come to Mars, following in the trail left by the loud frontiersmen, the aromatic sophisticates, and the professional travellers and romantic lecturers in search of new grist.

And so the dry and crackling people, the people who spent their time listening to their hearts and feeling their pulses and spooning syrups into their wry mouths, these people who had once taken chair cars to California in November and third-class steamers to Italy in April, the dried-apricot people, the mummy people, came at last to Mars . . .

# *The Martian*

The blue mountains lifted into the rain and the rain fell down into the long canals and old LaFarge and his wife came out of their house to watch.

'First rain this season,' LaFarge pointed out.

'It's good,' said his wife.

'Very welcome.'

They shut the door. Inside, they warmed their hands at a fire. They shivered. In the distance, through the window, they saw rain gleaming on the sides of the rocket which had brought them from Earth.

'There's only one thing,' said LaFarge, looking at his hands.

'What's that?' asked his wife.

'I wish we could have brought Tom with us.'

'Oh, now, Lafe!'

'I won't start again; I'm sorry.'

'We came here to enjoy our old age in peace, not to think of Tom. He's been dead so long now, we should try to forget him and everything on Earth.'

'You're right,' he said, and turned his hands again to the heat. He gazed into the fire. 'I won't speak of it any more. It's just I miss driving out to Green Lawn Park every Sunday to put flowers on his marker. It used to be our only excursion.'

The blue rain fell upon the house.

At nine o'clock they went to bed and lay quietly, hand in hand, he fifty-five, she sixty, in the raining darkness.

'Anna?' he called softly.

'Yes?' she replied.

'Did you hear something?'

They both listened to the rain and the wind.

'Nothing,' she said.

'Someone whistling,' he said.

'No, I didn't hear it.'

'I'm going to get up and see, anyhow.'

He put on his robe and walked through the house to the front door. Hesitating, he pulled the door wide, and rain fell cold upon his face. The wind blew.

In the dooryard stood a small figure.

Lightning cracked the sky, and a wash of white colour illumined the face looking in at old LaFarge there in the doorway.

'Who's there?' called LaFarge, trembling.

No answer.

'Who is it? What do you want!'

Still not a word.

He felt very weak and tired and dumb. 'Who are you?' he cried.

His wife entered behind him and took his arm. 'Why are you shouting?'

'A small boy's standing in the yard and won't answer me,' said the old man, trembling. 'He looks like Tom!'

'Come to bed, you're dreaming.'

'But he's there; see for yourself.'

He pulled the door wider to let her see. The cold wind blew and the thin rain fell upon the soil and the figure stood looking at them with distant eyes. The old woman held to the doorway.

'Go away!' she said, waving one hand. 'Go away!'

'Doesn't it look like Tom?' asked the old man.

The figure did not move.

'I'm afraid,' said the old woman. 'Lock the door and come to bed. I won't have anything to do with it.'

She vanished, moaning to herself, into the bedroom.

The old man stood with the wind raining coldness on his hands.

'Tom,' he called softly. 'Tom, if that's you, if by some chance it is you, Tom, I'll leave the door unlatched. And if you're cold and want to come in to warm yourself, just come in later and lie by the hearth; there're some fur rugs there.'

He shut but did not lock the door.

His wife felt him return to bed, and shuddered. 'It's a terrible night. I feel so old,' she said, sobbing.

'Hush, hush,' he gentled her, and held her in his arms. 'Go to sleep.'

After a long while she slept.

And then, very quietly, as he listened, he heard the front door open, the rain and wind come in, the door shut. He heard soft footsteps on the hearth and a gentle breathing. 'Tom,' he said to himself.

Lightning struck in the sky and broke the blackness apart.

In the morning the sun was very hot.

Mr LaFarge opened the door into the living-room and glanced all about, quickly.

The hearthrugs were empty.

LaFarge sighed. 'I'm getting old,' he said.

He went out to walk to the canal to fetch a bucket of clear water to wash in. At the front door he almost knocked young Tom down carrying in a bucket already filled to the brim. 'Good morning, Father!'

'Morning, Tom.' The old man fell aside. The young boy, barefooted, hurried across the room, set the bucket down, and turned, smiling. 'It's a fine day!'

'Yes, it is,' said the old man incredulously. The boy acted as if nothing was unusual. He began to wash his face with the water.

The old man moved forward. 'Tom, how did you get here? You're alive?'

'Shouldn't I be?' The boy glanced up.

'But, Tom, Green Lawn Park, every Sunday, the flowers

and . . .' LaFarge had to sit down. The boy came and stood before him and took his hand. The old man felt the fingers, warm and firm. 'You're really here, it's not a dream?'

'You *do* want me to be here, don't you?' The boy seemed worried.

'Yes, yes, Tom!'

'Then why ask questions? Accept me!'

'But your mother; the shock . . .'

'Don't worry about her. During the night I sang to both of you, and you'll accept me more because of it, especially her. I know what the shock is. Wait till she comes, you'll see.' He laughed, shaking his head of coppery, curled hair. His eyes were very blue and clear.

'Good morning, Lafe, Tom.' Mother came from the bedroom, putting her hair up into a bun. 'Isn't it a fine day?'

Tom turned to laugh in his fathers face. 'You *see*?'

They ate a very good lunch, all three of them in the shade behind the house. Mrs LaFarge had found an old bottle of sunflower wine she had put away, and they all had a drink of that. Mr LaFarge had never seen his wife's face so bright. If there was any doubt in her mind about Tom she didn't voice it. It was a completely natural thing to her. And it was also becoming natural to LaFarge himself.

While Mother cleared the dishes LaFarge leaned towards his son and said confidentially, 'How old are you now, Son?'

'Don't you know, Father? Fourteen, of course.'

'Who are you, *really*? You can't be Tom, but you are *someone*. Who?'

'Don't.' Startled, the boy put his hands to his face.

'You can tell me,' said the old man. 'I'll understand. You're a Martian, aren't you? I've heard tales of the Martians; nothing definite. Stories about how rare Martians are and when they come among us they come as Earth Men. There's something about you — you're Tom and yet you're not.'

'Why can't you accept me and stop talking?' cried the

boy. His hands completely shielded his face. Don't doubt, please don't doubt me!' He turned and ran from the table.

'Tom, come back!'

But the boy ran off along the canal towards the distant town.

'Where's Tom going!' asked Anna, returning for more dishes. She looked at her husband's face. 'Did you say something to bother him?'

'Anna,' he said, taking her hand. 'Anna, do you remember anything about Green Lawn Park, a market, and Tom having pneumonia?'

'What *are* you talking about?' She laughed.

'Never mind,' he said quietly.

In the distance the dust drifted down after Tom had run along the canal rim.

At five in the afternoon, with the sunset, Tom returned. He looked doubtfully at his father. 'Are you going to ask me anything?' he wanted to know.

'No questions,' said LaFarge.

The boy smiled his white smile. 'Swell.'

'Where've you been?'

'Near the town. I almost didn't come back. I was almost' — the boy sought for a word — 'trapped.'

'How do you mean, "trapped"?'

'I passed a small tin house by the canal and I was almost made so I couldn't come back here ever again to see you. I don't know how to explain it to you, there's no way, I can't tell you, even *I* don't know; it's strange, I don't want to talk about it.'

'We won't then. Better wash up, boy. Supper-time.'

The boy ran.

Perhaps ten minutes later a boat floated down the serene surface of the canal, a tall, lank man with black hair poling it along with leisurely drives of his arms. 'Evening, Brother LaFarge,' he said, pausing at his task.

'Evening, Saul. What's the word?'

'All kinds of words tonight. You know that fellow named Nomland who lives down the canal in the tin hut?'

LaFarge stiffened. 'Yes?'

'You know what sort of rascal he was?'

'Rumour had it he left Earth because he killed a man.'

Saul leaned on his wet pole, gazing at LaFarge. 'Remember the name of the man he killed?'

'Gillings, wasn't it?'

'Right. Gillings. Well, about two hours ago Mr Nomland came running to town crying about how he had seen Gillings, alive, here on Mars, today, this afternoon! He tried to get the jail to lock him up safe. The jail wouldn't. So Nomland went home, and twenty minutes ago, as I get the story, blew his brains out with a gun. I just came from there.'

'Well, well,' said LaFarge.

'The darnedest things happen,' said Saul. 'Well, good night, LaFarge.'

'Good night.'

The boat drifted on down the serene canal waters.

'Supper's hot,' called the old woman.

Mr LaFarge sat down to his supper and, knife in hand, looked over at Tom. 'Tom,' he said, 'what did you do this afternoon?'

'Nothing,' said Tom, his mouth full. 'Why?'

'Just wanted to know.' The old man tucked his napkin in.

At seven that night the old woman wanted to go to town. 'Haven't been there in months,' she said. But Tom desisted. 'I'm afraid of the town,' he said. 'The people. I don't want to go there.'

'Such talk for a grown boy,' said Anna. 'I won't listen to it. You'll come along. *I* say so.'

'Anna, if the boy doesn't want to . . .' started the old man.

But there was no arguing. She hustled them into the canal-boat, and they floated up the canal under the evening stars,

Tom lying on his back, his eyes closed; asleep or not, there was no telling. The old man looked at him steadily, wondering. Who is this, he thought, in need of love as much as we? Who is he and what is he, that, out of loneliness, he comes into the alien camp and assumes the voice and face of memory and stands among us, accepted and happy at last? From what mountain, what cave, what small last race of people remaining on this world when the rockets came from Earth? The old man shook his head. There was no way to know. This, to all purposes, was Tom.

The old man looked at the town ahead and did not like it, but then he returned to thoughts of Tom and Anna again, and he thought to himself: Perhaps this is wrong to keep Tom but a little while, when nothing can come of it but trouble and sorrow, but how are we to give up the very thing we've wanted, no matter if it stays only a day and is gone, making the emptiness emptier, the dark nights darker, the rainy nights wetter? You might as well force the food from our mouths as take this one from us.

And he looked at the boy slumbering so peacefully at the bottom of the boat. They boy whimpered with some dream. 'The people,' he murmured in his sleep. 'Changing and changing. The trap.'

'There, there, boy.' LaFarge stroked the boy's soft curls and Tom ceased.

LaFarge helped wife and son from the boat.

'Here we are!' Anna smiled at all the lights, listening to the music from the drinking-houses, the pianos, the phonographs, watching people, arm in arm, striding by in the crowded streets.

'I wish I was home,' said Tom.

'You never talked that way before,' said the mother. 'You always liked Saturday nights in town.'

'Stay close to me,' whispered Tom. 'I don't want to get trapped.'

Anna overheard. 'Stop talking that way; come along!'

LaFarge noticed that the boy held his hand. LaFarge squeezed it. 'I'll stick with you, Tommy-boy.' He looked at the throngs coming and going, and it worried him also. 'We won't stay long.'

'Nonsense, we'll spend the evening,' said Anna.

They crossed a street, and three drunken men careened into them. There was much confusion, a separation, a wheeling about, and then LaFarge stood stunned.

Tom was gone.

'Where is he?' asked Anna irritably. 'Him always running off alone any chance he gets. Tom!' she called.

Mr LaFarge hurried through the crowd, but Tom was gone.

'He'll come back; he'll be at the boat when we leave,' said Anna certainly, steering her husband back towards the motion-picture theatre. There was a sudden commotion in the crowd, and a man and a woman rushed by LaFarge. He recognized them. Joe Spaulding and his wife. They were gone before he could speak to them.

Looking back anxiously, he purchased the tickets for the theatre and allowed his wife to draw him into the unwelcome darkness.

Tom was not at the landing at eleven o'clock. Mrs LaFarge turned very pale.

'Now, Mother,' said LaFarge, 'don't worry. I'll find him. Wait here.'

'Hurry back.' Her voice jaded into the ripple of the water.

He walked through the night streets, hands in pockets. All about, lights were going out one by one. A few people were still leaning out their windows, for the night was warm, even though the sky still held storm-clouds from time to time among the stars. As he walked he recalled the boy's constant references to being trapped, his fear of crowds and cities. There was no sense in it, thought the old man tiredly.

Perhaps the boy was gone forever, perhaps he had never been. LaFarge turned in at a particular alley, watching the numbers.

'Hello there, LaFarge.'

A man sat in his doorway, smoking a pipe.

'Hello, Mike.'

'You and your woman quarrel? You out walking it off?'

'No. Just walking.'

'You look like you lost something. Speaking of lost things,' said Mike, 'somebody got found this evening. You know Joe Spaulding? You remember his daughter Lavinia?'

'Yes.' LaFarge was cold. It all seemed a repeated dream. He knew which words would come next.

'Lavinia came home tonight,' said Mike, smoking. 'You recall, she was lost on the dead sea-bottoms about a month ago? They found what they thought was her body, badly deteriorated, and ever since the Spaulding family's been no good. Joe went around saying she wasn't dead, that wasn't really her body. Guess he was right. Tonight Lavinia showed up.'

'Where?' LaFarge felt his breath come swiftly, his heart pounding.

'On Main Street. The Spauldings were buying tickets for a show. And there, all of a sudden, in the crowd, was Lavinia. Must have been quite a scene. She didn't know them first off. They followed her half down a street and spoke to her. Then she remembered.'

'Did you see her?'

'No, but I heard her singing. Remember how she used to sing "The Bonnie Banks of Loch Lomond"? I heard her trilling out for her father a while ago over there in their house. It was good to hear; her such a beautiful girl. A shame, I thought, her dead; and now with her back again it's fine. Here now, you look weak yourself. Better come in for a spot of whisky . . .'

'Thanks, no, Mike.' The old man moved away. He heard

Mike say good night and did not answer, but fixed his eyes upon the two-storey building where rambling clusters of crimson Martian flowers lay upon the high crystal roof. Around back, above the garden, was a twisted iron balcony, and the windows above were lighted. It was very late, and still he thought to himself: What will happen to Anna if I don't bring Tom home with me? This second shock, this second death, what will it do to her? Will she remember the first death, too, and this dream and the sudden vanishing? O God, I've got to find Tom or what will become of Anna? Poor Anna, waiting there at the landing. He paused and lifted his head. Somewhere above, voices bade other soft voices good night, doors turned and shut, lights dimmed, and a gentle singing continued. A moment later a girl no more than eighteen, very lovely, came out upon the balcony.

LaFarge called up through the wind that was blowing.

The girl turned and looked down. 'Who's there?' she cried.

'It's me,' said the old man, and realizing this reply to be silly and strange, fell silent, his lips working. Should he call out, 'Tom, my son, this is your father?' How to speak to her? She would think him quite insane and summon her parents.

The girl bent forward in the blowing light. 'I know you,' she replied softly. 'Please go; there's nothing you can do.'

'You've got to come back!' It escaped LaFarge before he could prevent it.

The moonlit figure above drew into shadow, so there was no identity, only a voice. 'I'm not your son any more,' it said. 'We should never have come to town.'

'Anna's waiting at the landing!'

'I'm sorry,' said the quiet voice. 'But what can I do? I'm happy here, I'm loved, even as you loved me. I am what I am, and I take what can be taken; it's too late now, they've caught me.'

'But Anna, the shock to her. Think of that.'

'The thoughts are too strong in this house; it's like being imprisoned. I can't change myself back.'

'You are Tom, you were Tom, weren't you? You aren't joking with an old man; you're not really Lavinia Spaulding?'

'I'm not anyone, I'm just myself; wherever I am, I am something, and now I'm something you can't help.'

'You're not safe in the town. It's better out on the canal where no one can hurt you,' pleaded the old man.

'That's true.' The voice hesitated. 'But I must consider these people now. How would they feel if, in the morning, I was gone again, this time for good? Anyway, the mother knows what I am; she guessed, even as you did. I think they all guessed, but didn't question. You don't question Providence. If you can't have the reality, a dream is just as good. Perhaps I'm not their dead one back, but I'm something almost better to them; an ideal shaped by their minds. I have a choice of hurting them or your wife.'

'They're a family of five. They can stand your loss better!'

'Please,' said the voice. 'I'm tired.

The old man's voice hardened. 'You've got to come. I can't let Anna be hurt again. You're our son. You're my son, and you belong to us.'

'No, please!' The shadow trembled.

'You don't belong to this house or these people!'

'No, don't do this to me!'

'Tom, Tom, Son, listen to me. Come back, slip down the vines, boy. Come along, Anna's waiting; we'll give you a good home, everything you want.' He stared and stared upward, willing it to be.

The shadows drifted, the vines rustled.

At last the quiet voice said, 'All right, Father.'

'Tom!'

In the moonlight the quick figure of a boy slid down though the vines. LaFarge put up his arms to catch him.

The room lights above flashed on. A voice issued from one of the grilled windows. 'Who's down there?'

'Hurry, boy!'

More lights, more voices. 'Stop, I have a gun! Vinny, are you all right?' A running of feet.

Together the old man and the boy ran across the garden.

A shot sounded. The bullet struck the wall as they slammed the gate.

'Tom, you go that way; I'll go here and lead them off! Run to the canal; I'll meet you there in ten minutes, boy!'

They parted.

The moon hid behind a cloud. The old man ran in darkness.

'Anna, I'm here!'

The old woman helped him, trembling, into the boat. 'Where's Tom?'

'He'll be here in a minute,' panted LaFarge.

They turned to watch the alleys and the sleeping town. Late strollers were still out: a policeman, a night watchman, a rocket pilot, several lonely men coming home from some nocturnal rendezvous, four men and women issuing from a bar, laughing. Music played dimly somewhere.

'Why don't he come?' asked the old woman,

'He'll come, he'll come.' But LaFarge was not certain. Suppose the boy had been caught again, somehow, someway, in his travel down to the landing, running through the midnight streets between the dark houses. It was a long run, even for a young boy. But he should have reached here first.

And now, far away, along the moonlit avenue, a figure ran.

LaFarge cried out and then silenced himself, for also far away was the sound of voices and running feet. Lights blazed on in window after window. Across the open plaza leading to the landing, the one figure ran, It was not Tom; it was only a running shape with a face like silver shining in the light of the globes clustered about the plaza, And as it rushed nearer, nearer, it became more familiar, until when it reached the landing it was Tom! Anna flung up her hands, LaFarge hurried to cast off. But already it was too late.

For out of the avenue and across the silent plaza now came one man, another, a woman, two other men, Mr Spaulding, all running. They stopped, bewildered. They stared about, wanting to go back because this could be only a nightmare, it was quite insane. But they came on again, hesitantly, stopping, starting.

It was too late. The night, the event, was over. LaFarge twisted the mooring-rope in his fingers. He was very cold and lonely. The people raised and put down their feet in the moonlight, drifting with great speed, wide-eyed, until the crowd, all ten of them, halted at the landing. They peered wildly into the boat. They cried out.

'Don't move, Lafarge!' Spaulding had a gun.

And now it was evident what had happened. Tom flashing through the moonlit streets, alone, passing people. A policeman seeing the figure dart past. The policeman pivoting, staring at the face, calling a name, giving pursuit. '*You*, stop!' Seeing a criminal face. All along the way, the same thing, men here, women there, night watchmen, rocket pilots. The swift figure meaning everything to them, all identities, all persons, all names. How many different names had been uttered in the last five minutes? How many different faces shaped over Tom's face, all wrong?

All down the way the pursued and the pursuing the dream and the dreamers, the quarry and the hounds. All down the way the sudden revealment, the flash of familiar eyes, the cry of an old, old name, the remembrances of other times, the crowd multiplying. Everyone leaping forward as, like an image reflected from ten thousand mirrors, ten thousand eyes, the running dream came and went, a different face to those ahead, those behind, those yet to be met, those unseen.

And here they all are now, at the boat, wanting the dream for their own, just as we want him to be Tom, not Lavinia or William or Roger or any other, thought LaFarge. But it's all done now. The thing has gone too far.

'Come up, all of you!' Spaulding ordered them.

Tom stepped up from the boat, Spaulding seized his wrist. 'You're coming home with me. I *know*.'

'Wait,' said the policeman. 'He's my prisoner. Name's Dexter: wanted for murder.'

'No!' a woman sobbed. 'It's my husband! I guess I know my husband!'

Other voices objected. The crowd moved in.

Mrs LaFarge shielded Tom. 'This is my son; you have no right to accuse him of anything. We're going home right now!'

As for Tom, he was trembling and shaking violently. He looked very sick. The crowd thickened about him, putting out their wild hands, seizing and demanding.

Tom screamed.

Before their eyes he changed. He was Tom and James and a man named Switchman, another named Butterfield; he was the town mayor and the young girl Judith and the husband William and the wife Clarisse. He was melting wax shaping to their minds. They shouted, they pressed forward, pleading. He screamed, threw out his hands, his face dissolving to each demand, 'Tom!' cried LaFarge. 'Alice!' another. 'William!' They snatched his wrists, whirled him about, until with one last shriek of horror he fell.

He lay on the stones, melted wax cooling, his face all faces, one eye blue, the other golden, hair that was brown, red, yellow, black, one eyebrow thick, one thin, one hand large, one small.

They stood over him and put their fingers to their mouths. They bent down.

'He's dead,' someone said at last.

It began to rain.

The rain fell upon the people, and they looked up at the sky.

Slowly, and then more quickly, they turned and walked away and then started running, scattering from the scene. In a minute the place was desolate. Only Mr and Mrs LaFarge remained, looking down, hand in hand, terrified.

The rain fell upon the upturned, unrecognizable face.

Anna said nothing but began to cry.

'Come along home, Anna, there's nothing we can do,' said the old man.

They climbed down into the boat and went back along the canal in the darkness. They entered their house and lit a small fire and warmed their hands. They went to bed and lay together, cold and thin, listening to the rain returned to the roof above them.

'Listen,' said LaFarge at midnight. 'Did you hear something?'

'Nothing, nothing.'

'I'll go look anyway.'

He fumbled across the dark room and waited by the outer door for a long time before he opened it.

He pulled the door wide and looked out.

Rain poured from the black sky upon the empty dooryard, into the canal and among the blue mountains.

He waited five minutes and then softly, his hands wet, he shut and bolted the door.

## *The Luggage Store*

It was a very remote thing, when the luggage-store proprietor heard the news on the night radio, received all the way from Earth on a light-sound beam. The proprietor felt how remote it was.

There was going to be a war on Earth.

He went out to peer into the sky.

Yes, there it was, Earth, in the evening heavens, following the sun into the hills. The words on the radio and that green star were one and the same.

'I don't believe it,' said the proprietor.

'It's because you're not there,' said Father Peregrine, who had stopped by to pass the time of evening.

'What do you mean, Father?'

'It's like when I was a boy,' said Father Peregrine. 'We heard about wars in China. But we never believed them. It was too far away. And there were too many people dying. It was impossible. Even when we saw the motion-pictures we didn't believe it. Well, that's how it is now. Earth is China. It's so far away it's unbelievable. It's not here. You can't touch it. You can't even see it. All you see is a green light. Two billion people living on that light? Unbelievable! War? We don't hear the explosions.'

'We will,' said the proprietor. 'I keep thinking about all those people that were going to come to Mars this week. What was it? A hundred thousand or so coming up in the next month or so. What about *them* if the war starts?'

'I imagine they'll turn back. They'll be needed on Earth.'

'Well,' said the proprietor, 'I'll get my luggage dusted off. I got a feeling there'll be a rush sale here any time.'

'Do you think everyone now on Mars will go back to

Earth if this *is* the Big War we've all been expecting for years?'

'It's a funny thing, Father, but yes, I think we'll *all* go back. I know, we came up here to get away from things — politics, the atom bomb, war, pressure groups, prejudice, laws — I know. But it's still home there. You wait and see. When the first bomb drops on America the people up here'll start thinking. They haven't been here long enough. A couple years is all. If they'd been here forty years, it'd be different, but they got relatives down there, and their home towns. Me, I can't believe in Earth any more; I can't imagine it much. But I'm old. I don't count. I might stay on here.'

'Yes, I guess you're right.'

They stood on the porch watching the stars. Finally Father Peregrine pulled some money from his pocket and handed it to the proprietor. 'Come to think of it, you'd better give me a new valise. My old one's in pretty bad condition . . .'

# The Off Season

Sam Parkhill motioned with the broom, sweeping away the blue Martian sand.

'Here we are,' he said. 'Yes, sir, look at that!' He pointed. 'Look at that sign. SAM'S HOT DOGS! Ain't that beautiful, Elma.'

'Sure, Sam,' said his wife.

'Boy, what a change for me! If the boys from the Fourth Expedition could see me now. Am I glad to be in business myself while all the rest of them guys're off soldiering around still. We'll make thousands, Elma, thousands.'

His wife looked at him for a long time, not speaking. 'Whatever happened to Captain Wilder?' she asked finally. 'That captain that killed the guy who thought he was going to kill off every other Earth Man, what was his name?'

'Spender, that nut. He was too damn particular. Oh, Captain Wilder? He's off on a rocket to Jupiter, I hear. They kicked him upstairs. I think he was a little batty about Mars too. Touchy, you know. He'll be back down from Jupiter and Pluto in about twenty years if he's lucky. That's what he gets for shooting off his mouth. And while he's freezing to death, look at me, look at this place!'

This was a crossroads where two dead highways came and went in darkness. Here Sam Parkhill had flung up this riveted aluminium structure, garish with white light, trembling with juke-box melody.

He stooped to fix a border of broken glass he had placed on the footpath. He had broken the glass from some old Martian buildings in the hills. 'Best hot dogs on two worlds!

First man on Mars with a hot-dog stand! The best onions and chili and mustard! You can't say I'm not alert. Here's the main highways, over there is the dead city and the mineral deposits. Those trucks from Earth Settlement 101 will have to pass here twenty-four hours a day! Do I know my locations, or don't I?'

His wife looked at her fingernails.

'You think those ten thousand new-type work rockets will come through to Mars?' she said at last.

'In a month,' he said loudly. 'Why you look so funny?'

'I don't trust those Earth people,' she said. 'I'll believe it when I see them ten thousand rockets arrive with the one hundred thousand Mexicans and Chinese on them.'

'Customers.' He lingered on the word. 'One hundred thousand hungry people.'

'If,' said his wife slowly, watching the sky, 'there's no atomic war. I don't trust no atom bombs. There's so many of them on Earth now, you never can tell.'

'Ah,' said Sam and went on sweeping.

From the corners of his eyes he caught a blue flicker. Something floated in the air gently behind him. He heard his wife say, 'Sam. A friend of yours to see you.'

Sam whirled to see the mask seemingly floating in the wind.

'So you're back again!' And Sam held his broom like a weapon.

The mask nodded. It was cut from pale blue glass and was fitted above a thin neck, under which were blowing loose robes of thin yellow silk. From the silk two mesh silver hands appeared. The mask mouth was a slot from which musical sounds issued now as the robes, the mask, the hands increased to a height, decreased.

'Mr Parkhill, I've come back to speak to you again,' the voice said from behind the mask.

'I thought I told you I don't want you near here!' cried Sam. 'Go on, I'll give you the Disease!'

'I've already had the Disease,' said the voice. 'I was one of the few survivors. I was sick a long time.'

'Go on and hide in the hills; that's where you belong, that's where you've been. Why you come on down and bother me? Now, all of a sudden. Twice in one day.'

'We mean you no harm.'

'But I mean you harm!' said Sam backing up. 'I don't like strangers. I don't like Martians. I never seen one before. It ain't natural. All these years you guys hide, and all of a sudden you pick on me. Leave me alone.'

'We come for an important reason,' said the blue mask.

'If it's about this land, it's mine. I built this hot-dog stand with my own hands.'

'In a way it *is* about the land.'

'Look here,' said Sam. 'I'm from New York City. Where I come from there's ten million others just like me. You Martians are a couple dozen left, got not cities, you wander around in the hills, no leaders, no laws, and now you come tell me about this land. Well, the old got to give way to the new. That's the law of give and take. I got a gun here. After you left this morning I got it out and loaded it.'

'We Martians are telepathic,' said the cold, blue mask. 'We are in contact with one of your towns across the dead sea. Have you listened on your radio?'

'My radio's busted.'

'Then you don't know. There's big news. It concerns Earth—'

A silver hand gestured. A bronze tube appeared in it.

'Let me show you this.'

'A gun,' cried Sam Parkhill.

An instant later he had yanked his own gun from his hip holster and fired into the mist, the robe, the blue mask.

The mask sustained itself a moment, Then, like a small circus tent pulling up its stakes and dropping soft fold on fold, the silks rustled, the mask descended, the silver claws tinkled on the stone path. The mask lay on a small huddle of silent white bones and material.

Sam stood gasping.

His wife swayed over the huddled pile.

'That's no weapon,' she said bending down. She picked up the bronze tube. 'He was going to show you a message. It's all written out in snake-script, all the blue snakes. I can't read it. Can you?'

'No, that Martian picture-writing, it wasn't anything. Let it go!' Sam glanced hastily around. 'There may be others! We've got to get him out of sight. Get the shovel!'

'What're you going to do?'

'Bury him, of course!'

'You shouldn't have shot him.'

'It was a mistake. Quick!'

Silently she fetched him the shovel.

At eight o'clock he was back sweeping the front of the hot-dog stand self-consciously. His wife stood, arms folded, in the bright doorway.

'I'm sorry what happened,' he said. He looked at her, then away. 'You know it was purely the circumstances of Fate.'

'Yes,' said his wife.

'I hated like hell to see him take out that weapon.'

'What weapon?'

'Well, I thought it was one! I'm sorry, I'm sorry ! How many times do I say it!'

'Ssh,' said Elma, putting one finger to her lips. 'Ssh.'

'I don't care,' he said. 'I got the whole Earth Settlements, Inc, back of me!' he snorted. 'These Martians won't dare—'

'Look,' said Elma.

He looked out on to the dead sea-bottom. He dropped his broom. He picked it up and his mouth was open, a little free drop of saliva flew on the air, and he was suddenly shivering.

'Elma, Elma, Elma!' he said.

'Here they come,' said Elma.

Across the ancient sea floor a dozen tall, blue-sailed Martian sand-ships floated, like blue ghosts, like blue smoke.

'Sand-ships! But there aren't any more, Elma, no more sand-ships.'

'Those seem to be sand-ships,' she said.

'But the authorities confiscated all of them! They broke them up, sold some at auction! I'm the only one in this whole damn territory's got one and knows how to run one.'

'Not any more,' she said, nodding at the sea.

'Come on, let's get out of here!'

'Why?' she asked slowly, fascinated with the Martian vessels.

'They'll kill me! Get in our truck, quick!'

Elma didn't move.

He had to drag her around back of the stand where the two machines stood: his truck, which he had used steadily until a month ago, and the old Martian sand-ship which he had bid for at auction, smiling, and which, during the last three weeks, he had used to carry supplies back and forth over the glassy sea floor. He looked at his truck now and remembered. The engine was out on the ground; he had been puttering with it for two days.

'The truck don't seem to be in running condition,' said Elma.

'The sand-ship. Get in!'

'And let you drive me in a sand-ship? Oh no.'

'Get in! I can do it!'

He shoved her in, jumped in behind her, and flapped the tiller, let the cobalt sail up to take the evening wind.

The stars were bright and the blue Martian ships were skimming across the whispering sands. At first his own ship would not move, then he remembered the sand anchor and yanked it in.

'There!'

The wind hurled the sand-ship keening over the dead sea-bottom, over long-buried crystals, past up-ended pillars, past deserted docks of marble and brass, past dead white chess cities, past purple foothills, into distance. The figures of the Martian ships receded and then began to pace Sam's ship.

'Guess I showed them, by God!' cried Sam. 'I'll report to the Rocket Corporation. They'll give me protection! I'm pretty quick.'

'They could have stopped you if they wanted,' Elma said tiredly. 'They just didn't bother.'

He laughed. 'Come off it. Why should they let me get off? No, they weren't quick enough, is all.'

'Weren't they?' Elma nodded behind them.

He did not turn. He felt a cold wind blowing. He was afraid to turn. He felt something in the seat behind him, something as frail as your breath on a cold morning, something as blue as hickory-wood smoke at twilight, something like old white lace, something like a snowfall, something like the icy rime of winter on the brittle sedge.

There was a sound as of a thin plate of glass broken — laughter. Then silence. He turned.

The young woman sat at the tiller bench quietly. Her wrists were thin as icicles, her eyes as clear as the moon and as large, steady and white. The wind blew at her and, like an image on cold water, she rippled, silk standing out from her frail body in tatters of blue rain.

'Go back,' she said.

'No.' Sam was quivering, the fine, delicate fear-quivering of a hornet suspended in the air, undecided between fear and hate. 'Get off my ship!'

'This isn't your ship,' said the vision. 'It's old as our world. It sailed the sand seas ten thousand years ago when the seas were whispered away and the docks were empty, and you came and took it, stole it. Now turn it around, go back to the crossroad place. We have need to talk with you. Something important has happened.'

'Get off my ship!' said Sam. He took a gun from his

holster with a creak of leather. He pointed it carefully.
'Jump off before I count three or—'

'Don't!' cried the girl. 'I won't hurt you. Neither will the
others. We come in peace!'

'One,' said Sam.

'Sam!' said Elma.

'Listen to me,' said the girl.

'Two,' said Sam firmly, cocking the gun-trigger.

'Sam!' cried Elma.

'Three,' said Sam.

'We only—' said the girl.

The gun went off.

In the sunlight, snow melts, crystals evaporate into a
steam, into nothing. In the firelight, vapours dance and
vanish. In the core of a volcano, fragile things burst and
disappear. The girl, in the gunfire, in the heat, in the
concussion, folded like a soft scarf, melted like a crystal
figurine. What was left of her, ice, snowflake, smoke, blew
away in the wind. The tiller seat was empty.

Sam holstered his gun and did not look at his wife.

'Sam,' she said after a minute more of travelling,
whispering over the moon-coloured sea of sand, 'stop the
ship.'

He looked at her, and his face was pale. 'No you don't.
Not after all this time, you're not pulling out on me.'

She looked at his hand on his gun. 'I believe you would,'
she said. 'You actually would.'

He jerked his head from side to side, hand tight on the
tiller bar. 'Elma, this is crazy. We'll be in town in a minute,
we'll be okay!'

'Yes,' said his wife, lying back cold in the ship.

'Elma, listen to me.'

'There's nothing to hear, Sam.'

'Elma!'

They were passing a little white chess city, and in his
frustration, in his rage, he sent six bullets crashing among

the crystal towers. The city dissolved in a shower of ancient glass and splintered quartz. It fell away like carved soap, shattered. It was no more. He laughed and fired again, and one last tower, one last chess-piece, took fire, ignited, and in blue flinders went up to the stars.

'I'll show them! I'll show everybody!'

'Go ahead, show us, Sam.' She lay in the shadows.

'Here comes another city!' Sam reloaded the gun. 'Watch me fix it!'

The blue phantom ships loomed up behind them, drawing steadily apace. He did not see them at first. He was only aware of a whistling and a high windy screaming, as of steel on sand, and it was the sound of the sharp razor prows of the sand-ships preening the sea-bottoms, their red pennants, blue pennants unfurled. In the blue light ships were blue dark images, masked men, men with silvery faces, men with blue stars for eyes, men with carved golden ears, men with tinfoil cheeks and ruby-studded lips, men with arms folded, men following him, Martian men.

One, two, three. Sam counted. The Martian ships closed in.

'Elma, Elma, I can't hold them all off!'

Elma did not speak or rise from where she had slumped.

Sam fired his gun eight times. One of the sand-ships fell apart, the sail, the emerald body, the bronze hull points, the moon-white tiller, and all the separate images in it. The masked men, all of them, dug into the sand and separated out into orange and then smoke-flame.

But the other ships closed in.

'I'm outnumbered, Elma!' he cried. 'They'll kill me!'

He threw out the anchor. It was no use. The sail fluttered down, folding unto itself, sighing. The ship stopped. The wind stopped. Travel stopped. Mars stood still as the majestic vessels of the Martians drew around and hesitated over him.

'Earth Man,' a voice called from a high seat somewhere.

A silverine mask moved. Ruby-rimmed lips glittered with the words.

'I didn't do anything!' Sam looked at all the faces, one hundred in all, that surrounded him. There weren't many Martians left on Mars – one hundred, one hundred and fifty, all told. And most of them were here now, on the dead seas, in their resurrected ships, by their dead chess cities, one of which had just fallen like some fragile vase hit by a pebble. The silverine masks glinted.

'It was all a mistake,' he pleaded, standing out of his ship, his wife slumped behind him in the deeps of the hold, like a dead woman. 'I came to Mars like any honest enterprising business-man. I took some surplus material from a rocket that crashed, and I built the finest little stand you ever saw right there on that land by the crossroads – you know where it is. You've got to admit it's a good job of building.' Sam laughed, staring around. 'And that Martian – I know he was a friend of yours – came. His death was an accident, I assure you. All I wanted to do was have a hot-dog stand, the only one on Mars, the first and most important one. You understand how it is? I was going to serve the best darned hot dogs there, with chili and onions and orange-juice.'

The silver masks did not move. They burned in the moonlight. Yellow eyes shone upon Sam. He felt his stomach clench in, wither, become a rock. He threw his gun in the sand.

'I give up.'

'Pick up your gun,' said the Martians in chorus.

'What?'

'Your gun.' A jewelled hand waved from the prow of a blue ship. 'Pick it up. Put it away.'

Unbelieving, he picked up the gun.

'Now,' said the voice, 'turn your ship and go back to your stand.'

'Now?'

'Now,' said the voice. 'We will not harm you. You ran away before we were able to explain. Come.'

Now the great ships turned as lightly as moon thistles. Their wing-sails flapped with a sound of soft applause on the air. The masks were coruscating, turning, firing the shadows.

'Elma!' Sam tumbled into the ship. 'Get up, Elma. We're going back.' He was excited. he almost gibbered with relief. 'They aren't going to hurt me, kill me, Elma. Get up, honey, get up.'

'What — what?' Elma blinked around slowly as the ship was sent into the wind again, she helped herself, as in a dream, back up to a seat and slumped there like a sack of stones, saying no more.

The sand slid under the ship. In half an hour they were back at the crossroads, the ships planted, all of them out of the ships.

The Leader stood before Sam and Elma, his mask beaten of polished bronze, the eyes only empty slits of endless blue-black, the mouth a slot out of which words drifted into the wind.

'Ready your stand,' said the voice. A diamond-gloved hand waved. 'Prepare the viands, prepare the foods, prepare the strange wines, for tonight is indeed a great night!'

'You mean,' said Sam, 'you'll let me stay on here?'

'Yes.'

'You're not mad at me?'

The mask was rigid and carved and cold and sightless.

'Prepare your place of food,' said the voice softly. 'And take this.'

'What is it?'

Sam blinked at the silver-foil scroll that was handed him, upon which, in hieroglyph, snake-figures danced.

'It is the land grant to all the territory from the silver mountains to the blue hills, from the dead salt sea there to the distant valleys of moonstone and emerald,' said the Leader.

'M-mine?' said Sam, incredulous.

'Yours.'

'One hundred thousand miles of territory?'

'Yours.'

'Did you hear that, Elma?'

Elma was sitting on the ground, leaning against the aluminium hot-dog stand, eyes shut.

'But why, why – why are you giving me all this?' asked Sam, trying to look into the metal slots of the eyes.

'That is not all. Here.' Six other scrolls were produced. The names were declared, the territories announced.

'Why, that's half of Mars! I own half of Mars!' Sam rattled the scrolls in his fists. He shook them at Elma, insane with laughing. 'Elma, did you hear?'

'I heard,' said Elma, looking up at the sky.

She seemed to be watching for something. She was becoming a little more alert now.

'Thank you, oh, thank you,' said Sam to the bronze mask.

'Tonight is the night,' said the mask. 'You must be ready.'

'I will be. What is it – a surprise? Are the rockets coming through earlier than we thought, a month earlier from Earth? All ten thousand rockets, bringing the settlers, the miners, the workers and their wives, all hundred thousand of them? Won't that be swell, Elma? You see, I told you. I told you, that town there won't always have just one thousand people in it. There'll be fifty thousand more coming, and the month after that a hundred thousand more, and by the end of the year five million Earth Men. And me with the only hot-dog stand staked out on the busiest highway to the mines!'

The mask floated on the wind. 'We leave. Prepare. The land is yours.'

In the blowing moonlight, like metal petals of some ancient flower, like blue plumes, like cobalt butterflies immense and quiet, the old ships turned and moved over the shifting sands, the masks beaming and glittering, until the last shine, the last blue colour, was lost among the hills.

'Elma, why did they do it? Why didn't they kill me? Don't they know anything? What's wrong with them? Elma, do you understand?' He shook her shoulder. 'I own half of Mars!'

She watched the night sky, waiting.

'Come on,' he said. 'We've got to get the place fixed. All the hot dogs boiling, the buns warm, the chili cooking, the onions peeled and diced, the relish laid out, the napkins in the clips, the place spotless! Hey!' He did a little wild dance, kicking his heels. 'Oh boy, I'm happy; yes, sir, I'm happy,' he sang, off key. 'This is my lucky day!'

He boiled the hot dogs, cut the buns, sliced the onions in a frenzy.

'Just think, that Martian said a surprise. That can only mean one thing, Elma. Those hundred thousand people coming in ahead of schedule, tonight, of all nights! We'll be flooded! We'll be working long hours for days, what with tourists riding around seeing things, Elma. Think of the money!'

He went out and looked at the sky. He didn't see anything.

'In a minute, maybe,' he said snuffing the cool air gratefully, arms up, beating his chest. 'Ah!'

Elma said nothing. She peeled potatoes for French fries quietly, her eyes always on the sky.

'Sam,' she said half an hour later. 'There it is. Look.'

He looked and saw it.

Earth.

It rose full and green, like a fine-cut stone above the hills.

'Good old Earth,' he whispered lovingly. 'Good old wonderful Earth. Send me your hungry and your starved. Something, something — how does the poem go? Send me your hungry, old Earth. Here's Sam Parkhill, his hot dogs all boiled, his chili cooking, everything neat as a pin. Come on, you Earth, send me your rockets!'

He went out to look at his place. There it sat, perfect as a fresh-laid egg on the dead sea-bottom, the only nucleus of light and warmth in hundreds of miles of lonely wasteland. It was like a heart beating alone in a great dark body. He felt almost sorrowful with pride, gazing at it with wet eyes.

'It sure makes you humble,' he said among the cooking odours of wieners, warm buns, rich butter. 'Step up,' he invited the various stars in the sky. 'Who'll be the first to buy?'

'Sam,' said Elma.

Earth changed in the black sky.

It caught fire.

Part of it seemed to come apart in a million pieces, as if a gigantic jigsaw had exploded. It burned with an unholy dripping glare for a minute, three times normal size, then dwindled.

'What was that?' Sam looked at the green fire in the sky.

'Earth,' said Elma, holding her hands together.

'That can't be Earth, that's not Earth! No, that ain't Earth! It can't be.'

'You mean it couldn't be Earth,' said Elma, looking at him. 'That just isn't Earth. No, that's not Earth; is that what you mean?'

'Not Earth – oh no, it *couldn't* be,' he wailed.

He stood there, his hands at his sides, his mouth open, his eyes wide and dull, not moving.

'Sam.' She called his name. For the first time in days her eyes were bright. 'Sam?'

He looked up at the sky.

'Well,' she said. She glanced around for a minute or so in silence. Then briskly she flapped a wet towel over her arm. 'Switch on more lights, turn up the music, open the doors.

There'll be another batch of customers along in about a million years. Gotta be ready, yes, sir.'

Sam did not move.

'What a swell spot for a hot-dog stand,' she said. She reached over and picked a toothpick out of a jar and put it between her front teeth. 'Let you in on a little secret, Sam,' she whispered, leaning towards him. 'This looks like it's going to be an off season.'

## The Watchers

They all came out and looked at the sky that night. They left their suppers or their washing-up or their dressing for the show, and they came out upon their now-not-quite-as-new porches and watched the green star of Earth there. It was a move without conscious effort; they all did it, to help them understand the news they had heard on the radio a moment before. There was Earth and there the coming war, and there hundreds of thousands of mother or grandmothers or fathers or brothers or aunts or uncles or cousins. They stood on the porches and tried to believe in the existence of Earth, much as they had once tried to believe in the existence of Mars; it was a problem reversed. To all intents and purposes, Earth now was dead; they had been away from it for three or four years. Space was anaesthetic; seventy million miles of space numbed you, put memory to sleep, depopulated Earth, erased the past, and allowed these people here to go on with their work. But now, tonight, the dead were risen, Earth was reinhabited, memory awoke, a million names were spoken: What was so-and-so doing tonight on Earth? What about this one and that one? The people on the porches glanced sidewise at each other's faces.

At nine o'clock Earth seemed to explode, catch fire, and burn.

The people on the porches put up their hands as if to beat the fire out.

They waited.

By midnight the fire was extinguished. Earth was still there. There was a sigh, like an autumn wind, from the porches.

'We haven't heard from Harry for a long time.'

'He's all right.'

'We should send a message to Mother.'

'She's all right.'

'*Is* she?'

'Now, don't worry.'

'Will she be all right, do you think?'

'Of course, of course; now come back to bed.'

But nobody moved. Late dinners were carried out on to the night lawns and set upon collapsible tables, and they picked at these slowly until two o'clock and the light-radio message flashed from Earth. The could read the great Morse-code flashes which flickered like a distant firefly:

AUSTRALIAN CONTINENT ATOMIZED IN PREMATURE EXPLOSION OF ATOMIC STOCKPILE. LOS ANGELES, LONDON BOMBED. WAR. COME HOME. COME HOME. COME HOME.

They stood up from their tables.

COME HOME. COME HOME. COME HOME.

'Have you heard from your brother Ted this year?'

'You know. With mail rates five bucks a letter to Earth, I don't write much.'

COME HOME.

'I've been wondering about Jane; you remember Jane, my kid sister?'

COME HOME.

At three in the chilly morning the luggage-store proprietor glanced up. A lot of people were coming down the street.

'Stayed open late on purpose. What'll it be, mister?'

By dawn the luggage was gone from his shelves.

# The Silent Towns

There was a little white silent town on the edge of the dead Martian sea. The town was empty. No one moved in it. Lonely lights burned in the stores all day. The shop doors were wide, as if people had run off without using their keys. Magazines, brought from Earth on the silver rocket a month before, fluttered, untouched, burning brown, on wire racks fronting the silent drug-stores.

The town was dead. Its beds were empty and cold. The only sound was the power hum of electric lines and dynamos, still alive, all by themselves. Water ran in forgotten bathtubs, poured out into living-rooms, on to porches, and down through little garden plots to feed neglected flowers. In the dark theatres gum under the many seats began to harden with tooth impressions still in it.

Across town was a rocket port. You could still smell the hard scorched smell where the last rocket blasted off when it went back to Earth. If you dropped a dime in the telescope and pointed it at Earth, perhaps you could see the big war happening there. Perhaps you could see New York explode. Maybe London could be seen, covered with a new kind of fog. Perhaps then it might be understood why this small Martian town is abandoned. How quick was the evacuation? Walk in any store, bang the NO SALE key. Cash drawers jump out, all bright and jingly with coins. The war on Earth must be very bad . . .

Along the empty avenues of this town, now, whistling softly, kicking a tin can ahead of him in deepest concentration came a tall, thin man. His eyes glowed with a dark, quiet look of loneliness. He moved his bony hands in his pockets, which were tinkling with new dimes.

Occasionally he tossed a dime to the ground. He laughed temperately, doing this, and walked on, sprinkling bright dimes everywhere.

His name was Walter Gripp. He had a placer mine and a remote shack far up in the blue Martian hills and he walked to town once every two weeks to see if he could marry a quiet and intelligent woman. Over the years he had always returned to his shack, alone and disappointed. A week ago, arriving in town, he had found it this way!

That day he had been so surprised that he rushed to a delicatessen, flung wide a case, and ordered a triple-decker beef sandwich.

'Coming up!' he cried, a towel on his arm.

He flourished meats and bread baked the day before, dusted a table, invited himself to sit, and ate until he had to go find a soda-fountain, where he ordered a bicarbonate. The druggist, being one Walter Gripp, was astoundingly polite and fizzed one right up for him!

He stuffed his jeans with money, all he could find. He loaded a boy's wagon with ten-dollar bills and ran lickety-split through town. Reaching the suburbs, he suddenly realized how shamefully silly he was. He didn't need money. He rode the ten-dollar bills back to where he'd found them, counted a dollar from his own wallet to pay for the sandwiches, dropped it in the delicatessen till, and added a quarter tip.

That night he enjoyed a hot Turkish bath, a succulent fillet carpeted with delicate mushrooms, imported dry sherry, and strawberries in wine. He fitted himself for a new blue flannel suit, and a rich grey Homburg which balanced oddly atop his gaunt head. He slid money into a juke-box which played 'That Old Gang of Mine.' He dropped nickels in twenty boxes all over town. The lonely streets and the night were full of the sad music of 'That Old Gang of Mine' as he walked, tall and thin and alone, his new shoes clumping softly, his cold hands in his pockets.

But that was a week past. He slept in a good house on Mars Avenue, rose mornings at nine, bathed, and idled to town for ham and eggs. No morning passed that he didn't freeze a ton of meats, vegetables, and lemon-cream pies, enough to last ten years, until the rockets came back from Earth, if they ever came.

Now, tonight, he drifted up and down, seeing the wax women in every colourful shop window, pink and beautiful. For the first time he knew how dead the town was. He drew a glass of beer and sobbed gently.

'Why,' he said, 'I'm all *alone*.'

He entered the Elite Theatre to show himself a film, to distract his mind from his isolation. The theatre was hollow, empty, like a tomb with phantoms crawling grey and black on the vast screen. Shivering, he hurried from the haunted place.

Having decided to return home, he was striking down the middle of a side street, almost running, when he heard the phone.

He listened.

'Phone ringing in someone's house.'

He proceeded briskly.

'Someone should answer that phone,' he mused.

He sat on the kerb to pick a rock from his shoe, idly.

'Someone!' he screamed, leaping. 'Me! Good Lord, what's wrong with me!' he shrieked. He whirled. Which house? That one!

He raced over the lawn, up the steps, into the house, down a dark hall.

He yanked up the receiver.

'Hello!' he cried.

*Buzzzzzzzz.*

'Hello, hello!'

They had hung up.

'Hello!' he shouted, and banged the phone. 'You stupid

idiot!' he cried to himself. 'Sitting on that kerb, you fool! Oh, you damned and awful fool!' He squeezed the phone. 'Come on, ring again. Come *on*!'

He had never thought there might be others left on Mars. In the entire week he had seen no one. He had figured that all other towns were as empty as this one.

Now, staring at this terrible little black phone, he trembled. Interlocking dial systems connected every town on Mars. From which of thirty cities had the call come?

He didn't know.

He waited. He wandered to the strange kitchen, thawed some iced huckleberries, ate them disconsolately.

'There wasn't anyone on the other end of that call,' he murmured. 'Maybe a pole blew down somewhere and the phone rang by itself.'

But hadn't he heard a click, which meant someone had hung up far away?

He stood in the hall the rest of the night. 'Not because of the phone,' he told himself. 'I just haven't anything else to do.'

He listened to his watch tick.

'She won't phone back,' he said. 'She won't *ever* call a number that didn't answer. She's probably dialling other houses in town *now*! And here I sit— Wait a minute!' He laughed. 'Why do I keep saying "she"?'

He blinked. 'It could as easily be a "he", couldn't it?'

His heart slowed. He felt very cold and hollow.

He wanted very much for it to be a 'she'.

He walked out of the house and stood in the centre of the early, dim morning street.

He listened. Not a sound. No birds. No cars. Only his heart beating. Beat and pause and beat again. His face ached with strain. The wind blew gently, oh so gently, flapping his coat.

'Sh,' he whispered. '*Listen*.'

He swayed in a slow circle, turning his head from one silent house to another.

She'll phone more and more numbers, he thought. It must be a woman. Why? Only a woman would call and call. A man wouldn't. A man's independent. Did I phone anyone? No! Never thought of it. It must be a woman. It *has* to be, by God!

Listen.

Far away, under the stars, a phone rang.

He ran. He stopped to listen. The ringing, soft. He ran a few more steps. Louder. he raced down an alley. Louder still! He passed six houses, six more. Much louder! He chose a house and its door was locked.

The phone rang inside.

'Damn you!' He jerked the door-knob.

The phone screamed.

He heaved a porch chair through the parlour window, leaped in after it.

Before he even touched the phone, it was silent.

He stalked through the house then and broke mirrors, tore down drapes, and kicked in the kitchen stove.

Finally, exhausted, he picked up the thin directory which listed every phone on Mars. Fifty thousand names.

He started with number one.

Amelia Ames. He dialled her number in New Chicago, one hundred miles over the dead sea.

No answer.

Number two lived in New New York, five thousand miles across the blue mountains.

No answer.

He called three, four, five, six, seven, eight, his fingers jerking, unable to grip the receiver.

A woman's voice answered, 'Hello?'

Walter cried back at her, 'Hello, oh Lord, hello!'

'This is a recording,' recited the woman's voice. 'Miss Helen Arasumian is not home. Will you leave a message on

the wire spool so she may call you when she returns? Hello?
This is a recording. Miss Arasumian is not home. Will you
leave a message—'

He hung up.

He sat with his mouth twitching.

On second thought he redialled that number.

'When Miss Helen Arasumian comes home,' he said, 'Tell
her to go to hell!'

He phoned Mars Junction, New Boston, Arcadia, and
Roosevelt City exchanges, theorizing that they would be
logical places for persons to dial from; after that he
contacted local city halls and other public institutions in each
town. He phoned the best hotels. Leave it to a woman to
put herself up in luxury.

Suddenly he stopped, clapped his hands sharply together,
and laughed. Of course! He checked the directory and
dialled a long-distance call through to the biggest beauty
parlour in New Texas City. If ever there was a place where
a woman would putter around, patting mud-packs on her
face and sitting under a drier, it would be a velvet-soft,
diamond-gem beauty parlour!

The phone rang. Someone at the other end lifted the
receiver.

A woman's voice, 'Hello?'

'If this is a recording,' announced Walter Gripp, 'I'll
come over and blow the place up.'

'This isn't a record,' said the woman's voice. 'Hello! Oh,
hello, there *is* someone alive! Where *are* you?' She gave a
delighted scream.

Walter almost collapsed. '*You!*' He stood up jerkily, eyes
wild. 'Good Lord, what luck, what's your name?'

'Genevieve Selsor!' She wept into the receiver. 'Oh, I'm
so glad to hear from you, whoever you are!'

'Walter Gripp!'

'Walter, hello, Walter!'

'Hello, Genevieve!'

'Walter. It's such a nice name. Walter, Walter!'

'Thank you.'

'Walter, where *are* you?'

Her voice was so kind and sweet and fine. He held the phone tight to his ear so she could whisper sweetly into it. He felt his feet drift off the floor. His cheeks burned.

'I'm in Marlin Village,' he said 'I —'

*Buzz.*

'Hello?' he said.

*Buzz.*

He jiggled the hook. Nothing.

Somewhere a wind had blown down a pole. As quickly as she had come, Genevieve Selsor was gone.

He dialled, but the line was dead.

'I know where she is, anyway.' He ran out of the house. The sun was rising as he backed a beetle-car from the stranger's garage, filled its back seat with food from the house, and set out at eighty miles an hour down the highway, heading for New Texas City.

A thousand miles, he thought. Genevieve Selsor, sit tight, you'll hear from me!

He honked his horn on every turn out of town.

At sunset, after an impossible day of driving, he pulled to the roadside, kicked off his tight shoes, laid himself out in the seat, and slid the grey Homburg over his weary eyes. His breathing became slow and regular. The wind blew and the stars shone gently upon him in the new dusk. The Martian mountains lay all around, millions of years old. Starlight glittered on the spires of a little Martian town, no bigger than a game of chess, in the blue hills.

He lay in the half-place between awakeness and dreams. He whispered. Genevieve. *Oh, Genevieve, sweet Genevieve*, he sang softly, *the years may come, the years may go. But,*

*Genevieve, sweet Genevieve* . . . There was a warmth in him. He heard her quiet, sweet, cool voice sighing. *Hello, oh, hello, Walter! This is no record. Where are you, Walter, where are you?*

He sighed, putting up a hand to touch her in the moonlight. Long dark hair shaking in the wind; beautiful it was. And her lips like red peppermints. And her cheeks like fresh-cut wet roses. And her body like a clear vaporous mist, while her soft, cool, sweet voice crooned to him once more the words to the old sad song, *Oh, Genevieve, sweet Genevieve, the years may come, the years may go* . . .

He slept.

He reached New Texas City at midnight.

He halted before the Deluxe Beauty Salon, yelling.

He expected her to rush out, all perfume, all laughter.

Nothing happened.

'She's asleep.' He walked to the door. 'Here I am,' he called. 'Hello, Genevieve!'

The town lay in double moonlit silence. Somewhere a wind flapped a canvas awning.

He swung the glass door wide and stepped in.

'Hey!' He laughed uneasily. 'Don't hide! I know you're here!'

He searched every booth.

He found a tiny handkerchief on the floor. It smelled so good he almost lost his balance. 'Genevieve,' he said.

He drove the car through the empty streets but saw nothing. 'If this is a practical joke . . .'

He slowed the car. 'Wait a minute. We were cut off. Maybe *she* drove to Marlin Village while I was driving here! She probably took the old Sea Road. We missed each other during the day. How'd she know I'd come get her? I didn't *say* I would. And she was so afraid when the phone died that she rushed to Marlin Village to find me! And here I am, by God, what a fool *I* am!'

Giving the horn a blow, he shot out of town.

He drove all night. He thought, What if she isn't in Marlin Village waiting when I arrive?

He wouldn't think of that. She *must* be there. And he would run up and hold her and perhaps even kiss her, once, on the lips.

*Genevieve, sweet Genevieve*, he whistled, stepping it up to one hundred miles an hour.

Marlin Village was quiet at dawn. yellow lights were still burning in several stores, and a juke-box that had played steadily for one hundred hours finally, with a crackle of electricity, ceased, making the silence complete. The sun warmed the streets and warmed the cold and vacant sky.

Walter turned down Main Street, the car lights still on, honking the horn a double toot, six times at one corner, six times at another. He peered at the store names. His face was white and tired, and his hands slid on the sweaty steering wheel.

'Genevieve!' he called in the empty street.

The door to a beauty salon opened.

'Genevieve!' He stopped the car.

Genevieve Selsor stood in the open door of the salon as he ran across the street. A box of cream chocolates lay open in her arms. Her fingers, cuddling it, were plump and pallid. Her face, as she stepped into the light, was round and thick, and her eyes were like two immense eggs stuck into a white mess of bread dough. Her legs were as big around as the stumps of trees, and she moved with an ungainly shuffle. Her hair was an indiscriminate shade of brown that had been made and re-made, it appeared, as a nest for birds. She had no lips at all and compensated this by stencilling on a large red, greasy mouth that now popped open in delight, now shut in sudden alarm. She had plucked her brows to thin antenna lines.

Walter stopped. His smile dissolved. He stood looking at her.

She dropped her candy box to the sidewalk.

'Are you — Genevieve Selsor?' His ears rang.

'Are you Walter Griff?' she asked.

'Gripp.'

'Gripp,' she corrected herself.

'How do you do,' he said with a restrained voice.

'How do you do.' She shook his hand.

Her fingers were sticky with chocolate.

'Well,' said Walter Gripp.

'What?' asked Genevieve Selsor.

'I just said, "Well," ' said Walter.

'Oh.'

It was nine o'clock at night. They had spent the day picnicking, and for supper he had prepared a filet mignon which she didn't like because it was too rare, so he broiled it some more and it was too much broiled or fried or something. He laughed and said, 'We'll see a movie!' She said okay and put her chocolaty fingers on his elbow. But all she wanted to see was a fifty-year-old film of Clark Gable. 'Doesn't he just kill you?' She giggled. 'Doesn't he *kill* you, now?' The film ended. 'Run it off again, ' she commanded. 'Again?' he asked. 'Again,' she said. And when he returned she snuggled up and put her paws all over him. 'You're not quite what I expected, but you're nice,' she admitted. 'Thanks,' he said, swallowing. 'Oh, that Gable,' she said, and pinched his leg. 'Ouch,' he said.

After the film they went shopping down the silent streets. She broke a window and put on the brightest dress she could find. Dumping a perfume bottle on her hair, she resembled a drowned sheep-dog. 'How old are you?' he inquired. 'Guess.' Dripping, she led him down the street. 'Oh, thirty,' he said. 'Well,' she announced stiffly, 'I'm only twenty-seven, so there!'

'Here's another candy store!' she said. 'Honest, I've led the life of Reilly since everything exploded. I never liked my folks, they were fools. They left for Earth two months ago. I was supposed to follow on the last rocket, but I stayed on; you know why?'

'Why?'

'Because everyone picked on me. So I stayed where I could throw perfume on myself all day and drink ten thousand malts and eat candy without people saying. "Oh, that's full of calories!" So here I *am*!'

'Here you are.' Walter shut his eyes.

'It's getting late,' she said, looking at him.

'Yes.'

'I'm tired,' she said.

'Funny. I'm wide awake.'

'Oh,' she said.

'I feel like staying up all night,' he said. 'Say, there's a good record at Mike's. Come on, I'll play it for you.'

'I'm tired.' She glanced up at him with sly, bright eyes.

'I'm very alert,' he said. 'Strange.'

'Come back to the beauty shop,' she said. 'I want to show you something.'

She took him in through the glass door and walked him over to a large white box. 'When I drove from Texas City,' she said, 'I brought this with me.' She untied the pink ribbon. 'I thought: Well, here I am the only lady on Mars, and here is the only man, and, well . . .' She lifted the lid and folded back crisp layers of whispery pink tissue-paper. She gave it a pat. 'There.'

Walter Gripp stared.

'What is it?' he asked, beginning to tremble.

'Don't you know, silly? It's all lace and all white and all fine and everything.'

'No, I don't know what it is.'

'It's a wedding dress, silly!'

'Is it?' His voice cracked.

He shut his eyes. Her voice was still soft and cool and sweet, as it had been on the phone. But when he opened his eyes and looked at her . . .

He backed up. 'How nice,' he said.

'Isn't it?'

'Genevieve.' He glanced at the door.

'Yes?'

'Genevieve, I've something to tell you.'

'Yes?' She drifted towards him, the perfume smell thick about her round white face.

'The thing I have to say to you is . . .' he said.

'Yes?'

'Good-bye!'

And he was out of the door and into his car before she could scream.

She ran and stood on the kerb as he swung the car about.

'Walter Griff, come back here!' she wailed, flinging up her arms.

'Gripp,' he corrected her.

'Gripp!' she shouted.

The car whirled away down the silent street, regardless of her stampings and shriekings. The exhaust from it fluttered the white dress she crumpled in her plump hands, and the stars shone bright, and the car vanished out on to the desert and away into blackness.

He drove all night and all day for three nights and days. Once he thought he saw a car following, and he broke into a shivering sweat and took another highway, cutting off across the lonely Martian world, past little dead cities, and he drove for a week and a day, until he had put ten thousand miles between himself and Marlin Village. Then he pulled into a small town named Holtville Springs, where there were some tiny stores he could light up at night and restaurants to sit in, ordering meals. And he's lived there ever since, with two deep freezes packed with food to last him one hundred years, and enough cigars to last ten thousand days, and a good bed with a soft mattress.

And when once in a while over the long years the phone rings — he doesn't answer.

# The Long Years

Whenever the wind came through the sky, he and his small family would sit in the stone hut and warm their hands over a wood fire. The wind would stir the canal waters and almost blow the stars out of the sky, but Mr Hathaway would sit contented and talk to his wife, and his wife would reply, and he would speak to his two daughters and his son about the old days on Earth, and they would all answer neatly.

It was the twentieth year after the Great War. Mars was a tomb planet. Whether or not Earth was the same was a matter for much silent debate for Hathaway and his family on the long Martian nights.

This night one of the violent Martian dust-storms had come over the low Martian graveyards, blowing through ancient towns and tearing away the plastic walls of the newer, American-built city that was melting down into the sand, desolated.

The storm abated. Hathaway went out into the cleared weather to see Earth burning green on the windy sky. He put his hand up as one might reach to adjust a dimly burning globe in the ceiling of a dark room. He looked across the long-dead sea-bottoms. Not another living thing on this entire planet, he thought. Just myself. And *them*. He looked back within the stone hut.

What was happening on Earth now? He had seen no visible sign of change in Earth's aspect through his thirty-inch telescope. Well, he thought, I'm good for another twenty years if I'm careful. Someone might come. Either across the dead seas or out of space in a rocket on a little thread of red flame.

He called into the hut, 'I'm going to take a walk.'

'All right,' his wife said.

He moved quietly down through a series of ruins. 'Made in New York,' he read from a piece of metal as he passed. 'And all these things from Earth will be gone long before the Old Martian towns.' He looked towards the fifty-centuries-old village that lay among the blue mountains.

He came to a solitary Martian graveyard, a series of small hexagonal stones on a hill swept by the lonely wind.

He stood looking down at four graves with crude wooden crosses on them, and names. Tears did not come to his eyes. They had dried long ago.

'Do you forgive me for what I've done?' he asked of the crosses. 'I was very much alone. You do understand, don't you?'

He returned to the stone hut and once more, just before going in, shaded his eyes, searching the black sky.

'You keep waiting and waiting and looking,' he said, 'and one night perhaps—'

There was a tiny red flame on the sky.

He stepped away from the light of the hut.

'—and you look *again*,' he whispered.

The tiny red flame was still there.

'It wasn't there last night,' he whispered.

He stumbled and fell, picked himself up, ran behind the hut, swivelled the telescope, and pointed it at the sky.

A minute later, after a long, wild staring, he appeared in the low door of the hut. The wife and the two daughters and the son turned their heads to him. Finally he was able to speak.

'I have good news,' he said. 'I have looked at the sky. A rocket is coming to take us all home. It will be here in the early morning.'

He put his hands down and put his head into his hands and began to cry gently.

He burned what was left of New New York that morning at three.

He took a torch and moved into the plastic city and with the flame touched the walls here or there. The city bloomed up in great tosses of heat and light. It was a square mile of illumination, big enough to be seen out in space. It would beckon the rocket down to Mr Hathaway and his family.

His heart beating rapidly with pain, he returned to the hut. 'See?' he held up a dusty bottle into the light. 'Wine I saved, just for tonight. I knew that someday someone would find us! Well have a drink to celebrate!'

He poured five glasses full.

'It's been a long time,' he said, gravely looking into his drink. 'Remember the day the war broke? Twenty years and seven months ago. And all the rockets were called home from Mars. And you and I and the children were out in the mountains, doing archaeological work, research on the ancient surgical methods of the Martians. We ran our horses, almost killing them, remember? But we got here to the city a week late. Everyone was gone. America had been destroyed; every rocket had left without waiting for stragglers, remember, remember? And it turned out we were the *only* ones left? Lord, Lord, how the years pass! I couldn't have stood it without you here, all of you. I'd have killed myself without you. But with you, it was worth waiting. Here's to us, then.' He lifted his glass. 'And to our long wait together.' He drank.

The wife and the two daughters and the son raised their glasses to their lips.

The wine ran down over the chins of all four of them.

By morning the city was blowing in great black soft flakes across the sea-bottom. The fire was exhausted, but it had served its purpose; the red spot on the sky grew larger.

From the stone hut came the rich brown smell of baked gingerbread. His wife stood over the table, setting down the hot pans of new bread as Hathaway entered. The two daughters were gently sweeping the bare stone floor with stiff brooms, and the son was polishing the silverware.

'We'll have a huge breakfast for them,' laughed Hathaway. 'Put on your best clothes!'

He hurried across his land to the vast metal storage shed. Inside was the cold-storage unit and power plant he had repaired and restored with his efficient, small, nervous fingers over the years, just as he had repaired clocks, telephones, and spool recorders in his spare time. The shed was full of things he had built, some senseless mechanisms, the functions of which were a mystery even to himself now as he looked upon them.

From the deep freeze he fetched rimed cartons of beans and strawberries, twenty years old. Lazarus come forth, he thought, and pulled out a cool chicken.

The air was full of cooking odours when the rocket landed.

Like a boy, Hathaway raced down the hill. He stopped once because of a sudden sick pain in his chest. He sat on a rock to regain his breath, then ran all the rest of the way.

He stood in the hot atmosphere generated by the fiery rocket. A port opened. A man looked down.

Hathaway shielded his eyes and at last said, 'Captain Wilder!'

'Who is it?' asked Captain  der, and jumped down and stood there looking at the old man. He put his hand out. 'Good Lord, it's Hathaway!'

'That's right.' They looked into each other's faces.

'Hathaway, from my old crew, from the Fourth Expedition.'

'It's been a long time, Captain.'

'Too long. It's good to see you.'

'I'm old,' said Hathaway simply.

'I'm not young myself any more. I've been out to Jupiter and Saturn and Neptune for twenty years.'

'I heard they had kicked you upstairs so you wouldn't

interfere with colonial policy here on Mars.' The old man looked around. You've been gone so long you don't know what's happened—'

Wilder said, 'I can guess. We've circled Mars twice. Found only one other man, name of Walter Gripp, about ten thousand miles from here. We offered to take him with us, but he said no. The last we saw of him he was sitting in a rocking-chair in the middle of the highway, smoking a pipe, waving to us. Mars is pretty well dead, not even a Martian alive. What about Earth?'

'You know as much as I do. Once in a while I get the Earth radio, very faintly. But it's always in some other language. I'm sorry to say I only know Latin. A few words come through. I take it most of Earth's a shambles, but the war goes on. Are you going back, sir?'

'Yes. We're curious, of course. We had no radio contact so far out in space. We'll want to see Earth, no matter what.'

'You'll take us with you?'

The captain started. 'Of course, your wife, I remember her. Twenty-five years ago, wasn't it? When they opened First Town and you quit the service and brought her up here. And there were children—'

'My son and two daughters.'

'Yes, I remember. They're here?'

'Up at our hut. There's a fine breakfast waiting all of you up the hill. Will you come?'

'We would be honoured, Mr Hathaway.' Captain Wilder called to the rocket, 'Abandon ship!'

They walked up the hill, Hathaway and Captain Wilder, the twenty crew members following, taking deep breaths of the thin, cool morning air. The sun rose and it was a good day.

'Do you remember Spender, Captain?'

'I've never forgotten him.'

'About once a year I walk up past his tomb. It looks like he got his way at last. He didn't want us to come here, and I suppose he's happy now that we've all gone away.'

'What about — what was his name? — Parkhill, Sam Parkhill?'

'He opened a hot-dog stand.'

'It sounds just *like* him.'

'And went back to Earth the next week for the war.' Hathaway put his hand to his chest and sat down abruptly upon a boulder. 'I'm sorry. The excitement. Seeing you again after all these years. Have to rest.' He felt his heart pound. He counted the beats. It was very bad.

'We've got a doctor,' said Wilder. 'Excuse me, Hathaway, I know you are one, but we'd better check you with our own—' The doctor was summoned.

'I'll be all right,' insisted Hathaway. 'The waiting, the excitement.' He could hardly breathe. His lips were blue. 'You know,' he said as the doctor placed a stethoscope to him, 'it's as if I kept alive all these years just for this day, and now you're here to take me back to Earth, I'm satisfied and I can just lie down and quit.'

'Here.' The doctor handed him a yellow pellet. 'We'd better let you rest.'

'Nonsense. Just let me sit a moment. It's good to see all of you. Good to hear new voices again.'

'Is the pellet working?'

'Fine. Here we go!'

They walked on up the hill.

'Alice, come see who's here!'

Hathaway frowned and bent into the hut. 'Alice, did you hear?'

His wife appeared. A moment later the two daughters, tall and gracious, came out followed by an even taller son.

'Alice, you remember Captain Wilder?'

She hesitated and looked at Hathaway as if for instructions and then smiled. 'Of course, Captain Wilder!'

'I remember, we had dinner together the night before I took off for Jupiter, Mrs Hathaway.'

She shook his hand vigorously. 'My daughters, Marguerite and Susan. My son, John. You remember the captain, surely?'

Hands were shaken amid laughter and much talk.

Captain Wilder sniffed the air, 'Is that *gingerbread*?'

'Will you have some?'

Everyone moved. Folding tables were hurried out while hot foods were rushed forth and plates and fine damask napkins and good silverware were laid. Captain Wilder stood looking first at Mrs Hathaway and then at her son and her two tall, quiet-moving daughters. He looked into their faces as they darted past and he followed every move of their youthful hands and every expression of their wrinkleless faces. He sat upon a chair the son brought. 'How old are you, John?'

The son replied, 'Twenty-three.'

Wilder shifted his silverware clumsily. His face was suddenly pale. The man next to him whispered, 'Captain Wilder, that can't be right.'

The son moved away to bring more chairs.

'What's that, Williamson?'

'I'm forty-three myself, Captain. I was in school the same time as young John Hathaway there, twenty years ago. He says he's only twenty-three now; he only *looks* twenty-three. But that's wrong. He should be forty-two, at least. What's it mean, sir?'

'I don't know.'

'You look kind of sick, sir.'

'I don't feel well. The daughters, too, I saw them twenty years or so ago; they haven't changed, not a wrinkle. Will you do me a favour? I want you to run an errand, Williamson. I'll tell you where to go and what to check. Late in the breakfast, slip away. It should take you only ten minutes. The place isn't far from here. I saw it from the rocket as we landed.'

'Here! What are you talking about so seriously?' Mrs Hathaway ladled quick spoons of soup into their bowls. 'Smile now; we're all together, the trip's over, and it's like home!'

'Yes.' Captain Wilder laughed. 'You certainly look very well and young, Mrs Hathaway!'

'Isn't that like a man!'

He watched her drift away, drift with her pink face warm, smooth as an apple, unwrinkled and colourful. She chimed her laugh at every joke, she tossed salads neatly, never once pausing for breath. And the bony son and curved daughters were brilliantly witty, like their father, telling of the long years and their secret life, while their father nodded proudly to each.

Williamson slipped off down the hill.

'Where's *he* going?' asked Hathaway.

'Checking the rocket,' said Wilder. 'But, as I was saying, Hathaway, there's nothing on Jupiter, nothing at all for men. That includes Saturn and Pluto.' Wilder talked mechanically, not hearing his words, thinking only of Williamson running down the hill and climbing back to tell what he had found.

'Thanks.' Marguerite Hathaway was filling his water-glass. Impulsively he touched her arm. She did not even mind. Her flesh was warm and soft.

Hathaway, across the table, paused several times, touched his chest with his fingers, painfully, then went on listening to the murmuring talk and sudden loud chattering, glancing now and again with concern at Wilder, who did not seem to like chewing his gingerbread.

Williamson returned. He sat picking at his food until the captain whispered aside to him, 'Well?'

'I found it, sir.'

'And?'

Williamson's cheeks were white. He kept his eyes on the laughing people. The daughters were smiling gravely and the son was telling a joke. Williamson said, 'I went into the graveyard.'

'The four crosses were there?'

'The four crosses were there, sir. The names were still on them. I wrote them down to be sure.' He read from a white paper: 'Alice, Marguerite, Susan, and John Hathaway. Died of unknown virus. July 2007.'

'Thank you, Williamson.' Wilder closed his eyes.

'Nineteen years ago, sir.' Williamson's hand trembled. 'Yes.'

'Then who are *these*?'

'I don't know.'

'What are you going to do?'

'I don't know that either.'

'Will we tell the other men?'

'Later. Go on with your food as if nothing happened.'

'I'm not very hungry now, sir.'

The meal ended with wine brought from the rocket. Hathaway arose. 'A toast to all of you; it's good to be with friends again. And to my wife and children, without whom I couldn't have survived alone. It is only through their kindness in caring for me that I've lived on, waiting for your arrival.' He moved his wine-glass towards his family, who looked back self-consciously, lowering their eyes at last as everyone drank.

Hathaway drank down his wine. He did not cry out as he fell forward on to the table and slipped to the ground. Several men eased him to rest. The doctor bent to him and listened. Wilder touched the doctor's shoulder. The doctor looked up and shook his head. Wilder knelt and took the old man's hand. 'Wilder?' Hathaway's voice was barely audible. 'I spoiled the breakfast.'

'Nonsense.'

'Say good-bye to Alice and the children for me.'

'Just a moment, I'll call them.'

'No, no, don't!' gasped Hathaway. 'They wouldn't understand. I wouldn't want them to understand! Don't!'

Wilder did not move.

Hathaway was dead.

Wilder waited for a long time. Then he arose and walked away from the stunned group around Hathaway. He went to Alice Hathaway, looked into her face, and said, 'Do you know what has just happened?'

'Something about my husband?'

'He's just passed away; his heart,' said Wilder, watching her.

'I'm sorry,' she said.

'How do you feel?' he asked.

'He didn't want us to feel badly. He told us it would happen one day and he didn't want us to cry. He didn't teach us how, you know. He didn't want us to know. He said it was the worst thing that could happen to a man to know how to be lonely and know how to be sad and then to cry. So we're not to know what crying is, or being sad.'

Wilder glanced at her hands, the soft warm hands and the fine manicured nails and the tapered wrists. He saw her slender, smooth white neck and her intelligent eyes. Finally he said, 'Mr Hathaway did a fine job on you and your children.'

'He would have liked to hear you say that. He was so proud of us. After a while he even forgot that he had made us. At the end he loved and took us as his real wife and children. And, in a way, we *are*.'

'You gave him a good deal of comfort.'

'Yes, for years on end we sat and talked. He so much loved to talk. He liked the stone hut and the open fire. We would have lived in a regular house in the town, but he liked it up here, where he could be primitive if he liked, or modern if he liked. He told me all about his laboratory and the things he did in it. He wired the entire dead American town below with sound speakers. When he pressed a button the town lit up and made noises as if ten thousand people lived in it. There were airplane noises and car noises and the sounds of people talking. He would sit and light a cigar and talk to us, and the sounds of the town would come up to us, and once in a while the phone would ring and a recorded voice would ask Mr Hathaway scientific and surgical questions and he would answer them. With the phone ringing and us here and the sounds of the town and his cigar, Mr Hathaway was quite happy. There's only one thing he couldn't make us do,' she said. 'And that was to grow old. He got older every day, but we stayed the same. I guess he didn't mind. I guess he wanted us this way.'

'We'll bury him down in the yard where the other four crosses are. I think he would like that.'

She put her hand on his wrist, lightly. 'I'm sure he would.'

Orders were given. The family followed the little procession down the hill. Two men carried Hathaway on a covered stretcher. They passed the stone hut and the storage shed where Hathaway, many years before, had begun his work, Wilder paused within the workshop door.

How would it be, he wondered, to live on a planet with a wife and three children and have them die, leaving you alone with the wind and silence? What would a person do? Bury them with crosses in the graveyard and then come back up to the workshop and, with all the power of mind and memory and accuracy of finger and genius, put together, bit by bit, all those things that were wife, son, daughter. With an entire American city below from which to draw needed supplies, a brilliant man might do anything.

The sound of their footsteps was muffled in the sand. At the graveyard, as they turned in, two men were already spading out the earth.

*

They returned to the rocket in the late afternoon.

Williamson nodded at the stone hut. 'What are we going to do about *them*?'

'I don't know,' said the captain.

'Are you going to turn them off?'

'Off?' The captain looked faintly surprised. 'It never entered my mind.'

'You're not taking them back with us?'

'No, it would be useless.'

'You mean you're going to leave them here, like *that*, as they *are*!'

The captain handed Williamson a gun. 'If you can do anything about this, you're a better man than I.'

Five minutes later Williamson returned from the hut, sweating. 'Here, take your gun. I understand what you mean now. I went in the hut with the gun. One of the daughters smiled at me. So did the others. The wife offered me a cup of tea. Lord, it'd be murder!'

Wilder nodded. 'There'll never be anything as fine as them again. They're built to last; ten, fifty, two hundred years. Yes, they've as much right to – to life as you or I or any of us.' He knocked out his pipe. 'Well, get aboard. We're taking off. This city's done for, we'll not be using it.'

It was late in the day. A cold wind was rising. The men were aboard. The captain hesitated. Williamson said, 'Don't tell me you're going back to say – good-bye – to them?'

The captain looked at Williamson coldly. 'None of your business.'

Wilder strode up towards the hut through the darkening wind. The men in the rocket saw his shadow lingering in the stone-hut doorway. They saw a woman's shadow. They saw the captain shake her hand.

Moments later he came running back to the rocket.

On nights when the wind comes over the dead sea-bottoms and through the hexagonal graveyard, over four old crosses and one new one, there is a light burning in the low stone hut, and in that hut, as the wind roars by and the dust whirls and the cold stars burn, are four figures, a woman, two daughters, a son, tending a low fire for no reason and talking and laughing.

Night after night for every year and every year, for no reason at all, the woman comes out and looks at the sky, her hands up, for a long moment, looking at the green burning of Earth, not knowing why she looks, and then she goes back and throws a stick on the fire, and the wind comes up and the dead sea goes on being dead.

# *There Will Come Soft Rains*

In the living-room the voice-clock sang, *Tick-tock, seven
o'clock, time to get up, time to get up, seven o'clock!* as
if it were afraid that nobody would. The morning house lay
empty. The clock ticked on, repeating its sounds into the
emptiness. *Seven-nine, breakfast time, seven-nine!*

In the kitchen the breakfast stove gave a hissing sigh and
ejected from its warm interiors eight pieces of perfectly
browned toast, eight eggs sunny-side up, sixteen slices of
bacon, two coffees, and two cool glasses of milk.

'Today is August 4, 2026,' said a second voice from the
kitchen ceiling, 'in the city of Allendale, California.' It
repeated the date three times for memory's sake. 'Today
is Mr Featherstone's birthday. Today is the anniversary of
Tilita's marriage. Insurance is payable, as are the water, gas,
and light bills.'

Somewhere in the walls, relays clicked, memory tapes
glided under electric eyes.

*Eight-one, tick-tock, eight-one o'clock, off to school, off
to work, run, run, eight-one!* but no doors slammed, no
carpets took the soft tread of rubber heels. It was raining
outside. The weather box on the front door sang quietly:
'Rain, rain, go away; rubbers, raincoats for today . . .' And
the rain tapped on the empty house, echoing.

Outside, the garage chimed and lifted its door to reveal
the waiting car. After a long wait the door swung down
again.

At eight-thirty the eggs were shrivelled and the toast was
like stone. An aluminium wedge scraped them into the sink,
where hot water whirled them down a metal throat which
digested and flushed them away to the distant sea. The dirty

dishes were dropped into a hot washer and emerged twinkling dry.

*Nine-fifteen*, sang the clock, *time to clean*.

Out of warrens in the wall, tiny robot mice darted. The rooms were a-crawl with the small cleaning animals, all rubber and metal. They thudded against chairs, whirling their moustached runners, kneading the rug nap, sucking gently at hidden dust. Then, like mysterious invaders, they popped into their burrows. Their pink electric eyes faded. The house was clean.

*Ten o'clock*. The sun came out from behind the rain. The house stood alone in a city of rubble and ashes. This was the one house left standing. At night the ruined city gave off a radioactive glow which could be seen for miles.

*Ten-fifteen*. The garden sprinklers whirled up in golden founts, filling the soft morning air with scatterings of brightness. The water pelted window-panes, running down the charred west side where the house had been burned evenly free of its white paint. The entire west face of the house was black, save for five places. Here the silhouette in paint of a man mowing a lawn. Here, as in a photograph, a woman bent to pick flowers. Still farther over, their images burned on wood in one titanic instant, a small boy, hands flung into the air; higher up, the image of a thrown ball, and opposite him a girl, hands raised to catch a ball which never came down.

The five spots of paint – the man, the woman, the children, the ball – remained. The rest was a thin charcoaled layer.

The gentle sprinkler rain filled the garden with falling light.

Until this day, how well the house had kept its peace! How carefully it had inquired, 'Who goes there? What's the password?' and, getting no answer from lonely foxes and whining cats, it had shut up its windows and drawn shades in an old-maidenly preoccupation with self-protection which bordered on a mechanical paranoia.

It quivered at each sound, the house did. If a sparrow brushed a window, the shade snapped up. The bird, startled, flew off! No, not even a bird must touch the house!

The house was an altar with ten thousand attendants, big, small, servicing, attending, in choirs. But the gods had gone away, and the ritual of the religion continued senselessly, uselessly.

*Twelve noon*.

A dog whined, shivering, on the front porch.

The front door recognized the dog voice and opened. The dog, once huge and fleshy, but now gone to bone and covered with sores, moved in and through the house, tracking mud. Behind it whirred angry mice, angry at having to pick up mud, angry at inconvenience.

For not a leaf fragment blew under the door but what the wall-panels flipped open and the copper scrap rats flashed swiftly out. The offending dust, hair or paper, seized in miniature steel jaws, was raced back to the burrows. There, down tubes which fed into the cellar, it was dropped into the sighing vent of an incinerator which sat like evil Baal in a dark corner.

The dog ran upstairs, hysterically yelping to each door, at last realizing, as the house realized, that only silence was here.

It sniffed the air and scratched the kitchen door. Behind the door, the stove was making pancakes which filled the house with a rich baked odour and the scent of maple syrup.

The dog frothed at the mouth, lying at the door, sniffing, its eyes turned to fire. It ran wildly in circles, biting at its tail, spun in a frenzy, and died. It lay in the parlour for an hour.

*Two o'clock*, sang a voice.

Delicately sensing decay at last, the regiments of mice hummed out as softly as blow grey leaves in an electrical wind.

*Two-fifteen.*

The dog was gone.

In the cellar, the incinerator glowed suddenly and a whirl of sparks leaped up the chimney.

*Two thirty-five.*

Bridge tables sprouted from patio walls. Playing-cards fluttered on to pads in a shower of pips. Martinis manifested on an oaken bench with egg-salad sandwiches. Music played.

But the tables were silent and the cards untouched.

At four o'clock the tables folded like great butterflies back through the panelled walls.


*Four-thirty.*

The nursery walls glowed.

Animals took shape: yellow giraffes, blue lions, pink antelopes, lilac panthers cavorting in crystal substance. The walls were glass. They looked out upon colour and fantasy. Hidden films clocked through well-oiled sprockets, and the walls lived. The nursery floor was woven to resemble a crisp, cereal meadow. Over this ran aluminium roaches and iron crickets, and in the hot, still air butterflies of delicate red tissue wavered among the sharp aromas of animal spoors! There was the sound like a great matted yellow hive of bees within a dark bellows, the lazy bumble of a purring lion. And there was the patter of okapi feet and the murmur of a fresh jungle rain, like other hoofs, falling upon the summer-starched grass. Now the walls dissolved into distances of parched weed, mile on mile, and warm, endless sky. The animals drew away into thornbrakes and water-holes.

It was the children's hour.

*

*Five o'clock*. The bath filled with clear hot water.

*Six, seven, eight o'clock*. The dinner dishes manipulated like magic tricks, and in the study a *click*. In the metal stand opposite the hearth where a fire now blazed up warmly, a cigar popped out, half an inch of soft grey ash on it, smoking, waiting.

*Nine o'clock*. The beds warmed their hidden circuits, for nights were cool here.

*Nine-five*. A voice spoke from the study ceiling: 'Mrs McClellan, which poem would you like this evening?'

The house was silent.

The voice said at last, 'Since you express no preference, I shall select a poem at random.' Quiet music rose to back the voice. 'Sara Teasdale. As I recall, your favourite . . .

'There will come soft rains and the smell of the ground,
The swallows circling with their shimmering sound;

And frogs in the pools singing at night,
And wild plum-trees in tremulous white;

Robins will wear their feathery fire,
Whistling their whims on a low fence-wire;

And not one will know of the war, not one
Will care at last when it is done.

Not one would mind, neither bird nor tree,
If mankind perished utterly;

And Spring herself, when she woke at dawn,
Would scarcely know that we were gone.'

The fire burned on the stone hearth and the cigar fell away into a mound of quiet ash on its tray. The empty chairs faced each other between the silent walls, and the music played.

At ten o'clock the house began to die.

The wind blew. A falling tree-bough crashed through the

kitchen window. Cleaning solvent, bottled, shattered over the stove. The room was ablaze in an instant!

'Fire!' screamed a voice. The house-lights flashed, water-pumps shot water from the ceilings. But the solvent spread on the linoleum, licking, eating, under the kitchen door, while the voices took it up in chorus: 'Fire, fire, fire!'

The house tried to save itself. Doors sprang tightly shut, but the windows were broken by the heat, and the wind blew and sucked upon the fire.

The house gave ground as the fire in ten billion angry sparks moved with flaming ease from room to room and then up the stairs. While scurrying water-rats squeaked from the walls, pistolled their water, and ran for more. And the wall-sprays let down showers of mechanical rain.

But too late. Somewhere, sighing, a pump shrugged to a stop. The quenching rain ceased. The reserve water supply which had filled baths and washed dishes for many quiet days was gone.

The fire crackled up the stairs. It fed upon the Picassos and Matisses in the upper halls, like delicacies, baking off the oily flesh, tenderly crisping the canvases into black shavings.

Now the fire lay in beds, stood in windows, changed the colours of drapes!

And then, reinforcements.

From attic trap-doors, blind robot faces peered down with faucet mouths gushing green chemical.

The fire backed off, as even an elephant must at the sight of a dead snake. Now there were twenty snakes whipping over the floor, killing the fire with a clear, cold venom of green froth.

But the fire was clever. It had sent flame outside the house, up through the attic to the pumps there. An explosion! The attic brain which directed the pumps was shattered into bronze shrapnel on the beams.

The fire rushed back into every closet and felt the clothes hung there.

The house shuddered, oak bone on bone, its bared skeleton cringing from the heat, its wire, its nerves revealed as if a surgeon had torn the skin off to let the red veins and capillaries quiver in the scalded air. Help, help! Fire! Run, run! Heat snapped mirrors like the first brittle winter ice. And the voices wailed Fire, fire, run, run, like a tragic nursery rhyme, a dozen voices, high, low, like children dying in a forest, alone, alone. And the voices fading as the wires popped their sheathings like hot chestnuts. One, two, three, four, five voices died.

In the nursery the jungle burned. Blue lions roared, purple giraffes bounded off. The panthers ran in circles, changing colour, and ten million animals, running before the fire, vanished off towards a distant steaming river . . .

Ten more voices died. In the last instant under the fire avalanche, other choruses, oblivious, could be heard announcing the time, playing music, cutting the lawn by remote control mower, or setting an umbrella frantically out and in the slamming and opening front door, a thousand things happening, like a clock-shop when each clock strikes the hour insanely before or after the other, a scene of maniac confusion, yet unity; singing, screaming, a few last cleaning mice darting bravely out to carry the horrid ashes away! And one voice, with sublime disregard for the situation, read poetry aloud in the fiery study, until all the film-spools burned, until all the wires withered and the circuits cracked.

The fire burst the house and let it slam flat down, puffing out skirts of spark and smoke.

In the kitchen, an instant before the rain of fire and timber, the stove could be seen making breakfasts at a psychopathic rate, ten dozen eggs, six loaves of toast, twenty dozen bacon strips, which, eaten by fire, started the stove working again, hysterically hissing!

The crash. The attic smashing into kitchen and parlour. The parlour into cellar, cellar into sub-cellar. Deep freeze, arm-chair, film tapes, circuits, beds, and all like skeletons thrown in a cluttered mound deep under.

Smoke and silence. A great quantity of smoke.

Dawn showed faintly in the east. Among the ruins, one wall stood alone. Within the wall, a last voice said, over and over again and again, even as the sun rose to shine upon the heaped rubble and steam:

'Today is August 5, 2026, today is August 5, 2026, today is . . .'

# The Million-Year Picnic

Somehow the idea was brought up by Mom that perhaps the whole family would enjoy a fishing trip. But they weren't Mom's words; Timothy knew that. They were Dad's words, and Mom used them for him somehow.

Dad shuffled his feet in a clutter of Martian pebbles and agreed. So immediately there was a tumult and a shouting, and very quickly the camp was tucked into capsules and containers, Mom slipped into travelling jumpers and blouse, Dad stuffed his pipe full with trembling hands, his eyes on the Martian sky, and the three boys piled yelling into the motorboat, none of them really keeping an eye on Mom and Dad, except Timothy.

Dad pushed a stud. The water-boat sent a humming sound up into the sky. The water shook back and the boat nosed ahead, and the family cried, 'Hurrah!'

Timothy sat in the back of the boat with Dad, his small fingers atop Dad's hairy ones, watching the canal twist, leaving the crumbled place behind where they had landed in their small family rocket all the way from Earth. He remembered the night before they left Earth, the hustling and hurrying, the rocket that Dad had found somewhere, somehow, and the talk of a vacation on Mars. A long way to go for a vacation, but Timothy said nothing because of his younger brothers. They came to Mars and now, first thing, or so they said, they were going fishing.

Dad had a funny look in his eyes as the boat went up-canal. A look that Timothy couldn't figure. It was made of strong light and maybe a sort of relief. It made the deep wrinkles laugh instead of worry or cry.

So there went the cooling rocket, around a bend, gone.

'How far are we going?' Robert splashed his hand. It looked like a small crab jumping in the violet water.

Dad exhaled. 'A million years.'

'Gee,' said Robert.

'Look, kids.' Mother pointed one soft, long arm. 'There's a dead city.'

They looked with fervent anticipation, and the dead city lay dead for them alone, drowsing in a hot silence of summer made on Mars by a Martian weather-man.

And Dad looked as if he was pleased that it was dead.

It was a futile spread of pink rocks sleeping on a rise of sand, a few tumbled pillars, one lonely shrine, and then the sweep of sand again. Nothing else for miles. A white desert around the canal and a blue desert over it.

Just then a bird flew up. Like a stone thrown across a blue pond, hitting, falling deep, and vanishing.

Dad got a frightened look when he saw it. 'I thought it was a rocket.'

Timothy looked at the deep ocean sky, trying to see Earth and the war and the ruined cities and the men killing each other since the day he was born. But he saw nothing. The war was as removed and far off as two flies battling to the death in the arch of a great high and silent cathedral. And just as senseless.

William Thomas wiped his forehead and felt the touch of his son's hand on his arm, like a young tarantula, thrilled. He beamed at his son. 'How goes it Timothy?'

'Fine, Dad.'

Timothy hadn't quite figured out what was ticking inside the vast adult mechanism beside him. The man with the immense hawk nose, sunburnt, peeling — and the hot blue eyes like agate marbles you play with after school in summer back on Earth, and the long, thick columnar legs in the loose riding-breeches.

'What are you looking at so hard, Dad?'

'I was looking for Earthian logic, common sense, good government, peace and responsibility.'

'All that up there?'

'No. I didn't find it. It's not there any more. Maybe it'll never be there again. Maybe we fooled ourselves that it was ever there.'

'Huh?'

'See the fish,' said Dad, pointing.

There rose a soprano clamour from all three boys as they rocked the boat in arching their tender necks to see. They *oohed* and *ahed*. A silver ring fish floated by them, undulating, and closing like an iris, instantly, around food particles, to assimilate them.

Dad looked at it. His voice was deep and quiet.

'Just like war. War swims along, see food, contracts. A moment later — Earth is gone.'

'William,' said Mom.

'Sorry,' said Dad.

They sat still and felt the canal water rush cool, swift, and glassy. The only sound was the motor hum, the glide of water, the sun expanding the air.

'When do we see the Martians?' cried Michael.

'Quite soon, perhaps,' said Father. 'Maybe tonight.'

'Oh, but the Martians are a dead race now,' said Mom.

'No, they're not. I'll show you some Martians, all right,' Dad said presently.

Timothy scowled at that but said nothing. Everything was odd now. Vacations and fishing and looks between people.

The other boys were already engaged making shelves of their small hands and peering under them towards the seven-foot banks of the canal, watching for Martians.

'What do they look like?' demanded Michael.

'You'll know them when you see them.' Dad sort of laughed, and Timothy saw a pulse beating time in his cheek.

Mother was slender and soft, with a woven plait of spun-gold hair over her head in a tiara, and eyes the colour of the deep, cool canal water, where it ran in shadow, almost purple, with flecks of amber caught in it. You could see her thoughts swimming around in her eyes, like fish — some bright, some dark, some fast, quick, some slow and easy, and sometimes, like when she looked up where Earth was, being nothing but colour and nothing else. She sat in the boat's prow, one hand resting on the side lip, the other on the lap of her dark blue breeches, and a line of sunburnt soft neck showing where her blouse opened like a white flower.

She kept looking ahead to see what was there, and, not being able to see it clearly enough, she looked backward towards her husband, and through his eyes, reflected then, she saw what was ahead; and since he added part of himself to this reflection, a determined firmness, her face relaxed and she accepted it and she turned back, knowing suddenly what to look for.

Timothy looked too. But all he saw was a straight pencil line of canal going violet through a wide, shallow valley penned by low, eroded hills, and on until it fell over the sky's edge. And this canal went on and on, through cities that would have rattled like beetles in a dry skull if you shook them. A hundred or two hundred cities dreaming hot summer-day dreams and cool summer-night dreams . . .

They had come millions of miles for this outing — to fish. But there had been a gun on the rocket. This was a vacation. But why all the food, more than enough to last them years and years, left hidden back there near the rocket? Vacation. Just behind the veil of the vacation was not a soft face of laughter, but something hard and bony and perhaps terrifying. Timothy could not lift the veil, and the two other boys were busy being ten and eight years old, respectively.

'No Martians yet. Nuts.' Robert put his V-shaped chin on his hands and glared at the canal.

Dad had brought an atomic radio along, strapped to his

wrist. It functioned on an old-fashioned principle: you held it against the bones near your ear and it vibrated singing or talking to you. Dad listened to it now. His face looked like one of those fallen Martian cities, caved in, sucked dry, almost dead.

Then he gave it to Mom to listen. Her lips dropped open.

'What—' Timothy started to question, but never finished what he wished to say.

For at that moment there were two titanic, marrow-jolting explosions that grew upon themselves, followed by a half-dozen minor concussions.

Jerking his head up, Dad notched the boat speed higher immediately. The boat leaped and jounced and spanked. This shook Robert out of his funk and elicited yelps of frightened but ecstatic joy from Michael, who clung to Mom's legs and watched the water pour by his nose in a wet torrent.

Dad swerved the boat, cut speed, and ducked the craft into a little branch canal and under an ancient, crumbling stone wharf that smelled of crab-flesh. The boat rammed the wharf hard enough to throw them all forward, but no one was hurt, and Dad was already twisted to see if the ripples on the canal were enough to map their route into hiding. Water-lines went across, lapped the stones and rippled back to meet each other, settling, to be dappled by the sun. It all went away.

Dad listened. So did everybody.

Dad's breathing echoed like fists beating against the cold, wet, wharf stones. In the shadow Mom's cat eyes just watched Father for some clue to what next.

Dad relaxed and blew out a breath, laughing at himself.

'The rocket, of course. I'm getting jumpy. The rocket.'

Michael said, 'What happened, Dad, what happened?'

'Oh, we just blew up our rocket, is all,' said Timothy, trying to sound matter-of-fact. 'I've heard rockets blown up before. Ours just blew.'

'Why did we blow up our rocket?' asked Michael. 'Huh, Dad?'

'It's part of the game, silly!' said Timothy.

'A game!' Michael and Robert loved the word.

'Dad fixed it so it would blow up and no one'd know where we landed or went! In case they ever came looking, see?'

'Oh, boy, a secret!'

'Scared by my own rocket,' admitted Dad to Mom. 'I *am* nervous. It's silly to think there'll ever be any more rockets. Except *one*, perhaps, if Edwards and his wife get through with *their* ship.'

He put his tiny radio to his ear again. After two minutes he dropped his hand as you would drop a rag.

'It's over at last,' he said to Mom. 'The radio just went off the atomic beam. Every other world station's gone. They dwindled down to a couple in the last few years. Now the air's completely silent. It'll probably remain silent.'

'For how long?' asked Robert.

'Maybe — your great-grandchildren will hear it again,' said Dad. He just sat there, and the children were caught in the centre of his awe and defeat and resignation and acceptance.

Finally he put the boat out into the canal again, and they continued in the direction in which they had originally started.

It was getting late. Already the sun was down the sky, and a series of dead cities lay ahead of them.

Dad talked very quietly and gently to his sons. Many times in the past he had been brisk, distant, removed from them, but now he patted them on the head with just a word and they felt it.

'Mike, pick a city.'

'What, Dad?'

'Pick a city, Son. Any one of these cities we pass.'

'All right,' said Michael. 'How do I pick?'

'Pick the one you like the most. You, too, Robert and Tim. Pick the city you like best.'

'I want a city with Martians in it,' said Michael.

'You'll have that,' said Dad. 'I promise.' His lips were for the children, but his eyes were for Mom.

They passed six cities in twenty minutes. Dad didn't say anything more about the explosions; he seemed much more interested in having fun with his sons, keeping them happy, than anything else.

Michael liked the first city they passed, but this was vetoed because everyone doubted quick first judgments. The second city nobody liked. It was an Earth Man's settlement, built of wood and already rotting into sawdust. Timothy liked the third city because it was large. The fourth and fifth were too small, and the sixth brought acclaim from everyone, including Mother, who joined in the Gees, Goshes, and Look-at-thats!

There were fifty or sixty huge structures still standing, streets were dusty but paved, and you could see one or two old centrifugal fountains still pulsing wetly in the plazas. That was the only life – water leaping in the late sunlight.

'This is the city,' said everybody.

Steering the boat to a wharf, Dad jumped out.

'Here we are. This is ours. This is where we live from now on!'

'From now on?' Michael was incredulous. He stood up, looking, and then turned to blink back at where the rocket used to be. 'What about the rocket? What about Minnesota?'

'Here,' said Dad.

He touched the small radio to Michael's blond head. 'Listen.'

Michael listened.

'Nothing,' he said.

'That's right. Nothing. Nothing at all any more. No more Minneapolis, no more rockets, no more Earth.'

Michael considered the lethal revelations and began to sob little dry sobs.

'Wait a moment,' said Dad the next instant. 'I'm giving you a lot more in exchange, Mike!'

'What?' Michael held off the tears, curious, but quite ready to continue in case Dad's further revelation was as disconcerting as the original.

'I'm giving you this city, Mike. It's yours.'

'Mine?'

'For you and Robert and Timothy, all three of you, to own for yourselves.'

Timothy bounded from the boat. 'Look, guys, all for *us*! All of *that*!' He was playing the game with Dad, playing it large and playing it well. Later, after it was all over and things had settled, he could go off by himself and cry for ten minutes. But now it was still a game, still a family outing, and the other kids must be kept playing.

Mike jumped out with Robert. They helped Mom.

'Be careful of your sister,' said Dad, and nobody knew what he meant until later.

They hurried into the great pink-stoned city, whispering among themselves, because dead cities have a way of making you want to whisper, to watch the sun go down.

'In about five days,' said Dad quietly. 'I'll go back down to where our rocket was and collect the food hidden in the ruins there and bring it here; and I'll hunt for Bert Edwards and his wife and daughters there.'

'Daughters?' asked Timothy. 'How many?'

'Four.'

'I can see that'll cause trouble later.' Mom nodded slowly.

'Girls.' Michael made a face like an ancient Martian stone image. 'Girls.'

'Are they coming in a rocket too?'

'Yes. If they make it. Family rockets are made for travel to the Moon, not Mars. We were lucky we got through.'

'Where did you get the rocket?' whispered Timothy, for the other boys were running ahead.

'I saved it. I saved it for twenty years, Tim. I had it hidden away, hoping I'd never have to use it. I suppose I should have given it to the government for the war, but I kept thinking about Mars . . .'

'And a picnic!'

'Right. This is between you and me. When I saw everything was finishing on Earth, after I'd waited until the last moment, I packed us up. Bert Edwards had a ship hidden, too, but we decided it would be safer to take off separately, in case anyone tried to shoot us down.'

'Why'd you blow up the rocket, Dad?'

'So we can't go back, ever. And so if any of those evil men ever come to Mars they won't know we're here.'

'Is that why you look up all the time?'

'Yes, it's silly. They won't follow us, ever. They haven't anything to follow with. I'm being too careful, is all.'

Michael came running back. 'Is this really *our* city, Dad?'

'The whole darn planet belongs to us, kids. The whole darn planet.'

They stood there, King of the Hill, Top of the Heap, Ruler of All They Surveyed, Unimpeachable Monarchs and Presidents, trying to understand what it meant to own a world and how big a world really was.

Night came quickly in the thin atmosphere, and Dad left them in the square by the pulsing fountain, went down to the boat, and came walking back carrying a stack of paper in his big hands.

He laid the papers in a clutter in an old courtyard and set them afire. To keep warm, they crouched around the blaze and laughed, and Timothy saw the little letters leap like frightened animals when the flames touched and engulfed them. The papers crinkled like an old man's skin, and the cremation surrounded innumerable words:

'GOVERNMENT BONDS; Business Graph, 1999; Religious

Prejudice: An Essay; The Science of Logistics; Problems of the Pan-American Unity; Stock Report for July 3, 1998; The War Digest . . .'

Dad had insisted on bringing these papers for this purpose. He sat there and fed them into the fire, one by one, with satisfaction, and told his children what it all meant.

'It's time I told you a few things. I don't suppose it was fair, keeping so much from you. I don't know if you'll understand, but I have to talk, even if only part of it gets over to you.'

He dropped a leaf in the fire.

'I'm burning a way of life, just like that way of life is being burned clean of Earth right now. Forgive me if I talk like a politician. I am, after all, a former state governor, and I was honest and they hated me for it. Life on Earth never settled down to doing anything very good. Science ran too far ahead of us too quickly, and the people got lost in a mechanical wilderness, like children making over pretty things, gadgets, helicopters, rockets; emphasizing the wrong items, emphasizing machines instead of how to run the machines. Wars got bigger and bigger and finally killed Earth. That's what the silent radio means. That's what we ran away from.

'We were lucky. There aren't any more rockets left. It's time you knew this isn't a fishing trip at all. I put off telling you. Earth is gone. Interplanetary travel won't be back for centuries, maybe never. But that way of life proved itself wrong and strangled itself with its own hands. You're young. I'll tell you this again every day until it sinks in.'

He paused to feed more papers to the fire.

'Now we're alone. We and a handful of others who'll land in a few days. Enough to start over. Enough to turn away from it all back on Earth and strike out on a new line—'

The fire leaped up to emphasize his talking. And then all the papers were gone except one. All the laws and beliefs of Earth were burnt into small, hot ashes which soon would be carried off in a wind.

Timothy looked at the last thing that Dad tossed in the fire. It was a map of the World, and it wrinkled and distorted itself hotly and went − flimpf − and was gone like a warm, black butterfly. Timothy turned away.

'Now I'm going to show you the Martians,' said Dad. 'Come on, all of you. Here, Alice.' He took her hand.

Michael was crying loudly, and Dad picked him up and carried him, and they walked down through the ruins towards the canal.

The canal. Where tomorrow or the next day their future wives would come up in a boat, small, laughing girls now, with their father and mother.

The night came down around them, and there were stars. But Timothy couldn't find Earth. It had already set. That was something to think about.

A night bird called among the ruins as they walked. Dad said, 'Your mother and I will try to teach you. Perhaps we'll fail. I hope not. We've had a good lot to see and learn from. We planned this trip years ago, before you were born. Even if there hadn't been a war we would have come to Mars, I think, to live and form our own standard of living. It would have been another century before Mars would have been really poisoned by the Earth civilization. Now, of course—'

They reached the canal. It was long and straight and cool and wet and reflective in the night.

'I've always wanted to see a Martian,' said Michael. 'Where are they, Dad? You promised.'

'There they are,' said Dad, and he shifted Michael on his shoulder and pointed straight down.

The Martians were there. Timothy began to shiver.

The Martians were there − in the canal − reflected in the water. Timothy and Michael and Robert and Mom and Dad.

The Martians stared back at them for a long, long silent time from the rippling water . . .